Cantor's Dilemma

Cantor's Dilemma

CARL DJERASSI

DOUBLEDAY

NEW YORK LONDON TORONTO SYDNEY AUCKLAND

PUBLISHED BY DOUBLEDAY

a division of Bantam Doubleday Dell Publishing Group, Inc.
666 Fifth Avenue, New York, New York 10103

DOUBLEDAY and the portrayal of an anchor with a dolphin
are trademarks of Doubleday,
a division of Bantam Doubleday Dell Publishing Group, Inc.

"Castor's Dilemma," a short story by Carl Djerassi, on which *Cantor's Dilemma* is, in part, based, appeared in *The Hudson Review*.

Excerpts from "The Dry Salvages," "East Coker," "Little Gidding," and Burnt Norton" in *Four Quartets,* © 1943 by T. S. Eliot and renewed 1971 by Valerie Eliot, reprinted by permission of Harcourt Brace Jovanovich, Inc., and Faber and Faber Ltd.

Excerpt from "A Dedication to My Wife" in *Collected Poems 1909–1962* by T. S. Eliot, © 1936 by Harcourt Brace Jovanovich, Inc., © 1963, 1964 by T. S. Eliot, reprinted by permission of Harcourt Brace Jovanovich, Inc., and Faber and Faber Ltd.

Library of Congress Cataloging-in-Publication Data

Djerassi, Carl.
Cantor's dilemma / by Carl Djerassi. — 1st ed.
p. cm.
I. Title.
PS3554.J47C36 1989
813'.54—dc19 89-1125
CIP

ISBN 0-385-26183-7

BOOK DESIGN BY TASHA HALL

October 1989

FIRST EDITION

BG

FOR MY MOST FAITHFUL READERS,
DIANE AND LEAH MIDDLEBROOK,
AND FOR TERRENCE HOLT

It seems paradoxical that scientific research, in many ways one of the most questioning and skeptical of human activities, should be dependent on personal trust. But the fact is that without trust the research enterprise could not function.

ARNOLD S. RELMAN, Editor,
New England Journal of Medicine, 1983

Cantor's Dilemma

1

"Damn," he muttered as he pressed his hand against his throbbing knee. He hobbled to the bathroom, feeling his way with his right palm along the wall. It didn't take expertise in neurobiology to know that photochemical stimulation of the retina was the surest way of waking up.

At home, he was certain of his path: out on the right side of the bed; four steps along the edge while brushing the mattress with his left leg; three steps across no man's land with his right hand reaching for the wall; and then straight on to the bathroom door, left hand finding the washbasin and, finally, right foot cautiously feeling for the base of the toilet. Keeping his eyes closed as he squatted to empty his bladder, he used the time and the darkness to retain the last memory of whatever dream he had woken from. Focusing on the interrupted dream, like not turning on the light, was another step toward resumption of sleep.

This night, however, he was in unfamiliar territory: the Sheraton Commander in Cambridge, across Harvard Square, and he had really banged his knee. He was still rubbing it while sitting on the toilet, the sound of the last few pings of urine clearly audible in the silence. The pain had fully wakened him, and he began to think of the lecture. Suddenly it struck him. My God, he thought as he reached for the light switch, that's it! How could I've missed it? The light blinded him momentarily as he stretched for the robe hanging on the back of the door.

It was 3:14 A.M. when Professor I. Cantor sat at the small desk and started scribbling on the only piece of paper he could find in the desk drawer. It may have been the first time in history that a Nobel Prize-winning idea was set down on the back of a laundry list.

2

Not as ugly as Kaposi's, nor quite as famous as Rous's, Krauss's sarcoma was distinguished by the fact that its discoverer, Harvard cancer doyen Kurt Krauss, was still very much alive. His sarcoma had become one of the classic models against which most new chemotherapeutic agents were first tested. If the new compound didn't shrink Krauss's sarcoma, it stood little chance of being examined further.

Rumors in the cancer field had a way of ending up very quickly at Krauss's lab. The best way of converting rumor into reality—or sending it into oblivion—was to present one's conclusions at Krauss's lunch seminar. "I.C.," Krauss had phoned, "rumors have it you're dabbling with a new theory of tumorigenesis."

"I'd hardly call it dabbling," Cantor replied, "I'm damn serious about it, although it's still a hypothesis." On the face of it, Cantor's concept was relatively straightforward. In his view, the ubiquitous culprit had to be a protein. Before it could exert its damage, the protein had to enter a cell by penetrating one or, frequently, several cell membranes. With one rare exception, all such cell membranes permit translocation in only one direction. To Cantor, that was the key: what if a chemical change—presumably caused by mutation—allowed two-way passage of the carcinogen into normal cells? A single intruder could then break into a cell, cause the mischief, get out, enter the next cell and the next. . . . The signal responsible for one-way transport of proteins through cell membranes is always a structural segment near the "free amino" end of a protein. Of the twenty known amino acids making up a protein molecule, only one —arginine—has three such "free amino" groups attached to one carbon atom. Cantor's key assumption was that mutations causing changes in the arginine composition of proteins were responsible for suddenly opening up two-way channels for proteins.

"So? You have a way to test it?" Krauss had immediately put his finger on the man's weakness. Cantor had not yet come up with any experiment that might demonstrate the correctness of his hypothesis, and a hypothesis without proof is sometimes worse than useless—it can be dangerous. A man can spend the rest of his experimental life chasing after a rainbow.

Reluctantly, Cantor conceded as much. "No, I haven't yet figured out how to test the proposition. But I'm working on it."

"While you're working on it, why not come and tell us all about your serious hypothesis?" Krauss's chuckle could be heard clearly over the telephone. "Maybe we can save you the trouble of testing it."

When people were summoned to speak at Krauss's weekly seminar, they came. Three weeks later, Cantor banged his knee in Cambridge and now, the morning after, he was having breakfast in the Brandywine Cafe going over his notes. Originally, he'd been apprehensive about how his hypothesis would hold up to one of Krauss's notorious critiques—the man could be merciless even to his friends —but after this morning's brainstorm on the toilet, Cantor felt supremely confident. He was not going to mention his flash of insight —the experiment that would convert hypothesis into unassailable fact—to Krauss or anyone else at Harvard. That would have to wait until the experiment was done. But he was convinced it would work. He felt intuitively that it was too beautiful not to.

Krauss's empire was the Harvard Medical School in Boston. Cantor had decided to spend the night in Cambridge rather than Boston because he'd wanted to pay one of his rare visits to the chemistry department on the other side of Harvard Square—that academic moat separating several of the schools at Harvard. There, scholars in closely related disciplines sometimes worked for years with only an occasional lowering of the drawbridge between their neighboring academic fiefdoms. Cantor, who was pushing sixty, had an international reputation as a cell biologist. However, few people remembered that he'd earned his Ph.D. in organic chemistry and how he'd metamorphosed into a biologist: his postdoctoral research at the National Institutes of Health dealt with the use of radiolabeling techniques to determine the fate of a new class of tranquilizers in experimental animals, but he soon switched to working with isolated enzymes in tissue homogenates—a far cry from his synthetic chemistry in graduate school. The coup de grace to a career in chemical research was struck at the Pasteur Institute in Paris, where he was irrevocably drawn to the burgeoning field of cell biology. Proudly, he referred to this largely autodidactic conversion as *déformation professionelle.* An organic chemist's perspective—theoretical and experimental—focuses primarily on molecules. By contrast, the biologist looks at entire systems: a cell; a leaf; a tree. Cantor's earlier chemical experiences had contributed heavily to his evolution into a molecular cell biologist.

The original purpose of his visit to Harvard's chemistry department was purely a courtesy call on Konrad Bloch, an old friend from graduate school days. In view of his inspiration of a few hours ago, however, he changed his morning's schedule. Bloch had received the Nobel Prize in 1964 for elucidating the way in which the body synthesizes cholesterol by establishing the origin of each of its twenty-seven carbon atoms.

Lately, he had been studying the formation of artificial vesicles enclosed by phospholipid membranes very similar to that found in natural cells. Bloch's technique was crucial for conducting experiments in the laboratory on how a living cell permits certain molecules to enter without diffusing back out—a technique that Cantor planned to use for testing the validity of his hypothesis. Using that methodology, Bloch and others had demonstrated that cholesterol did not just serve as the body's source of steroids, such as the sex hormones or cortisone, but also had a second major function: the presence of cholesterol among the phospholipids reduces the fluidity of a cell membrane to provide it with the optimum viscosity for permitting the one-way passage of chemicals into the cell. Even more relevant to Cantor's present interest was the known fact that membranes of leukemia cells are more fluid than are those of normal lymph cells. Was that due to decreased amounts of cholesterol in the cancer cells? Patients with chronic lymphatic leukemia show diminished cholesterol blood levels. Furthermore, adding cholesterol to leukemia cells reduces their membrane fluidity and decreases their malignancy. Were these just coincidences? Cantor decided to convert the courtesy stop into a working session with Bloch, who was famous for his generosity in listening to his colleagues' problems. What better use of these morning hours than a free consultation with a Nobelist?

Krauss's seminar room was full of graduate students, postdoctoral fellows, and some visitors from other departments. A few were still eating but, judging from the empty cups, crumpled sandwich sacks, balled paper napkins, and other detritus, most had finished their lunch. Kurt Krauss was clearly irritated. As soon as Cantor reached the front of the room, Krauss rose. The room fell silent. "Professor Cantor hardly needs an introduction, so in view of the late hour"— he threw an accusatory glance at his guest—"and without further ado, I'll call on our speaker to enlighten us with his new theory. I.C."—he gestured toward Cantor—"the floor is yours."

No scientific lecture is ever given without slides or other visual aids, especially if chemical structures are to be shown. The fields have become so complicated, the topics so esoteric, that even specialists talking to their own peers need to resort to overhead or slide projectors. Cantor had requested only the former. Felt pens in hand —one black, the other red—he proceeded to draw on the roll of clear plastic mounted on the base of the overhead projector, his drawings appearing in greatly magnified form on a screen behind his back in the dimly lit room. Cantor prided himself on his lecture style: his carefully drawn figures and precisely spoken words flowed together effortlessly. His audiences were always grateful that they could follow his presentation and at the same time take notes—a task that was often difficult with speakers who rushed ahead to the accompaniment of percussive commands: "Next slide, please."

Kurt Krauss could be terrifying in a manner that was often compared to that of the late physicist Robert Oppenheimer. When Krauss whispered to his neighbor in the front row, "We must teach I.C. some humility in our hallowed halls, mustn't we?" just after Cantor had started his talk, his voice may well have carried to the podium. He was also famous—many victims would say notorious—for his interruptions. Their impeccable timing was usually designed to cause the maximum amount of ego deflation. In addition, Krauss almost never took his eyes off a speaker; many a subject of his scrutiny claimed never to have seen Krauss blink.

Cantor didn't subscribe to this belief, but even so, today he felt that extra caution was in order. His theory was truly original—so much so that professional jealousy might actually sharpen Krauss's tongue. Cantor's tardiness hadn't helped, especially when he realized that he'd committed a faux pas by mentioning in his introductory remarks that his late arrival had been due to an exciting session with Bloch. To Krauss, a visit to the Cambridge campus prior to an appearance in his laboratory across the Charles River was an act of lèse-majesté, especially when announced in public.

Cantor's use of two colors was usually highly effective: red was reserved for noting key points, which were then settled in black on the white surface. This time, within the first few minutes, he twice caught himself mixing up pens and having to interrupt the natural flow of his presentation by erasures. But it wasn't just the extra measure of caution that affected Cantor's usually polished lecture style. This was the first public unveiling of his hypothesis, and he suddenly found that his mental processes had to operate on two parallel tracks, one public and the other totally private. Out loud, he spoke about his hypothesis; to himself, he was testing each statement against the experimental proof that he was sure he'd provide in the near future. Yet he wasn't prepared to tell anyone that he was even thinking of such experimental verification.

As his lecture proceeded, however, Cantor's confidence in his proposed experiment grew to conviction. He recovered his poise and, as in the last movement of a symphony, built up to a crescendo. Krauss never even removed his verbal rapier from its sheath, silent out of true admiration: Cantor's hypothesis was indeed an intellectual tour de force. Krauss had mentally rehearsed an appropriate accolade when Cantor presented him with an opportunity that would go down in Harvard history as one of the most famous quips in Kraussian lore.

Cantor was moving back and forth, writing with uncharacteristic speed in black and red on the plastic sheets, then stepping backward to point at the projected images on the screen. As he approached the end of his talk, he underlined the word "arginine" twice in red and then drew its chemical structure to call attention to the three incriminating amino groups. In his summation he returned once more to this key amino acid and triumphantly slashed two exclamation points behind that word, this time in black, then turned from the screen, flushed and breathing heavily, to face his audience.

Etiquette at such scientific talks follows a standard ritual; it hardly matters whether the subject matter is chemistry or cell biology. Invariably, the speaker ends by flashing a credit slide—not unlike the microsecond exposure in movies citing the gaffers, best boy, master electricians and the like—with numerous names. "Let me thank my collaborators listed on this slide for the skill and dedication that made this work possible; the National Institutes of Health for financial support; and you for your attention." At this point, the projectionist turns off the projector and switches on the lights, the audience applauds perfunctorily or enthusiastically as the occasion may warrant, and while the speaker fumbles with the microphone cord around his neck, the chairman rises to whisper to the speaker. After the expected nod, the former turns to the audience. "Dr. X has kindly consented to answer questions. Does anybody have one?" and without taking another breath proceeds with the first, and frequently also the second and third.

This is the scenario for most scientific talks, but not what happened at this particular noon seminar at the Harvard Medical School. Professor I. Cantor, although he used the first person plural in his talk, did not thank any collaborators. After all, he hadn't discussed any experimental work. He'd been talking about a hypothesis, *his* hypothesis. There was no concluding slide with names. As the lights went on, instead of the expected applause, he was greeted by a few giggles that grew into bursts of laughter. Cantor looked stunned.

3

"Where've you been, Jerry?" asked Stephanie, Cantor's secretary. "Professor Cantor wants to see you."

"The Prof? I thought he wasn't coming back from Boston until this afternoon."

"He caught a plane last night. He was here before I came in this morning."

What's I.C. up to? wondered Stafford.

"He's in his office." Stephanie motioned with her head. "Better go in right away. I've never seen him so impatient."

"Come in and close the door." Cantor pointed to one of the chairs facing his desk. "I didn't know you were keeping banker's hours."

Stafford didn't mind the implied complaint, indeed he was grateful that it was couched in terms that in Cantor would pass for humor. Unlike most members of his research team, Cantor was not a nocturnal creature. Stafford and the rest of Cantor's group assumed he spent his evenings keeping up with the literature in his field. Stephanie, his secretary, and very few others knew better. He was always in his office by eight in the morning, and he expected his coworkers to be available. Graduate students in most institutions are notoriously late risers, who work way past conventional bedtime. Cantor had no objection to their working late; he even encouraged it. But he also wanted them there when he was. Stafford still didn't care for the routine, and, whenever possible, he tried to beat the system.

"Not banker's hours, I.C.," Stafford replied. "Postdoc's. And only when you're out of town, and even then only rarely."

A faint smile crossed Cantor's face. Stafford knew he was the professor's favorite and that he was permitted a certain amount of levity, provided it was displayed in private. For an American professor, Cantor was unusually formal. He was also a very private person. Ever since his divorce, nearly a dozen years ago, no student had been invited to his home. Not even Stafford. Cantor's wife used to hold a big turkey dinner buffet for the entire group at Thanksgiving, an open house around Christmastime, occasional small get-togethers for the foreign fellows' wives—but these events belonged to a past beyond the memory of his present students.

"I thought you weren't due until this afternoon, I.C." Except for Stafford, nobody in the laboratory ever called Cantor "I.C." to his face. "Professor Cantor" or, on occasion, "Prof" was established etiquette. Only outsiders or professional equals "eye-seed" Cantor. Nobody remembered when Stafford had joined this select club. It was not that he had been specifically invited; one day he was just there. "How did your talk go at the Krauss seminar? Were they duly impressed?"

Cantor swiveled sideways in his chair so that he was facing the window rather than Stafford. He had a striking profile, dominated by thick, bushy eyebrows and a large nose that some called semitic, while others claimed that it reminded them of the profile on a Greco-Roman coin. He wore his carefully combed, wavy hair, dark brown with tinges of gray, rather long. It curled over the back of his collar and partly hid his large ears. His lips were full and always moist. Still gazing out the window, Cantor said, "They broke into thunderous"—he paused for effect—"laughter."

That's when he veered toward Stafford. It was one of his tricks, to surprise his listeners. He'd succeeded: bewilderment was drawn all over his student's face. "Laughter?"

"Yes, laughter. A real outburst . . . as soon as the lights went on."

Stafford was momentarily at a loss. He found it difficult to comprehend for several reasons. He couldn't imagine one of Cantor's polished talks ever being greeted by laughter—Cantor, who never told a joke during a lecture. And even if the inconceivable had happened, and the professor had laid an egg, it was so unlike him to disclose such a personal humiliation.

Cantor nodded. "You look just like I must have. I was flabbergasted. But then I realized, after a glance at the audience, that they weren't laughing at me but at something behind me. Do you know what I saw when I turned around?"

Stafford shook his head.

"It seems that, toward the end, I'd gotten so enmeshed in my talk that instead of marking on the overhead transparency, I started to draw on the screen itself. When I turned off the overhead projector and the room lights went up, there were all those black and red marks on the screen."

"My God, I.C.," Stafford exclaimed, "I wish I'd been there. What did you do?"

"I was so embarrassed, I took out my handkerchief, spat into it and started to rub one of the ink marks. Of course, that made an even bigger mess, which caused more titters and giggles. But then, Jerry"—he'd raised his right hand to stop Stafford's laughter—"Krauss jumped up from his seat and did something that I'll never forget: he ran forward and grabbed my hand. 'Don't clean the screen,' he said, 'just sign it. We can always get a new one. This talk will go down in history.' That's when they all started to applaud. The people actually rose and applauded."

Stafford was impressed. He'd never seen Cantor speak so candidly about himself—or display a pride that was enthusiastic rather than stiff. "That must've pleased you, I.C. Especially coming from Krauss."

"It did, but that wasn't all. After the talk, after we were alone, he said that this was the kind of idea a scientist gets only once in a lifetime, like Watson and Crick's double helix. Of course he was exaggerating. But you know what he said then?" Cantor didn't wait for a reply. "He said, 'They didn't get the Nobel Prize for years. But you,' he said, 'if only you people can devise an experiment . . .' It wasn't obvious whether he meant it as a wish or a challenge."

"Did Krauss have any suggestions about an experiment?"

Cantor's reply was instantaneous. "Of course not. Nobody did to whom I spoke on this trip. All they produced were the usual objections, as if I hadn't thought of them myself dozens of times. I know perfectly well that metastases are not just a characteristic of malignant cells, spreading from organ to organ. Lymphocytes, our natural defenses, also infiltrate other tissues, but there it's life-saving, not lethal." Without realizing it, Cantor had switched to a lecturing style. "Nobody has to remind me that frequent cell division is not by itself malignancy. Take wound healing or embryonic development. It's the timing, the location, that's different. For that matter, it isn't even clear whether the capacity for rapid division is germane to all tumor cells. Some tumors seem to grow only because the cells don't degenerate. Krauss's sarcoma, for instance."

Stafford's thoughts started drifting to the first time he'd given a talk, during his second year as a graduate student. He'd been asked to report on the progress of his research at a seminar attended by students from all research groups in the department, not just Cantor's. The audience hadn't laughed; they'd applauded in a perfunctory way. But he still remembered the hidden yawns, the glazed looks and drooping eyelids. The prof had been damn decent about it. Instead of criticizing him in public, Cantor had called him into his office. "Jeremiah," he'd said—he hadn't yet started calling him Jerry—"your talk was awful. All you told them today was how you're repeating the work of that group out West, studying phospholipids from marine sponges, so that you'd get some of their material for your membrane work. How can you take such promising results and make them sound so ploddingly dull? For heaven's sake, Jeremiah, you've got to learn how to excite your audience, how to convince them that what you're doing is really important. I don't mean to fake enthusiasm—show them what I see in your eyes or hear in your tone when you talk in the lab. And you took too much for granted by assuming your audience was familiar with sponges. *Never* make such an assumption. Many people don't even know that sponges are animals. I don't encourage the use of slides, but you could've jazzed up your presentation by a couple of those glorious underwater pictures we got with the sponge samples. Don't look so morose," he'd concluded, "you'll do fine—just remember what I'm telling you." Stafford had never forgotten.

Cantor had been gazing at the blackboard behind Stafford's back. Now he cleared his throat. "I know you're working on a project of your own. I've never before asked you to drop an experiment in midstream," he began, his eyes still fixed on some imaginary point behind Stafford, "but I'm going to do it now." Cantor's words had cut through Stafford's reverie, but the young man offered no response. Much as he respected his mentor, he always imagined himself in a subtle battle of strength in which he defended some private territory that Cantor would not be allowed to penetrate. "I've thought of an experiment," Cantor said slowly, eyes straying again to the blackboard. "It will transform my hypothesis into a theory of tumorigenesis to everybody's satisfaction—even Krauss's. It's an experiment that's going to work. I feel it in my bones and I want you to start on it—as of tomorrow." He stalked over to the blackboard and commenced to draw what he'd first set down on the back of the laundry form at the Hotel Sheraton Commander in Cambridge, Massachusetts: a fiendishly clever experiment with tagged proteins that involved no less than three different radioactive isotopes of carbon, hydrogen and sulfur as well as the nonradioactive, stable carbon isotope C-13. While the radioactive labels were intended to locate the protein in different cell fractions, the C-13 labeled arginine would shed light on the spatial arrangement of this amino acid within the protein molecule through its nuclear magnetic resonance spectrum. Only a cell biologist with a thorough background in chemistry would have come up with such an idea.

4

Branner, the exclusive girls' academy, was the only high school in Portland where the Latin class reached Ovid and even Virgil, and where one could take two years of calculus; it was one of the few obligatory stops in Oregon for Ivy League recruiters. It was also a school that believed truly in *mens sana in corpore sano* and insisted that each student concentrate seriously on at least one sport.

That is why in her senior year Celestine Price lost her virginity at the ungodly hour of 6:15 A.M. Competitive swimmers practiced three hours daily. Given Celestine's academic schedule, this meant entering the pool at six each morning for two hours of laps before classes and a third one at the end of the day. The regular gym teacher was a woman, but Branner's four top swimmers, groomed for statewide and Pacific Conference competitions, had a male coach. Eleven years ago, Glenn Larson had nearly made it onto the United States Olympic team. Now he was a computer programmer who moonlighted at Branner because, in addition to the extra income, it provided him with the opportunity to swim daily. He was always in the pool with the girls, and his superb body showed it.

The pool also offered ample opportunity for every sort of horseplay, which the girls—all but Celestine—exploited just so they could touch Larson's taut muscles. It was not that Celestine lacked a teenager's inclination for erotic play; rather it was her self-control. She wanted to be in sole charge of her innermost desires' ultimate realization, and that did not just apply to matters sexual. It was even truer of her professional ambitions, which were remarkably well planned out for a seventeen-year-old senior.

The Prices were Oregonians from way back, who had made their money originally in lumber but were now big in construction. Celestine's father, who died shortly after Celestine entered her teens, had been an engineer. She decided to follow in her father's footsteps. Her mother agreed, provided Celestine would accept the discipline of a Branner education with its full curriculum of Latin and math. In Mrs. Price's opinion, Latin was the only proper entry into the humanities, and math the door into the male world of science and engineering. By the time Celestine reached her senior year, she had switched from engineering to chemistry research as her career choice.

Celestine never got bored swimming laps. Once her arms and legs hit their pace, her mind tuned itself to her current fantasy list: accepting a medal for her latest discovery in science; breaking the 200-meter free-style Olympic record; selecting the man who would introduce her to the pleasures of sex. . . . Lately, she'd toyed with the idea that an older man, specifically Glenn Larson, might just be the right candidate. Larson had the body of Adonis; a small flower tattoo circled his navel, the thin stem disappearing into his bathing suit. One day, the waistband of his swimming trunks had slipped slightly and Celestine had caught sight of it. "So you like picking flowers?" she said. It was that question which led Larson to take a real chance—courting instant dismissal if they were caught.

"Celly," he replied, "we ought to work some more on your butterfly stroke. How about some extra practice? I could come next Saturday morning and spend a couple of hours with you."

"Next Saturday?" she asked slowly. "What time?"

"You name it."

Larson had never offered private coaching before. Was this the conscientious swimming coach speaking, or was there something else behind those words? She looked at the blue flower tattoo for a few seconds before replying, "The usual time. Nobody will disturb us at six o'clock on a Saturday morning. By the way, is it a bluebell?"

The pool and its locker rooms were in a separate building adjacent to the Branner gym. Larson arrived early to unlock the front door and changed quickly into his swimming trunks. In the water he started out on a fast crawl, then switched to a slower backstroke. Just as he turned to start a new lap, he saw Celestine leaning against the door of the coach's dressing room. She was wearing a long T-shirt with the words "A Woman's Place is on the Top" embossed across her chest—the logo of an all-girls group that had climbed Mount Hood that summer.

"Come in," he called, swimming in her direction, "I've been waiting for you."

She walked slowly toward the pool so that they reached the edge at the same time. "So have I," she said, "but I'm not ready yet. Why don't you come out?" Even though water was dripping from his body, Larson's mouth went dry as Celestine opened the door to his dressing room. By the time he entered, she was facing him with a towel.

"Here," she said, throwing the towel at him, "it's a pretty small room you've got here. And only one bench."

As a National Merit finalist, with her Virgil and calculus and swimming championships, Celestine had her choice of colleges. Her mother favored Bryn Mawr or Mount Holyoke, two Eastern women's colleges with strong science faculties. In the end, however, Celestine followed her Branner chemistry teacher's advice. "Both Holyoke and Bryn Mawr have excellent undergraduate programs in chemistry. Still, the union card for serious research is a Ph.D. Get it as quickly as possible. And if you ever want to get an academic position at a top university, you've got to get plucked into the old boys' network. The best way to accomplish this is to do postdoc work with two different mentors at two different institutions. If you turn out as well as I think you will, by the time you enter the job market, you'll have three men in three universities pushing for you. Make no mistake about it. Chemistry is still a man's world." To her mother's surprise, but not her teacher's, Celestine chose Johns Hopkins for its six-year combined B.S.-Ph.D. program.

In her second year at Johns Hopkins, Celestine took Professor Graham Lufkin's seminar on "Chemical Communication in Invertebrates." Lufkin lectured in exquisite detail, as only an expert who worked in the field could. The class was hushed as the professor talked about pheromones affecting the caste system among termites and described the death of the termite queen, who, after laying close to one hundred million eggs in ten or more years of spectacular productivity, finally turns infertile. "A crowd of workers surround her," Lufkin intoned, "and lick her—abrasively, not gently as they are wont to do during the prime of her life—for days on end, until her body has shrunk down to its shriveled skin." Celestine, the occasional romantic, never forgot that lecture.

But Celestine the chemist was particularly fascinated to learn about the isolation in 1959 of the first pheromone by the German chemist Butenandt and his associates. They had patiently collected and dissected nearly a million female silkworm moths over a period of twenty years to establish the chemical structure of their sex attractant. Now, using a technique developed by the Cornell chemist Wendell Roelofs, just a few hundred insects suffice for the identification of a pheromone in a matter of weeks. By attaching microelectrodes to the antennae of insects, Roelofs screened many chemicals for their capacity to elicit an electrically detectable response from a given insect, a signal exhibited strongly only for the bona fide sex attractant of its opposite sex. An entire new world had opened to Celestine: how to use chemical insight and apply it to biological problems.

Two days after she received an A+ in Lufkin's course, Celestine appeared in his office. "Did you come to find out about your grade, Miss Price?" he asked in his most formal manner. "You did very well."

"No, I've come to ask a favor."

"Go on." Lufkin moved his chair slightly closer, a sign that his own antennae were up.

"I'd like to do some independent reading about insect biochemistry. What do you recommend?"

Lufkin stroked his chin, as if contemplating her request. Actually he was inspecting Celestine in her white summer skirt, T-shirt and sandals—her long, bare legs; her muscular arms. She'd given up regular swimming—it was too time-consuming—but she stayed in shape by daily exercise. "Come back on Wednesday during my regular office hours," he finally replied. "I'll give you some relevant references."

Graham Lufkin was both a charmer and a rationalizer. He thought sexual contacts between faculty and students quite unprofessional. Contact with ex-students, on the other hand, was a different matter: a private relationship between consenting adults, which was nobody else's concern. His definition of "ex" was quite precise: the moment he signed the grade sheets for his course and sent them off to the registrar, the student became an "ex."

Lufkin kept his promise. Two days later, he presented Celestine with a list of papers: Bloch's work on sterol metabolism in insects; Nakanishi's isolation of phytoecdysones—insect molting hormones from plants, which probably act as defensive secretions; Röller's isolation and identification of the insect juvenile hormone, which keeps insects in their juvenile stages; the list went on. As he intoned the names and titles, Celestine was too excited to catch the change in Lufkin's voice when he concluded with, "By the way, I have an extra ticket to this Friday's Kronos Quartet performance. Would you like to join me?"

Celestine was still writing down the last reference. "Oh . . ." she said, "I have an aunt who plays chamber music. Yes, I'd love to."

He hadn't even offered to pick her up: they just met at the concert hall. Celestine knew little about the Kronos's specialty, modern chamber music, so she responded avidly to Lufkin's running commentary, delivered with fervor and knowledge in a low whisper, and shivered whenever his breath happened to blow ever so lightly into her ear. She had heard of Philip Glass, but not of Terry Riley or Alfred Schnittke; even Alban Berg's name—the fourth composer on the program—was only familiar by reputation. "Berg's most famous works are his two operas, *Wozzeck* and *Lulu*. Have you ever heard them?" She had not. Had Celestine ever been to an opera? No. "Ah, you should see *Lulu*. The type of character that almost convinces you that some human females secrete pheromones. Tell you what, Celestine"—she hadn't even noticed the sudden shift to her first name—"I live only fifteen minutes away. Stop at my house after the concert for some coffee and I'll play you the last act from *Lulu*, the part in which Jack the Ripper murders her. I've got the newest recording with Boulez conducting and Teresa Stratas in the lead role."

Celestine went and was again impressed: the ultramodern furniture, the books, the prints by artists even she had heard of, the conversation, the man's elegance and wit. After an hour, Lufkin drove her home.

He let her wait for a couple of weeks before telephoning one morning. "Celestine? This is Graham Lufkin. I hope I didn't wake you?" Upon learning that she'd just finished her weight-lifting exercises, he asked, "Weight lifting? So that's why you are in such wonderful shape. Do you do this every morning?"

"Except when I've got an eight o'clock class," she replied.

"What color leotard do you wear when you lift weights?"

Celestine looked down at her naked, glistening breasts, droplets of sweat running down to her belly. "Oh, just skin colored."

"How about having dinner with me at my place this Saturday? I'm a passable cook and I can be an entertaining host."

"I know that already," she said.

"Will you come?"

"Sure. Why not?"

The affair between Graham Lufkin and Celestine Price lasted for nearly a year. During that entire period Celestine didn't see another man. Lufkin never demanded monogamy from her and she had no idea whether he slept with other women. The nights and sometimes weekends—like the time he took her to New York to see her first opera—sufficed. She felt that the quality of intercourse with him—intellectual as well as sexual—was far superior to what her male peers could offer. At the end of her third year at Hopkins, she felt ready to begin her Ph.D. research.

Both Lufkin and Celestine agreed that their sexual intimacy

precluded any possibility of a more professional relationship. This did not stop Lufkin, however, from offering advice about picking a Ph.D. supervisor. "I know what the people in your department will tell you: work with one of the big-shot professors." He spoke with the gruff brevity of the self-assured. "They have more money, bigger research groups, and frequently they work on a variety of problems." His right index finger pointed at Celestine like a cocked pistol. "As a beginning graduate student, you're likely to be a small fish in a rather big pond. Don't reject out of hand the thought of working with a young hotshot assistant professor, somebody who'll still work in the lab. She's likely . . ."

"She?"

"Yes, she. I have somebody in mind for you—Jean Ardley. She's only been an assistant professor for two years, but she's got an excellent background. Got her Ph.D. in organic chemistry with another woman at Brown, and then did two postdocs." Lufkin had assumed his usual faculty adviser style, replete with authority and a surfeit of minutiae. "One at the Salk Institute in Guillemin's lab on peptides—he's the man who shared a Nobel Prize for his hypothalamic hormone work—and a couple of years in Texas with Röller. Remember, he's the insect physiologist who discovered the first juvenile hormone."

"How do you know so much about her? I've hardly run into her in our department."

He gave a dismissive shrug. "Chemistry is a big department. I don't even know whether she teaches any undergraduate courses."

Celestine eyed him curiously. "She isn't by any chance . . ."

"Celly! Don't say it." Lufkin was not smiling.

"Sorry."

"I got to know her a bit because she's come to me for some technical advice. She's starting on a damned interesting line of research—one that should suit a chemist like you with serious biological ambitions." Lufkin anchored her eyes before continuing. "You might as well get a female role model in graduate school and find out how she did it. What the costs are. How her male colleagues treat her." He pointed to himself. "There are still so few women in academic chemistry, you're unlikely to find one for your postdoc stint."

Celestine leaned forward. "Is that how you found your Ph.D. supervisor? Did somebody give you a sales talk . . ."

"Sales talk?" Lufkin started to pace back and forth. "Is that what you think this is? I wish somebody had given me some serious advice about the professors in the department when I arrived as a budding grad student. No, I did it the usual way: I shopped around, meeting faculty members, seeing which seemed the nicest. The trouble is that during those interviews they're usually on their best behavior. Few students realize that picking a Ph.D. mentor is probably the single most important decision they make when they start their graduate work. It's really like an orphan picking a new father . . ."

"Shouldn't you have said 'mother'?"

"Don't knock the fathers, Celly. Besides, there weren't any mothers in our department when I started out for my Ph.D."

5

They hadn't seen each other for over half a year. Not since that breakfast when, after a particularly passionate and long-drawn-out morning, Lufkin said apropos of nothing, "Celly, my lovely one, I don't think we should see each other anymore. At least not this way." He made an all-encompassing gesture with his hand. "What started out as a joyful affair between two adults has become complicated."

"Complicated?" She looked startled. "What do you mean?"

"I'm well on the way to falling in love with you."

"And what's complicated about that?"

"I'm some thirty years older than you."

"Thirty-five, to be precise."

"You're right, Celly, thirty-five. There you have it in a nutshell: when you reach the ripe old age of thirty-five, I'll be a doddering seventy."

"Don't be silly, Graham." She had never called him Graham before. "When I'm a doddering seventy, you'll be a horny hundred and five."

Lufkin leaned across the table and kissed her forehead. "You're a jewel. You may think I'm crazy . . . you may even be angry . . . but eventually, you'll understand that this is wiser."

Now she called him on the phone. "Graham," she said, "this is Celestine. I'd like to see you."

"Celly, how are you?" Lufkin's voice was uncharacteristically low.

"Working hard."

"It'd be tempting to see you again, but—"

Celestine cut him off. "Professor, I want to make an appointment in your office."

The moment Celestine sat down, she explained why she'd come. Last year, she reminded him, she'd followed his advice and had now completed her first year as a graduate student under Professor Jean Ardley. Her research project, the isolation and characterization of a newly discovered cockroach hormone, allatostatin, was going well. Lufkin started to tap his right middle finger on the desk. He knew all this. What was the real purpose of the visit? Seeing that he was getting impatient, Celestine sprung her surprise: a piece of academic scuttlebutt Lufkin had not known. Would it be wise for her to drop out of the six-year B.S.-Ph.D. program after her fourth year in order to follow her thesis preceptor to her new tenured associate professorship in the Midwest?

"I suppose I can't blame Jean for wanting to leave," Lufkin mused. "Getting tenure elsewhere after only three years as assistant professor at Hopkins isn't a bad move. But if you go with her, it means withdrawing from the fast track at Hopkins and entering a standard graduate curriculum. It could easily mean losing two years. Are you prepared to do that?"

"That's exactly why I came. You're the only one who knows why I started with Jean. It was good advice you gave me. But two extra years?"

She had shown good judgment in consulting Lufkin about her professional career. He wasn't a member of the chemistry department and had no vested interest in the possible loss of a very promising graduate student. Even their personal relationship had ended months ago. "You're working on a damned exciting project," he said. "You'd find it very difficult to continue your research here with Ardley hundreds of miles away. If she leaves, I bet they won't even maintain the insectary here. What would you do—have her ship you fresh cockroaches every few days? You might even end up starting on another project with a new thesis adviser. That would certainly cost you a year or two. Celly, if your research with Jean pans out, if you can establish the structure of the hormone, if . . ."

"What's your point?" Celestine's edginess showed.

"My point is that two years isn't much if you are successful with a project of this magnitude. And especially if you publish it with a professor who's not yet too well known."

That was all Celestine needed to hear. At the end of the school year, she packed her bags and followed Jean Ardley to her new university.

Celestine only pretended to be asleep. Actually, she'd been reflecting on how her two university choices had affected her experience with serious male companionship. Glenn Larson hardly counted. She'd been too blasé about him: when she decided at Branner that the time had come to lose her virginity, she'd treated that episode like an experiment rather than a romantic interlude. Lufkin had been different: more like a mentor. And now Stafford. Celestine couldn't help but compare the two. It wasn't that she didn't enjoy Jerry's hand moving up her thigh, its skin smooth as the shell of an egg. He just hadn't learned yet that deft touch of Graham Lufkin. But then Lufkin was a tenured professor of biology with years of experience, whereas Jeremiah Stafford—barely a Ph.D.—was only just shedding his Baptist repressions. She was certain, though, that Stafford would improve. This was only the second night they'd spent together, and this morning he'd really tried to take his time. The only thing she wasn't sure about was whether she'd be able to overcome his reluctance to utter barely a single word while making love. His Southern Baptist upbringing was still too ingrained. Even during prolonged foreplay, he used only one Baptist word to describe male and female genitalia or intercourse itself. The word was "it." Celestine, on the other hand, under the tutelage of Graham Lufkin, had become very much a verbal lover. She told Stafford with precise urgency what she wanted him to do next; she announced in lascivious detail what she intended to do to him; she cried out lustily and ended laughing at his silent nod, his answer to her question, "Wasn't that a good fuck?"

"Christ, do you know what time it is?" Celestine jumped out of bed, pulling the blanket off Stafford. "It's already eight-forty. You won't be in the lab before ten. I won't even have time to do my exercises."

"You've already had enough exercise this morning. Come on back to bed and give me the damn blanket. It's cold this morning."

"No, we can't, Jerry. I've got to go to the lab. We've got a new batch of *corpora cardiaca* from cockroaches and I've got to extract them this morning. Jean will be pissed off if I don't have the stuff lyophilized this afternoon."

"Damn the *corpora cardiaca*," he said in mock exasperation. "I don't even know what that is. I want your *corpora*."

"I've got only one *corpus*, Dr. Stafford. The cockroach has two *corpora cardiaca*, which are the organs that secrete my precious hormone. Haven't you ever had any Latin?"

In the shower, she asked, "How come you've got so much time all of a sudden? I thought your Professor Cantor was so demanding. The last time you were here . . ."

"What do you mean, last time? It was the only time I was here. I wish you didn't have a roommate."

"What's wrong with Leah? It was damn nice of her not to sleep here last night."

"That was last night. How often do you think she'll do that?" He was soaping her buttocks.

"This feels good," she purred. "Give me the soap, it's my turn."

As they were drying each other, she continued. "But seriously, how come you've got all this time? I thought you were always in the lab so early . . . or were you fibbing when you gave me that song and dance about how busy you people are in cell biology?"

Celestine had met Stafford in a chemistry department seminar dealing with spin labeling. The speaker was Harden McConnell from Stanford, the developer of a technique involving stable free radicals and electron spin resonance, which had turned out to be of considerable utility in cell membrane work. Cantor had wanted Stafford to learn about it. Unlike many biologists, the professor had never considered instruments as simply black boxes spilling out data. He insisted that his students learn the theory behind each instrumental technique. And so Stafford found himself sitting next to Celestine Price. He knew next to nothing about the properties of organic stable free radicals—he hadn't taken organic chemistry since his sophomore year at the University of South Carolina—and had turned to his neighbor for some enlightenment. Celestine immediately noticed his huge eyes, except that they seemed slightly off-beam, as if he were looking at two objects simultaneously. They were particularly striking set in his narrow face with its wide mouth.

That same evening, they met for coffee and dessert at the Student Union and two days later Stafford learned how to make love to Celestine Price. It was very different from his only other sexual encounter—a very brief and rather clumsy mutual exploration between two virgins in Columbia, South Carolina. Stafford was dazzled; he was hooked. Celestine's initial feelings could best be described as bemused affection: she was impressed by Stafford's scientific intellect, by the intensity with which he spoke about his research and academic ambitions, and touched by his sexual naiveté. Her new role as teacher excited her.

"I.C. isn't supposed to be back until this afternoon. He's giving a seminar at Harvard at Krauss's place. You know who Krauss is?"

Celestine shook her head. "Who?"

"In our field, probably the most powerful guy in the country. I'm surprised he hasn't won the Nobel. There's even a sarcoma named after him."

"Big deal. What's another sarcoma?"

"Don't say that. This one is important, like Peyton Rous's."

"And who is he?" Celestine sounded snappy. She didn't like scientific name dropping, at least not names that were totally unfamiliar to her. "He's not exactly a name in invertebrate biochemistry."

"He won the Nobel Prize. That ought to show you how important a sarcoma can be. Anyway, I.C.'s got this new idea about tumors and a two-way passage of proteins through the cell membrane, and it's the first time he's talking about it anywhere else other than the seminar he gave at our group lunch. He seemed nervous about presenting it at Harvard—I've never seen him that way before. It's a spectacular idea, but I guess he wants to see how the competition looks at it. That's why he's stopping to see some people on the way, Benacerraf at Harvard and Luria at MIT. They're friends of his. They've both got Nobel Prizes."

"What's all this Nobel Prize business?"

"What about it?" Stafford had turned defensive. "It's true. They all won the Nobel Prize."

"I believe you. It's just that I'm wondering why you have to mention it each time you get to a person's name."

They'd been dressing, and Stafford was about to put on his shoes. He straightened up to face Celestine. "I guess it's because we've been talking about it a lot recently in our group. If Cantor's hypothesis—that there's one cause to all cancer initiation—is right, he might get one. Of course, it's a big 'if.' "

"Listen, Jerry, I don't know anything about cancer. But isn't it awfully unlikely that there's one mechanism behind all tumors?"

"Unlikely, yes. But it's not impossible. I.C. thinks it all starts with a subtle change in the structure and composition of a certain protein. That's where the big 'if' comes in. He'll have to test it, of course, and right now nobody has the foggiest idea how. I'm glad I'm not working on it. I couldn't afford to take such a gamble. I've got to publish a few more papers on my own this year if I want to get the job I'm after."

"That I understand. But tell me, why are you doing your postdoc with the same man with whom you got your Ph.D.? Wouldn't it make more sense to go elsewhere?"

"Sure. But I.C. is special. He could have a research group three times our size—like the superstars at Berkeley or MIT. After all, he's in the same class. He sure has no problems getting grants from places like the NIH and the American Cancer Society. But the guy still does some work in the lab! Just name one other man in his position who does that."

"Jean Ardley still works in the lab. Almost every day."

"Jean Ardley?"

"Yes, Jean Ardley," she repeated firmly. Stafford could see her nostrils flaring.

"But, Celly." In his attempt to act conciliatory, he only made matters worse. "Ardley is not in I.C.'s class. She's just . . ." He was about to say "a young woman," but then he compromised. "She only started a few years ago."

6

"How was it?"

"It was very decent of you not to come home last night."

"That's not what I asked. How was your night? What's he like?"

"He's great." Celestine set the table. "We're having chicken Florentine and brown rice. And for dessert I got your favorite: Häagen-Dazs cherry vanilla. You really deserve it for last night."

Leah Woodeson hugged her roommate. "It was nothing. I wasn't exactly raised in a convent, you know. You said he was great. I know you scientists have a limited vocabulary, but what's 'great'? A great lay? A great conversationalist? A great what?"

Celestine, whose mouth was full, pointed by way of explanation at the flowers in the vase by the window.

"I missed them when I came in. Did he send them to you today?" asked Leah.

"Look at the note."

"You're certainly terse tonight," said Leah as she reached for the torn envelope.

> Dearest Celly: You're graceful and lovely. Your form is majestic, your constancy cardinal, your excellence royal. Studying you, I note your limpid gaze, felicitous expression, your dazzling waist. What unflawed throat, what masterly jaw, what phenomenal flesh! What a firmly rounded body, what well-favored flanks,

what a curved chest, what shapely legs, what solid breasts, what muscular arms, what longish fingers, what fast feet, what lower lip, what nibbling teeth, what wicked tongue! No wonder you're called Celestine. When will you open your door again?

Leah's reading was punctuated by titters, finally culminating in loud laughter.

"What's come over you?" Celestine sounded testy. "Don't you find it charming?"

"Charming? It's adorable, precious and . . . so funny. Don't get me wrong, Celly, you do have great flanks. But who wrote this? Not Jeremiah?"

Celestine nodded. "It's his note."

"Celly, he may have *written* that, but he couldn't have *composed* it. You told me he was a biologist. They don't write like that. In fact, nobody does, not near the end of the twentieth century. Trust me." Leah put one arm over her friend's shoulder. "Listen, it's charming, but I bet he copied it. Look here"—she pointed—" 'your form is majestic' . . . 'your constancy cardinal.' It's at least a couple of hundred years old. Actually, now that I read it again, I take that back. He didn't plagiarize, he just paraphrased. He must've gotten some out of the Norton and found the rest in a thesaurus. 'Masterful jaw' and 'phenomenal flesh' don't ring right next to 'cardinal constancy.' You've got to ask him, will you?"

Celestine shook her head. "You do it, the next time he comes." A smile started to appear on her face. "Does Richard ever write any love letters to you?"

"He hasn't yet. He's the oral type."

"I bet he's afraid to put anything on paper in case you take it apart. Knowing your talents as a deconstructionist, I'd be afraid."

"Deconstructionist? Celly, you didn't know the meaning of the word till you met me."

Ten days later, Leah Woodeson, in a bathrobe, was curled up in the only easy chair in their small living room, drinking her third cup of coffee and reading. She looked over the page as she heard the front door open. "Sneaking in at nine-fifteen in the morning, Miss Price? What's going to happen to the march of science?"

"It's marching right back to bed. I'm exhausted." As she passed by Leah's chair, Celestine looked over her friend's shoulder. "What are you reading?"

Leah held up the *London Review of Books*. "An article by Mitchell about the golden age of criticism. In case you don't know, the golden age is now and my type of work on dialogism is the cutting edge. Look what he wrote about literary criticism." She thrust the open page at Celestine. " 'Experimentalism is associated with the search for the new, the untried, the bizarre or the perverse.' Not bad, eh? So how was last night? Bizarre or perverse?"

"Actually, I want to talk to you about that."

"You do?" Leah mimicked a prurient leer. "Finally! When it comes to matters sexual, you're too secretive. I'm all ears."

"Leah, stop kidding, I'm serious. Last night, Jerry asked if I'd consider living with him."

"And what did you say?"

"I said I'd think about it."

"And would you really consider living with him?"

"Yes, I would," said Celestine after a pause. "He's a decent guy, he's honest. He says he's in love with me. Besides, Jerry made a good point. We're both at a stage in our research where we'll have to work our asses off. His Professor Cantor put him on some hush-hush super-urgent project, and Jean and I are about to start on the most difficult part of our research. He said having a stable relationship would be good for our science." Celestine fell silent; when she finally looked up and saw Leah's face, she asked, "What's the matter?"

"Who's going to teach you about Bakhtin?"

Celestine embraced her friend. "You're right, who will? If I mention Bakhtin around the lab, they'll probably ask, 'Where does he publish?' Until I met you a year ago, I didn't know anything about Bakhtin or, for that matter, semiotics, dialogism, poststructuralism, and all the other fancy isms you throw around. I'll miss them. And especially you, Leah." She gave her another hug.

"So you've made up your mind?"

Celestine nodded. "I haven't told Jerry, but yes, I have."

"Celly, why don't you have both cakes?"

"What do you mean?"

"Have you considered asking him to move in with us?"

"No." Celestine looked nonplussed. "You wouldn't mind?"

"In theory, no. All you'd have to do is to get a double bed. And I'd save some money on the rent. But first, I've got to interview him."

The interview dissolved into hilarity when Stafford's flower letter was "deconstructed." He admitted that its source was a Renaissance love letter he'd found in *Lives of the Courtesans* and even produced the original. He'd just changed the adjectives.

"Celly," Leah giggled, reading over the text, "did you know that, in your Renaissance existence, your constancy was 'papal,' your flesh 'miraculous'?" She turned to Stafford, poking him with her look. "How come you read *Lives of the Courtesans?*" she demanded.

"I ran into it when I went to the bookstore to buy a copy of the collected poems of T. S. Eliot." He raised his hand to stop her from interrupting. "I know. 'Why T. S. Eliot?' Professor Cantor told me to read him."

"That still leaves one question."

"Okay, okay. Why did Cantor suggest I buy a copy of Eliot's collected poems?"

"Of course. Even if I were not in lit crit, I'd still be curious about why one biologist tells another to read T. S. Eliot."

"When the prof first talked about a unifying theory of tumor generation, he quoted a line that stuck in my memory: 'We had the experience but missed the meaning,/ And approach to the meaning restores the experience. . . .' I asked him afterward where it came from, and he said Eliot's *Four Quartets*. He said you can find a lot of different meanings in the poem, like in a little Bible. So being a Bible-reading ex-Baptist, or maybe an ex-Bible-reading Baptist, I went out to buy a copy."

"And do you remember which quartet it came from?" asked Leah.

" 'The Dry Salvages,' " he said triumphantly, and then nudged Celestine. "You know, Celly, Eliot also won the Nobel Prize."

7

"Never run after it—just wait." Cantor didn't remember who'd first said that about the Nobel Prize. But why are we supposed to behave like maidens aspiring to become brides? he wondered. Why must prospective Nobelists always act like innocents, never acknowledging in public their eligibility?

Professor I. Cantor knew perfectly well that he was eligible for a Nobel Prize—in fact, in recent months the subject had never been far from his mind. Timing was critical: if he were to win the Prize, it would happen during the next three or, at most, four years, while his field was still red hot. These days, research in every area of molecular biology moved at such dazzling speed that results which only a few years ago were considered spectacular were now accepted as routine. Genetic engineering is only one example. How many beginning graduate students still remember the names of the two men who did the first recombinant DNA experiment but never got the Nobel for it? It's like struggling up a high mountain, where only recently two men had planted the first flag upon the peak, to find a ski resort under construction.

In the cancer field, however, a generalized theory of tumor production is Mount Everest or K-2. Only superstars climb such peaks, and even they use Sherpas. I. Cantor was such a superstar, and Stafford became his Sherpa. One aspect of this analogy between scientific research and mountain climbing—it's done because it's there—has been overworked. But there is another facet to the analogy, one less often noted: in either endeavor, the climber frequently moves sideways or even backward to get around a particularly aggravating obstacle. Cantor, who'd been working in the cancer field for years, had made many such moves in his time. Yet every once in a while the climber finds an unexpected route, never exploited by others, that appears to lead straight to the top. The pleasure of that discovery, though brief—after all, it must be followed by the actual assault—can be spine-tingling.

Yet Cantor differed in several respects from the superstars in universities that counted Nobel laureates by the dozen. Only one Nobel Prize had ever been won at Cantor's Midwestern university, and that was back in the 1930s. Getting a Nobel five decades later would put Cantor in a class all by himself. You couldn't do that at Harvard or Berkeley, where Nobels came in every few years. And although by ordinary standards Cantor had a respectably sized research group, by design his was much smaller than many Harvard-MIT-Berkeley operations, some of which exceeded thirty members, most of whom were treated simply as pairs of hands. There, the superstars heading the labs served primarily as fund raisers and as spokesmen for their groups at major scientific congresses; they certainly didn't do any lab work themselves. But Cantor had a private laboratory next to his office, and, even more importantly, still managed to spend a bit of time in it. "Just enough to keep me honest," he'd brag occasionally. Of course, Cantor also traveled all over the globe; he loved to talk about the latest accomplishments of his research group to colleagues and students. Yet he never worried about getting scooped, whereas some of the other laboratory heads ran their operations like the CIA. No wonder bright graduate students such as Stafford competed for the few vacancies in his lab. Usually, Cantor was both comfortable and informal with his favorite disciple —at least as informal as the very formal Cantor could ever get.

When Cantor began to sketch the plans for his experiment on the blackboard, however, something was different, and Stafford sensed it. The professor finished writing and Stafford stopped scribbling on the pad in his lap. Cantor, in his white lab coat—an affectation that most superstars (outside of hospitals) did not share—had returned to his desk. He'd started playing with some paper clips, slipping one into another to form a chain. It was long enough for a bracelet when he finally looked up. "Jerry," he said and then stopped. He lengthened the bracelet to a choker. "I must ask you something that will probably surprise you. I don't want you to talk about this project with anybody, even in my lab. You do understand why I want this to be kept quiet, don't you, Jerry?" Cantor almost seemed to be pleading as he leaned forward. The paper clip chain jingled faintly as it hung from his hand. "This is not the usual 'if' experiment: 'If it doesn't work we'll do this, and if it does, then we'll do that.' This"—he pointed to the blackboard—"has *got* to work, and when it's done, it's finished. Jerry"—Cantor gripped the side of his desk—"this experiment will be in all the textbooks; it's the sort you do once in a lifetime. Look how lucky you are: you aren't even twenty-eight years old, while I . . ."

Cantor's voice trailed off as he gazed at his young collaborator with affection and a tinge of envy. When it came to laboratory technique and perseverance, Stafford was absolutely tops, and to that extent deserved this chance. And what a chance it was! If only he'd been offered such an opportunity at the age of twenty-eight.

He wondered whether his old professor would have approached him under such circumstances. Probably not. But then Stafford was an exception—even among his own students. During the past couple of years, Jerry had practically become his younger alter ego. When Cantor resumed, his voice had recovered its customary briskness, business as usual. "Jerry, you know what's at stake here. It can't take longer than three months—not if you drop everything and start right away. Better head for the library now—and look into who else has used that Maeda technique. It's the usual density-gradient differential centrifugation but with a clever twist: he alternates between a stepwise and a continuous gradient. It ought to help you locate our protein in cellular plasma membranes. If I were you, I'd start with the *Citation Index*. You should thank God for it. When I was your age, all we had was *Index Medicus* or *Chemical Abstracts*."

It was true, the *Citation Index* simplified life. In contrast to all of the other bibliographic aids that searched the literature backward, this one did it forward. Maeda's original paper had been published in 1983. The *Citation Index* would list all publications *since* 1983 citing the Maeda paper and thus would lead Stafford quickly to other workers who had used the same method. It would save Stafford hours, but he knew all that, and Cantor knew that Jerry knew. Even though he suspected that the younger man would be irritated, Cantor could never resist the temptation to point out how much tougher research had been in the old days.

"I can't imagine how you managed, I.C.," said Stafford, and immediately felt sorry that he'd let himself be provoked. "It's a great experiment," he added. "I just hope I won't disappoint you."

8

Celestine had set the alarm for 6:55 A.M. She'd stayed up past midnight waiting for Stafford, but he hadn't appeared. In the five minutes before seven o'clock, she rolled over to his slumbering form. "Wake up, you creep," she murmured affectionately. "Where's all that regular sex life you promised?"

Stafford hardly stirred. "Hey, wake up." She shook him more vigorously. "Don't you have to go to the lab this morning?"

When she received no response, she rose from the bed. "Okay, I'll let you sleep while I exercise. But then watch out."

At 7:30 Celestine, dripping with sweat, returned to the bed where Stafford was still deep asleep. She ran her hands over her wet body, lifted the blanket and with her slippery hands started to massage him.

"Where were you last night, Jerry?" she asked as they were showering together. He still didn't seem fully awake: his eyes, puffy, weren't focusing on her. "I waited up until almost one and then I couldn't stay awake any more."

"I didn't get home until after three. I was in the lab."

"At 3 A.M.? Doing what, for God's sake? Fucking somebody in the stockroom?"

"Don't be crude, Celly. I'm so bushed these days, I'm not up to it."

"You're telling me." She soaped his flaccid penis. "What's really going on with you?"

While Stafford was still climbing toward the top, Celestine was ready to celebrate. She had achieved her first major success: determining the entire sequence of amino acids in the chain of the cockroach neurohormone allatostatin—an indispensable step toward discovering a new approach to insect control. "Allatostatin is like a necklace with sixty-four beads made of twenty precious stones," she'd explained to Leah at breakfast. "Before you can make another, you've got to figure out the exact order in which these stones are strung. That's exactly what I've done."

"Is that so tough?" asked Leah.

"Not in words or even on paper. These days, there are all kinds of techniques to accomplish the actual sequencing. Like using an amino acid analyzer: a machine that does this almost automatically by chopping off one amino acid—one stone of my necklace—at a time and identifying it. Or the technique I used: partial enzymatic cleavage and high-resolution mass spectrometry." Celestine reached for a pencil and smoothed out the crumpled paper napkin. In one stroke, she drew a circle and then added a series of small balls to mimic a bracelet. "The enzymes break the sixty-four-stone chain into a few smaller fragments"—she slashed the chain with her pencil as if the enzyme had already ruptured it—"and each of these— an incredibly small amount, picograms really—is then analyzed in a mass spectrometer. This not only gives me the exact number of different atoms in each amino acid molecule but also allows me to figure out the structure of the acid: how the atoms are actually arranged. Then all I had to do was determine how these few substrands are arranged within the necklace. That's what I finally did" —she drew three exclamation points on the napkin—"and that's why I've invited Jean Ardley for Thursday evening."

In the end, the party for four turned into dinner for three. Stafford telephoned at the last moment. "Don't wait for me, Celly. I can't leave yet, I'm in the middle of an experiment. I'll try to make it for coffee." Even though he sounded apologetic, Celestine slammed down the receiver.

To regain her composure, she opened the wine bottle in the

kitchen and took a sip. She could taste the tannin. The clerk in the liquor store had recommended that she let this red wine breathe before serving it. Right now the bitter taste matched her mood. With the bottle and three glasses on a tray Celestine marched into the living room. "Where is your Dr. Stafford?" asked her professor, noting the three glasses. "I was curious to meet the man who caught my favorite coworker."

" 'Caught' isn't exactly the right word, Professor Ardley. Nobody catches Celestine Price," said Leah, who for tonight's occasion wore a loose, soft skirt, freshly pressed blouse and loafers, rather than her usual uniform of jeans and Adidases. "Celly makes her own decisions."

"You're telling me," laughed the woman. "I certainly wasn't the one to persuade one of Hopkins's top chemistry candidates to jump off her Ph.D. express. It was her decision to join me out here on the slow lane. It wasn't such a bad choice, though, was it, Celly? By the way"—she turned back to Leah—"call me Jean. Only undergraduates call me 'Professor Ardley.' "

"All right, then," replied Leah, "come to the table, Jean."

Jean Ardley was a short woman, on the plump side, who favored pants, because they were more convenient in the lab, and relatively high heels. This evening, she wore smartly cut black slacks and a black silk blouse, against which her sandy hair looked almost blond. At work, it was usually arranged in a pony tail or tied in a knot on top of her head, but on more formal occasions, including lectures, she let it fall straight down to just below her shoulders. Her blue eyes and the chameleonlike fashion with which her face changed were her best features. Blue eye shadow and long earrings were her only adornments; her fingers were ringless.

After the three women finished eating, Leah brought a pot of coffee from the kitchen. "Jean," she said, "I hope you won't mind my asking this. You must be in your middle thirties. How old are you precisely?"

"Thirty-four. Why do you ask?"

"The usual reason for a woman aspiring to an academic career: how to combine it with motherhood. It seems that, at age thirty-four, you've pretty well made it—at least that's how it looks from where I'm sitting. You've even got tenure. So my question is this: do you plan to have any children?"

"I've never had the nerve to ask you that, Jean," Celly added, "but I've wondered. Leave it to Leah to ask the blunt questions."

Jean Ardley looked at the two young women, their eyes fixed on her. "I don't mind," she replied slowly. "I've still got a few years— maybe even ten. But I might as well tell you: last year, I had my tubes tied."

A long silence passed before Leah spoke up. "I know it's none of our business—"

"Go ahead."

"Why get sterilized? Why not—"

"Contraception? I'd been on the Pill for nearly eighteen years. I was an early starter, you see. I felt it was time to go off, even though I'm not a smoker. We could've switched to something else, condoms, for instance, but I finally decided that, given my professional ambitions, I just couldn't do justice to motherhood."

"Why didn't your husband have a vasectomy?" asked Leah.

"Why should he? It was my decision not to have children, not his. You never can tell. He might get married again. It could be twenty years later and he could still have children—"

"I don't get this about your professional ambitions," interrupted Leah. "Why couldn't you have a child, now that you have tenure?"

"You're right about tenure. It would've been impossible before. I'd say that in chemistry, or for that matter in most laboratory sciences, you just can't be a mother and get tenure during the six years you've got as an assistant professor. At least not in the big research universities. My male peers put in at least eighty hours a week. That's why many of their marriages don't work out—if they marry at all."

"Unless they marry another assistant professor on the same treadmill," interjected Celestine.

"And they're lucky enough to find jobs in the same university or at least within commuting distance of each other," Ardley rejoined. "Of course, you might be really fortunate enough to live with a man like my husband, who is professionally mobile. But I overstated the case: it's not impossible—just extremely difficult—to have a child and work toward tenure. Maybe it's easier in your field"—she motioned toward Leah—"because you can do some of your research at home. But what if you've got to be in the lab?" She shrugged. "Nowadays, the promotion committees are supposed to take pregnancy into consideration, but most of the people running them are still men, and older men at that. They've been taught about the legal aspects of sex discrimination, but they don't know beans about the real facts. Do you know that not a single chemistry department in any of the leading American universities has ever had a woman as chairperson? Except for the famous Chien-shiung Wu at Columbia it would also be true in physics. Isn't it funny that they usually call her 'Madame Wu' rather than 'Professor,' as if she were running a bordello?" Ardley picked up her cup.

"Jean, your coffee must be cold by now. Let me bring you a fresh cup," offered Celestine.

"But you did get tenure—and fairly early at that," observed Leah. "Wouldn't it be easier now to have a child?"

"That's exactly why I moved from Hopkins after only three years. When they offered me tenure here, I thought, Now I can have child after child and they can't do a thing about it. But Celestine"—she motioned with her head toward the kitchen—"can tell you that the realities are quite different. My entire group is now concentrating on a very exciting area—the chemistry of invertebrate neuropeptides—and I'm working harder than I ever did before, even though now I've got five grad students and even a couple of postdocs to help. I don't know if it's true in your field. I guess it wouldn't be, not in English literature—"

"Criticism," interrupted Celestine, who'd just arrived with fresh coffee, "in fact, dialogism."

"Dialogism?"

"I'll tell you later, Jean," offered Leah. "First finish what you were saying."

At that moment the door opened and Stafford entered. "I'm

sorry," he announced, breathing as if he'd run up the three flights of steps. "Professor Ardley, I'm Jeremiah Stafford," he said, approaching the table. "I've been wanting to thank you. If it weren't for you, I'd never have met Celly. Boy, I'm hungry. Is there anything left to eat?"

Celestine followed him into the kitchen. "Damn you, Jerry," she whispered, "I know what it's like to work hard in the lab. But why couldn't you make it for dinner tonight? You knew it was a special occasion—Jean has never been here before. Besides"—she grabbed him by the shoulders—"we were celebrating my cracking the allatostatin structure."

Stafford tried to mollify her. "Celly, I said I was sorry. You've no idea what pressure I.C. is putting on me. Every day now, he's after me: asking me how the experiment is doing, what stage of it I've gotten to, when it's going to be finished. Not *if* it's going to *work: when* it's going to be *finished*. I couldn't leave—"

"Hey, what's the matter with you two?" Leah stuck her head into the kitchen.

Ardley and Leah moved to the sofa; Celestine, still steaming, occupied the easy chair, while Stafford sat by the table wolfing down a plate of leftovers. Ardley was addressing him. "I've just been explaining to our literary critic here what a marvelous job Celly did. It's not just the sequencing. The really tough part was to isolate enough allatostatin in the first place. It took us well over a year. Every step in the isolation had to be followed by a complicated bioassay."

"What's allatostatin really good for?" asked Leah.

"For the cockroach or for us?" asked Ardley.

"Both."

"Well, let's start with the cockroach. Allatostatin serves as a hormonal signal, which at the appropriate time turns off the *corpora allata*—a pair of glands that are responsible for the secretion of another hormone, the so-called 'juvenile hormone.' It was characterized in the 1960s by Herbert Röller—I spent part of my postdoc with him. This hormone dictates the development and maintenance of larval characters in all insects. When the insect is ready to mature, juvenile hormone secretion must stop and allatostatin provides the signal. How's that for a snappy survey of invertebrate endocrinology?" She smiled at her audience.

"That's the good news for the insect, because otherwise it would never grow up and reproduce. The bad news for the cockroach is that we'd like to use allatostatin as a sort of roach Achilles' heel. Through some of the new genetic engineering techniques, we plan to clone an allatostatin gene into a virus which will then become an independent factory for the sixty-four-long amino acid sequence of allatostatin. The virus we've picked is quite specific for certain insects, but totally harmless to other organisms and, of course, to man. The continuous viral production of allatostatin should confuse the hormonal balance of the insects infected with it to such an extent that they'll die early and be unable to reproduce." She moved her hands like a boxing referee signaling a technical knockout. "If this idea works, we'll revolutionize the field of pest control. No more conventional insecticides.

"This brings me to what allatostatin will do for us. It will represent the bulk of Celly's Ph.D. thesis. That's good for her. As for me, I'll just become more famous." She grinned at Celestine.

Stafford had been listening with increasing attention. "Celly, you never told me about the virus angle of your allatostatin work. That's a really neat idea."

"Well, we haven't done it yet," Celestine retorted. "Besides, you've told me virtually nothing of what you've been doing during the past couple of months. Real hush-hush stuff," she informed Ardley. "He's not even telling the other people in the lab."

"Oh, come now," said her professor, "is that true, Dr. Stafford?"

Stafford looked embarrassed. "Professor Cantor asked me to keep it quiet," he mumbled.

She persisted. "Why would he do that? Are you people usually that secretive about your work?"

"No! The Prof has never done that before—he always said, 'If you're going to worry about being scooped, half the fun in research is gone.' "

"Isn't that precisely what you're doing now?"

"Yes, but this is—it's different." He looked up, around the room. "When and where are you going to publish Celly's results? Isn't there competition breathing down your neck?"

"There sure is. I've heard that Schooley's group in Palo Alto is nearly there. But we'll have the paper finished by the end of next week and then send it to *PNAS.*"

"Who'll submit the paper for you?"

"I thought I'd ask Roger Guillemin in La Jolla."

"Why Guillemin?" asked Stafford. "You need a Nobel Prize winner to do this for you?"

"Of course not. It's just that I know him well. I did my first postdoc stint with him; research in peptide hormones is his specialty."

"Still, why not pick someone close by? It would save you time. Why not Professor Cantor?"

"I never thought of him. He isn't working in our field. Besides, I've never met him. But I guess he'd do it, wouldn't he, especially if he knows it's your girl friend's work?"

Stafford flushed. "He doesn't know anything about Celly."

"You mean you never told him about us?" Celestine seemed astonished. "He doesn't know we're living together?"

Stafford shook his head. "Why should he? He doesn't discuss his private life with us, so why should I tell him about me?"

"Wait a minute, just wait a minute!" Leah couldn't hold back any longer. "Before you people jump to still another subject, what does *PNAS* stand for?"

"*Proceedings of the National Academy of Sciences,*" said Stafford, "I thought everybody knew that. It's only the most prestigious journal in our field."

"Now that we've taken care of the trivia"—she dismissed Stafford and turned to Ardley—"will you explain to me why you need somebody to submit your paper to the *PNAS?* If I want to send a paper to a journal in my field, to *Critical Inquiry* or *Semiotica* or *Diacritics,* I simply do so—I, Leah Woodeson, not my professor, and most certainly not some surrogate, who has nothing to do with my work. Before you answer that, I might as well ask my second question: how come you're publishing Celly's work with her?"

Leah didn't believe in camouflage—social or physical. "You'll have to learn to take me as I come," she had told Stafford on the day he moved in. She didn't pluck her eyebrows, paint her thin but otherwise near perfect lips, shave under her arms or cover her freckles with makeup. This last feature was special: the freckles were mostly bunched around the upper part of her cheeks and only when she became aroused did they stand out against her wheat-colored hair. Now her freckles showed.

"Why does your name even appear on the paper?" she continued full steam. "Wasn't Celly the one who did all the work? My adviser suggested the topic for my Ph.D. thesis but she isn't going to put her name on my articles. Why do you people do that in science? Why is it Ardley and Price; Cantor and Stafford . . . or is it the other way around?" She leaned back, looking first at Ardley and then the others.

Stafford remained silent, but he was clearly enjoying the direction in which the conversation had suddenly turned. "Leah," Celestine exclaimed, "what's come over you? You sound as if Jean were taking credit from me, as if—"

"Wait a moment, Celly." An edge of sharpness was noticeable in Ardley's voice. "Let me answer this. Let's start with the important question first: whose names should appear on the allatostatin paper or on the article describing Dr. Stafford's mysterious work? In what order should the authors be listed? These are real questions. They've probably created more ill will than anything else in science, except maybe the question of priority. Leah"—she reached over and touched her arm for emphasis—"I am the one who suggested the problem—"

"But so did my adviser," interrupted the younger woman.

"Please let me finish. I provided the facilities and Celly's fellowship through my research grant. I prepared the grant application to the National Institutes of Health. In it, I outlined in great detail what my research group was going to do, why it is important, what the earlier contributions were, and many other things. My application went through a committee of peers, a so-called study section, which examines hundreds of proposals. Maybe a quarter of them eventually get funded. Without such support, Celly could do nothing. I'm not just talking about her fellowship, I'm talking about all the instruments in my lab, the chemicals, the glassware. You do your work essentially alone—you're both architect and builder. You can even do much of your work at home. All you need is access to a library, which your thesis adviser does not provide, and paper and pencil—"

"Please! Even humanists use computers these days."

"Sorry about that. But even a PC is probably not provided by your professor; you either get it from the department or, more likely, you have to buy it yourself. Which is it?"

"My mom bought it."

"Well, there you are. The one Celly uses comes from my research grant. But to go on, I see Celly almost every day; we discuss the progress of the work; I suggest certain techniques; I call important references to her attention. There are other people in my lab who work on similar problems and with whom Celly interacts continuously. None of this occurs in the humanities. I bet you don't see your thesis adviser for weeks on end."

"Why should I see her? I do virtually all my research alone."

"Of course you do," countered Ardley. "But you don't have to learn new techniques, new methodology . . . you just need to be able to read. And use a word processor. I'm sorry I get so defensive, Leah. But in the laboratory sciences, there's both a teacher-apprentice relationship and collegiality which usually justify the professor's being one of the authors. In fact, most people in the field—including Celestine—would consider me the senior author.

"It's not necessarily the first name in a list of authors, although some senior researchers feel very strongly that their names must always appear first. Others always use an alphabetical order—"

"Especially if their names start with one of the early letters of the alphabet! Like *A* or *C!*" Stafford's outburst surprised Celestine.

"Jerry, you aren't fair! Jean always puts her name last when she publishes with her students."

"Well, it's not true in our lab," he mumbled, "it's always alphabetical." This was the only serious bone of contention in Cantor's group. Lab gossip had it that no Allens or Browns had ever worked with Cantor. There had been an exchange fellow from Prague, named Czerny, but that was the closest alphabetical proximity to "Cantor" that anyone remembered until Doug Catfield had arrived last year.

"Let me confess something to the three of you, but promise not to spread it around." Jean Ardley had calmed down, a conciliatory smile across her face. "Dr. Stafford, you do have a point about the alphabetical standing of names. When I was a senior at Brown —and a very ambitious one, almost unpleasantly so—I paid very much attention to where my name would ultimately appear. Of course, I'd never published a paper; I hadn't even decided where to go to graduate school. To my father's shock, I announced one day that I would change my name from Jean Yardley to Jean Ardley. Just like that!"

"You did that?" stuttered Stafford.

"Yes. I went to the courthouse and did it legally. I told the judge, 'It's best to be first, it's been true since prehistoric times.' Instead of asking how I knew that, he broke out laughing. The funny part of the story is that it was totally unnecessary. In the end, I stayed on at Brown. Everybody urged me to go elsewhere—you know how it is in American science: we're so afraid of inbreeding, we always recommend that our undergraduates go elsewhere for their graduate training. But I wanted a female role model and Brown was one of the very few American universities that had a female organic chemistry professor, Caitlin Barker. So I picked her."

"Lucky you changed your name," said Stafford. "Otherwise, you would have published as Barker and Yardley."

"Wrong. That's why I said I could've stayed with Yardley. You see, Professor Barker always puts her name last. I've done this myself ever since. I think that putting your younger collaborators and students first is a nice gesture of encouragement—and even appreciation. So it will be Price and Ardley in the *PNAS.*"

Leah broke in from her corner of the couch. "Thanks for telling me all this. But why can't you submit your own paper to that journal?"

"*PNAS* is the only journal to which you can't do that. To publish there, you've got to be a member of the National Academy of Sciences or find a member who'll submit it on your behalf and vouch for its contents, so to speak."

"And you're not a member of the National Academy?"

"Are you kidding?"

"Why do you say that? Aren't women allowed?"

Jean Ardley shrugged her shoulders. "Oh, they're *allowed.* At last count, out of 1610 members there were 50 women—one of them in the chemistry section. I bet all 50 of them are postmenopausal." She caught herself. "Now that was a nasty crack. I shouldn't have said that. The men are equally old—their mean age must be in the sixties. But I'll make it one of these days. That's probably one of the reasons I don't have children—I'd like to become the youngest woman member of the Academy. Then I'll submit our own papers to the *PNAS.* In the meantime, why do I put up with this snobbery?"

Leah grinned. "Because, underneath it all, you're also a snob."

"You're right! But aren't we all?"

Stafford was still sitting at the table, chin supported by his folded hands. He'd been paying careful attention without smiling once. "What do you think it'll take for you to get into the Academy?"

Ardley's reply was sarcastic. "Oh, several allatostatins, a successful virus incorporation or two, a demonstration that this idea actually works in practice . . . a few medals or awards . . . giving lots of invited lectures . . . publishing a great deal . . . and then finding two members of the National Academy, preferably very distinguished ones, to prepare and sign my nomination papers."

"Jean, why are there so few women in the National Academy of Sciences?" continued Leah.

"The reason why you have only one woman out of 171 members in the chemistry section—"

"You sure seem to know the precise figures," remarked Stafford.

"I wanted to calculate the odds." She turned to Leah. "So far there are very few women in tenured positions in chemistry in the top universities. None at Harvard, none at Princeton, none at Yale, one at Stanford. And that's where people get elected from. They don't come from Idaho or Kentucky."

"I hadn't realized there are so few women in chemistry," mused Leah. "It's certainly different in my field."

"I didn't say there were so few women in chemistry: it's only true at the top. These days, almost a quarter of our entering graduate students are women. I have three in my group. But, Leah, let's hear about your field. I seem to have done most of the talking, or maybe even lecturing, this evening. You promised to tell me about dialogism."

"Fair enough. I've been thinking about which instrument in my critical tool kit to use on you."

Stafford rose. "Will you people excuse me? I'm bushed. I think I'll hit the hay."

"You mean you don't want to learn about dialogism?" Ardley sounded surprised.

"I've heard Leah explain metadiscourse and Bakhtinian dialogism and the semiotics of gender and metaphor and metonymy"— Stafford sounded slightly hysterical—"it's one of the obligatory fringe benefits of living here." He nudged Leah as he passed by the sofa.

"Hold it!" Leah said, grabbing him by the sleeve. "And sit down. You haven't heard this explanation; it'll do you some good. Actually it'll do all of you some good. Ready?"

"All right," said Stafford with a mock groan, "but make it snappy. Metadiscourse has a tendency to become maxidiscourse." He sat on the arm of the easy chair and ran his hand through Celestine's short hair.

"Stay here"—she glanced up affectionately—"and behave yourself."

Leah was mollified. "Allow me to provide a deconstruction of your pronouns."

"First Bakhtinian dialogism and now 'deconstruction'?"

"Tsk, tsk. Professor Ardley, you've never heard of Mikhail Bakhtin, the famous Russian"—Stafford gave the R an exaggerated roll—"literary theoretician, the father of dialogism, the present rage among academic elitists? Why, Professor Ardley, I'm amazed. Celly and I know all about him. In this house, we hear Bakhtin's name at least twice a day."

Leah gave him an indulgent look. "Sorry, Jerry. This time you're getting a Frenchman, Derrida. But the pedigree of this idea is beside the point. Professor Ardley," she continued in the same jocular vein as Stafford, "now that you've had the twenty-second description of Bakhtin, let me give you the five-second explanation of deconstruction: it uncovers meanings that are veiled or 'repressed' in a user's language." Leah used her fingers to draw the quotation marks in the air. "I know this sounds like a lecture, but let me deconstruct what you scientists have been talking about all evening." She looked at her three listeners, one at a time, gathering their attention.

"Jean, earlier on, when you were explaining your insect work, the question of senior authorship, and why you thought it appropriate for a chemistry professor to add her name to a paper, you always said 'we.' "

"What should I've said?"

"What's wrong with the first person singular?"

"But we"—she caught herself and winced—"never do that in science. We're taught never to do that in a scientific paper or talk—even in the absence of any coworkers."

"But who's that 'we'? Whom are you addressing? Is it some ideal community of science? Or is it the royal 'we' of presidents or politicians or editors? I doubt whether it's that simple. It seems to me that the nature of that 'we' has to depend on the audience. If it's a lecture, you probably have a spectrum of listeners, ranging from your collaborators—your Celestine Prices—and students to your professional peers. To Celestine, you want to make it plain in front of everybody that you're acknowledging her contribution. But what about the big wheel up in front, who one day is supposed to nominate you for election to the National Academy of Sciences? The one who's supposed to know that you're really the senior author? I bet, with him, the 'we' signifies something else. Here, the 'we' clearly means: 'Never mind the mob, you and I know that it was really *my* idea'—"

"Now wait a moment, Leah, that isn't fair."

Leah held up her hand. "Wait, Jean, don't take it personally. Suppose this were a real lecture audience, and by 'we' you actually meant *we*. How would different listeners interpret your 'we'? Of course, it's even more difficult with writing: you don't know the precise composition of your readership. It changes all the time. That's the wonderful thing about that 'we': how it is taken depends on the listeners' investment in your work—and *your* investment in *their* investment. Have I made myself clear?"

Celestine had remained totally silent, her eyes moving as in a tennis match between her professor and Leah. Jean Ardley finally broke the silence. "But that's just words, of course. It's different in the real world. We all *know* what we mean." She frowned. "Tell me, what made you decide to go into this field of criticism?"

"It didn't happen overnight. In my sophomore year at Oberlin, I switched my major from English lit to feminist studies. My father nearly blew his top. 'How are you going to earn a living with that?' he asked. 'This is even worse than English literature.' "

"So what did you say?"

Leah shrugged her shoulders. "Nothing earth-shaking. I told him it was really about power relations. Right now, the most exciting movement in contemporary critical theory is poststructural feminism. That's what I'm concentrating on in my thesis. Virginia Woolf and dialogism suit me just fine. We'll see who gets the better academic job, Celly or I."

"Is that the first person plural or another type of royal 'we'?" asked Jean Ardley. "Never mind," she hastened on, "that's a silly question."

Leah gave her a long look. "Actually, it isn't."

9

Professor Cantor's office was always closed. Not locked, but closed. His students knew he was accessible. All it took was a knock on the door and they'd hear his "Yes?" or "Come in!" The shut door was simply a barrier to other interruptions.

Stafford had knocked at that door many times, of course, but he had always done so with a hint of trepidation, his knock two quiet, deferential taps: the sense of intruding was strong enough to rule out any more. This afternoon, however, his knock was almost peremptory; his entrance almost anticipated Cantor's response. He stood looking down at Cantor, writing at his desk. He waited to catch his eyes, to hear the standard question, "What's new in the lab, Jerry?"

"It's finished, I.C. I checked the final arginine assay twice, just to be sure. It came out exactly the way you expected: it's the key amino acid all right."

Cantor stared at the young man. It took a moment to penetrate. Then he jumped up to grasp Stafford by his shoulders. "So we did it, Jerry? I knew we would. We couldn't have been wrong!"

Stafford counted each "we." The Ardley dinner the week before had made more of an impact than he'd expected. Ever since, he had been comparing Cantor with Celestine's professor.

"Come on, let's go. Show me the results." Cantor hurried out of his office, through his secretary's anteroom, into the corridor. He turned around to see whether Stafford was following, and in his hurry bumped into a Dry Ice chest. "Look at this corridor," he exclaimed. "We ought to do something about this mess."

"But what?" Stafford said under his breath.

For someone who had just completed an incisive experiment, Stafford seemed remarkably subdued, even irritable. The corridor was indeed a mess, but not more than most others in the Life Sciences Building. The clutter of equipment rarely allowed two persons to walk side by side. Refrigerated centrifuges, unruly ranks of nitrogen, helium and oxygen tanks, two upright freezers containing tissue cultures, the Dry Ice chest with which Cantor had just collided— these were only some of the items that threw the fire marshal into fits during his periodic inspections. But Cantor's thoughts had already moved elsewhere. "Show me the scintillation counter results, show me . . ."

The list went on, but Stafford had anticipated most of it. The data were all ready for the professor's inspection. In fact, so many papers and graphs were piled up on the desk that Cantor never even asked to see Stafford's laboratory notebook. The overflowing desk with its disorganized pile of papers and printouts and Xerox copies of journal articles ("Students don't read anymore these days in the library," Cantor complained periodically, "they just photocopy") was in striking contrast to the immaculate laboratory bench. The tubes in the automatic fraction collector were meticulously labeled, with none of the usual felt-tip scribbles. A dozen or so small Erlenmeyer flasks were arranged in military order on the metal tray marked with the yellow warning sign RADIOACTIVE. Even the plastic gloves next to the tray were laid out carefully, as if the fingers were still in them.

Stafford quickly led Cantor through the key data—especially the scintillation counts associated with the radioactively tagged proteins. The professor was jubilant. "We're going to write this up for *Nature.*"

"Not *PNAS?*" Stafford was surprised.

"No, I'd like to string this out a bit. Just a preliminary communication first, without the experimental details, so that nobody can jump on the bandwagon right away. *Nature* is just fine for that." It was true; *Nature,* a weekly, was one of the two most widely read journals in the world for preliminary communications on biologically related subjects. Watson and Crick's first announcement of the double helix model for DNA had occupied a single page in *Nature.*

"In that case, why not *Science?* Why send the manuscript all the way to London? It'll take only a day to reach Washington."

"Come to my office." Cantor allowed himself a rare gesture of physical intimacy: he put his arm around Stafford's shoulder. "Jerry, you know I'm not a secretive man. But in this instance, I'd like to have as little advance notice as possible. I want . . . fireworks: a sudden explosion! Do you know how hard that is to bring off? I'm absolutely certain that, if we submit this to *Science,* Krauss will be one of the referees. If I were the editor, I'd certainly seek his advice. I'd like to surprise Kurt—after all, he's heard the theory; he as much as challenged me to test it experimentally. *We* did it in less than three months!

"What's the matter with you, Jerry?" Cantor smiled at his student. "You ought to be jumping with joy. Instead you just sit there and mope."

"I guess I'm just bushed, I.C. You do know how hard I worked."

"Of course, Jerry. Of course. You get a good night's sleep and, tomorrow, prepare the two tables summarizing the radioactivity and nuclear magnetic resonance data. I'll write the paper myself tonight. Then we'll go over the final text together."

"Thanks. I can use the sleep. But you haven't finished telling me why you don't want our paper in *Science.* Just because Krauss might be a referee?"

"No, that would be childish. I know I could always write Dan Koshland—he's the editor—and ask that he not send it to Krauss. He'd probably oblige me. Fireworks, Jerry! With a paper like ours, some referee will leak the news. *Nature* is in London. They're unlikely to send it to an American referee. Also, the English are more discreet. Of course, with something this unusual, you never can tell."

Stafford enjoyed these conversations with I.C.; from them he learned about grantsmanship, and now refereemanship—the sort of insight usually acquired only through bitter experience. And he got it from one of the champs, one who played the game with the best, and had done so for nearly three decades. The cancer problem and cell membrane proteins were only the latest triumph. Earlier on, he had won the Lasker Award for his work on the metabolic detoxification of tranquilizers. And then there was Cantor's research on cell membrane structure—"You can't have a cell without a membrane," he was fond of saying—which was still being pursued by some of the other people in his lab. In fact, it was Cantor's decade-long involvement with this topic that had led him to the cancer problem. Yet, in his last grant application to the National Cancer Institute, he had not even mentioned the tumorigenesis work.

"The problem is, Jerry, without money—lots of it these days—you can't do serious research; just think what it cost to get the instruments you used. When you send in your grant request, most of your competition sits on the study section that reviews your application," Cantor had explained. "They're like the journal referees, except here they're dealing with ideas, not completed work. I'm not saying they're dishonest. I don't think *I* was when I served my six-year term. But people don't take on such time-consuming duties solely out of noblesse oblige—some kind of intellectual philanthropy, you might say. There's always some element of self-interest, the most important component of which is first access to the latest news. You can't help but remember what you read, and after a while, say a few months or even weeks later, you forget where you first saw it and gradually you think it's your own idea. So the cognoscenti don't tell them everything; they put into their applications largely what they've already done but not yet published. Only beginners, who've never had a grant before, have to place all of their cards on the table. They haven't got any others. It's the usual business: those that have . . ."

In the end, their choice of the journal didn't make any difference. Just as Ardley could have remained Yardley, Cantor could have dispensed with his worries about premature release. "A Generalized

Theory of Tumorigenesis," by I. Cantor and J. P. Stafford, passed through *Nature*'s editorial process with no formal refereeing. John Maddox, *Nature*'s editor, though a physicist by training, had a nose for hot news in any field. It came from his former service as science editor for the *Guardian*, where he'd acquired a broad knowledge of science and of scientific practitioners. The day after the express envelope from America arrived in London, a messenger from Maddox's office was waiting at the National Institute for Medical Research in Mill Hill while one of Maddox's scientific confidants read the brief manuscript. His pithy notation—"Publish!"—was sufficient. That same evening, Maddox telephoned Cantor. "Professor Cantor, we don't usually bypass the refereeing process—you know, it's not just for our protection, it's also for the author's. But your paper is extraordinary. If it's true—"

"What do you mean, 'If it's true'?" exploded Cantor.

Maddox continued calmly. "I just mean this is the kind of experiment all kinds of people will eventually set out to verify. Of course, you'll have to publish your full paper elsewhere before they'll be able to do that. We haven't got the space for the experimental details. If your experiment is confirmed, it will be a sensational advance. If not . . ." He didn't have to finish the sentence. Cantor knew the depth of the trash can containing discarded hypotheses and discredited experiments in the cancer field.

Their article appeared in print within ten days of the manuscript's arrival in London, a fact that did not escape some of Cantor's colleagues, who usually waited months before their papers came out. In an enterprise as sensitive to priority as science, journal articles always include the actual date of the manuscript's receipt in the editorial office. In the States and in England, the length of time it takes a paper to appear is directly proportional to the number of hurdles raised by the referees. This is one area wherein meritocracy operates; where even giants can have their manuscripts taken apart by relative pipsqueaks. Every prolific scientific author, even one as distinguished and careful as Cantor, has had his share of bile-provoking arguments with some unknown critic.

Stafford learned that you could frequently tilt the choice of referee in your favor. Thus, frequent citation in your paper's bibliography of another scientist's work was likely to lead the journal editor to select that person as a particularly apposite referee. When you categorized that potential referee's work as "elegant," "thought-provoking," or even just "sound," he was likely to examine your paper in a mellower mood. "Flattery always helps," Cantor counseled.

He was full of nuggets of wisdom for budding academics. "Never insult a referee in your written rebuttal, however stupid his comments."

Cantor never told any jokes—at least not to his students—but he was full of anecdotes. Like the one about the *pli cacheté,* which he suddenly produced to focus on the root of the publication problem: the desire to establish priority. "We're all preoccupied by it," Cantor admitted. "If I learned that a month or even three days ago someone had submitted a paper on a similar theory of tumorigenesis to even so obscure a journal as *Neoplasma* or the *Japanese Journal of Medical Science,* I'd be livid. So imagine the conflict facing people who want to establish priority and at the same time keep their work secret."

"Like us?" asked Stafford.

"Come now. Just because we're first publishing a communication without experimental details? I'm not going through all this with *Nature* just for the sake of secrecy. I'm doing it for"—he searched for the right word but couldn't find it—"let's call it PR. How often in a scientist's life can one drop a bombshell such as this —an important problem, completely solved—on someone like Kurt Krauss? I just want to get the maximum . . . effect out of it, with the people who really count. No, when I talk about conflict, I'm talking about people who really want to keep their results from other scientists, yet claim priority if the competition should publish first."

Stafford looked nonplussed. "How on earth could you accomplish that?"

"Fortunately, you can't now," replied Cantor, "because it's completely contrary to what you're supposed to do with the results of your scientific research: you draw from a common pool of knowledge, and you better contribute back to it. But just a few decades ago, even as late as in my graduate school days, you could do that in some European journals. They had a device called the *pli cacheté*—"

Stafford raised his eyebrows. "A what? What does it mean?"

"It's French for 'sealed envelope'—truly sealed, with red wax or something equivalent. It meant that an article could be submitted so that the journal editor would date it upon receipt without, however, opening it until the author asked that the manuscript go through the editorial process. The author of a *pli cacheté* would generally request that that be done only when a competitor had published, or was about to publish, the same material. Of course, his article would most likely appear later, but it would have the original submission date of the *pli cacheté* and thus demonstrate priority."

"What sort of people did that?" asked Stafford.

"All kinds. Even Nobel Prize winners used them. I happen to recall one such paper on flower essences in *Helvetica Chimica Acta* by Leopold Ruzicka, who won the Prize in chemistry just before World War II. It was some smelly business in the perfume field that finally convinced the editorial board of that Swiss journal to abolish the *pli cacheté* system."

Cantor was up and pacing now, one hand in the pocket of his lab coat, in the manner Stafford knew from attending the man's classroom lectures.

"Rumor had it that sometime in the late forties a research chemist from a Swiss perfume company simultaneously filed two *plis cachetés* containing two different answers to the same problem. He wasn't sure which was correct, but he figured that in this manner he couldn't go wrong. Should somebody else publish an article that unequivocally confirmed one of the two possible conclusions, the man would simply demand that the editor open the envelope containing the right answer. He would then be able to claim priority for that work even though he hadn't really solved the problem."

"Come on, I.C.!" exclaimed Stafford. "I can't believe people tried that sort of thing. How do you know that really happened?"

"Well, I don't know it first hand," conceded Cantor, "but I did hear the story from a reliable source. Apparently the editor opened the wrong envelope by mistake and discovered what had transpired.

That was the last time that journal accepted a *pli cacheté.*" Cantor stopped in front of Stafford. "I wonder what made me think of the *pli cacheté* system? I hope it's not some unconscious wish of mine." Cantor chuckled. "By the way, there was actually a justification for the *pli cacheté:* it helped people who wanted to patent. In Europe, if you published your work first, you couldn't patent your discovery. Therefore, occasionally an inventor submitted his work in the form of a *pli cacheté* and published it only when his application was allowed by the Patent Office. A classic case of having your cake and eating it too."

"Have you ever patented any of your work, I.C.?"

Cantor had just passed Stafford's chair in his restless pacing. Now he stopped and pirouetted on his heels to face the question head on. "Once. But I find the idea of patenting work done in a university somewhat distasteful. I know that's considered old-fashioned, and I'm certainly in the minority. And I suppose there's nothing wrong or illegal with patenting one's discovery; it just opens a real can of worms. Not just the obvious problem: preoccupation with the financial rewards to the neglect of your research. Attribution of credit becomes even trickier—even tougher than deciding who should be a coauthor on a paper . . ." He looked down at Stafford with a wry smile. "Don't we all know what resentment that can cause? In the case of patents, it's much worse: one doesn't just apportion glory. You may be talking about real money."

Stafford was curious. Cantor had not talked to him—or any other students for that matter—about his attitude toward scientific credit and priority. Indirectly, perhaps, but not quite that openly. And money? The topic had never arisen, although his students often speculated about the source of his income. His Patek Philippe watch, BMW sedan, silk neckties in the laboratory—even the gold Mont Blanc fountain pen he unscrewed so deliberately, when others used disposable ballpoints—all of these suggested financial resources far beyond those of a Midwestern university salary.

"But you patented something, didn't you, I.C.? Why did you make an exception?"

"I really didn't. Several years before you came here, we'd developed a new cell-counting device. The university patent counsel had heard about it and thought it would make lots of money in clinical laboratories. So he insisted we take out a patent." Cantor shrugged his shoulders. "It actually made some money in royalties. We assigned the patent to the university. But even that created a quandary: one of my postdocs was a coinventor and he wasn't very happy when I insisted that all royalties go to the university. He felt it wasn't fair for a professor to impose his standards on a coworker. How do you feel about that, Jerry?"

Stafford gave a start. "You mean about the money?"

"No. The principle of a professor's standards being applicable to the student."

"I can't say," replied Stafford. "It would depend on the circumstances."

10

"God, you scared me," exclaimed Leah Woodeson as she unlocked the door to the apartment and caught sight of Stafford stretched out on the sofa, a magazine in hand. "What are you doing home this early? It's not even six. Don't tell me you're going to eat dinner with us tonight."

"I finished it," he said in a matter-of-fact tone, "now you'll see more of my charming self. You'll even understand why the gorgeous Celestine Price fell for this brilliant cell biologist." He motioned to Leah. "Come tell me what you've been up to."

"Why, you're a changed man, Jerry—so relaxed; polite even. What is it you've finally finished?"

"What you two so impertinently called my hush-hush experiment. It's done; I.C. is writing it up tonight. Tomorrow, I'll go over it with him and then he's sending it to a journal. He's picked one in England, so that nobody hears about it over here until it's actually in print."

Leah shook her head. "You scientists: first you work your ass off, day and night, and then you can actually write it all up in a few hours. I don't have anything to 'write up.' With me, I don't really know what I think about a given subject until after I've written about it. And even then, I wouldn't send it out until I'd shown it to my friends, my adviser. And once I sent it out, it would take a journal months to accept it—if they did—and after that, a year or two for it to come out. But what really gets me is this: you're in such a fantastic rush to get your work into print and you're still being secretive. Don't you know the Latin root *publicare*, 'to make generally known'? What *do* scientists want?"

"Don't be so judgmental, Leah." He tapped her lightly with the magazine. "It'll only be a secret a few more weeks. I think I.C. wants to impress Krauss at Harvard and a few other big guns."

"Say, what are you reading?" exclaimed Leah, looking at the journal in his hand. "My *London Review of Books?* What's come over you, Dr. Stafford?" She brushed back her hair, which had fallen over her eyes. It was one of her most frequent mannerisms and had caused Stafford to ask her once why she didn't have her hair cut short. "You scientists wouldn't understand: writers need something to do with their hands when they aren't writing. That's why so many of them smoke. I don't smoke, so I do this," she had replied. He just nodded and dropped the subject. He had learned to let Leah have the last word.

Now an impish smile crossed his face. "I just wanted to know what the literary critics are into now. And what do I find? Even here, you've got scientists publishing! And a Nobel Prize winner at that: Max Perutz."

"No kidding? Show me!"

He pointed to an article on Klaus Fuchs. "A real crook, but a fascinating article. You should read it."

"A crook? I thought scientists were paragons of truthfulness and never cheat."

"Fuchs didn't cheat in his science—there he was quite meticulous. He was a spy for the Soviets in Los Alamos, during the atomic bomb project. But enough of that. Let's do something about dinner. Tonight, I'll cook."

"Celly, let's take off for a couple of days. Look at all the snow out there. You can teach me cross-country skiing. You said you'd show this Southern boy some of those sports you muscle-bound women practice out West. How about ventilating our brains and exercising our bodies?"

"I'd love to, Jerry," she said, shaking her head, "but it'll just have to be in bed. I can't take off now, I'm just learning how to do virus incorporations. Jean is doing it with me—we're learning it together, so I'm pretty much committed to her schedule."

"You can't take off for even a couple of days? To celebrate my triumph?"

"I can't," she said firmly. "Remember, you couldn't even take off a few hours to celebrate mine. Besides, what will I.C. say? Is he going to let you out of the lab?"

"He won't mind this time. He told me that, after we send off the paper tomorrow, he'll take off Friday morning and not be back until Monday. Come on, let's go for it. We've never been away together for two solid days."

"I know we haven't," she murmured, thinking of Graham Lufkin, who had told her that thirty-six consecutive hours with a man—two nights and a day—were *sine qua non* if she wanted to get to know him intimately. Even now, she wasn't certain whether there was anything to that statement, but the weekend in New York with Graham had been fabulous. "I can't, Jerry. We're at a very important stage in our work. Maybe in a couple of weeks."

"What if the snow melts in the meantime?"

"If it does, we'll go to the big city for a cultural bash. I've got an aunt from Portland who has just moved to Chicago. She's told me I can stay at her place any time. I'm sure she won't mind if you share my bed. Speaking of beds—let's . . ."

"Let's," he said, "my brain is full."

"Let's be different, this weekend," said Cantor on the telephone. "I'm in the mood for celebrating. How about doing opus 6, number 6?"

"Haydn again? I.C., I thought you wanted to be different."

"Who's talking about Haydn, Sol? I mean Boccherini." Cantor was pleased to have put one over on their first violinist, Sol Minskoff. They had been classmates as undergraduates at City College of New York and had always stayed in touch. Minskoff was a first-class player; so good, in fact, that for a while he had debated whether to become a professional violinist or a lawyer. The bar won, but wherever Minskoff lived, he always had an amateur quartet going. He now had a flourishing practice in Chicago, and when he learned of Cantor's pied-à-terre in the city, he had grabbed him. Amateur violists were a rare breed—especially true violists, as distinct from disappointed violinists. There were plenty of the latter; finding a second violinist for the quartet, even on short notice, was easy.

"Ah," noted Minskoff, digesting this tidbit. "Boccherini. Even more productive than Haydn. Did you know he beat Haydn, 91 to 83, when it came to string quartets?"

"No, I didn't." Sol always has to win when it comes to music, thought Cantor.

"The 91 quartets were nothing. He wrote no less than 125 string quintets. If I ever find a second cellist, we'll try his opus 37, No. 7. What a rondo!" He hummed a few bars. "Speaking of cellists, you'll meet a new one: Paula Curry. . . ."

"Paula?" Cantor's accent fell heavily on the last letter. "I thought we were a stag group."

"Ah, I see: we haven't had a woman with us since you joined, have we? But you know it was a close thing, in your case . . . there was a woman violist that the other two were very keen on. I insisted on you. . . . Anyway, Herb had an accident and broke his leg. You can't play cello with a cast. Thank God, his cello wasn't in the car. And thank God, I found a cellist on such short notice. She's supposed to be good, although I haven't met her yet. She's new here."

"I'm sorry to hear about Herb. By the way, I wanted to suggest that this time we play at my place—the others have never been here before. I'll have a surprise after the Boccherini. And you better tell the rest about opus 6, number 6, just in case anyone wants to practice it. . . ."

"I.C., let's not start that all over again. We're amateurs, but we're not beginners. We can all sight-read. And we're playing for ourselves, not for the public. The first experience of a new piece; discovering some lovely section together; managing a difficult portion the very first time—you destroy all that when you practice. No, *nyet, nein!*"

"Who is it?" Cantor bellowed into the speaker phone. The loud ring had called him out of the bathroom, shaving cream still on his face. Who can that be? he wondered. The three quartet players were not due for another forty-five minutes.

"Paula." The static over the intercom was terrible. How many times have I told the super to fix it? wondered Cantor angrily. This is supposed to be an exclusive lakefront condominium, not some second-rate apartment building.

"Who?" Cantor had drawn a complete blank.

"Paula Curry," the voice repeated, "I'm the cellist. I'm afraid I'm somewhat early."

"Early?" Cantor muttered under his breath. He didn't even have a tie on. Feeling more undressed than he was, he pressed the button. "Come on up. Fifteenth floor. Turn left when you step out of the elevator."

Cantor quickly washed his face and grabbed a bow tie, one of his sartorial idiosyncrasies on weekends in the city; he tied it with quick expertise around the collar of his blue shirt. During the week, he always wore neckties under his white laboratory coat or suit jacket. He had just enough time to comb his hair before the doorbell sounded.

Paula Curry with a cello in her right arm towered above Cantor; as he looked at the woman framed by the open door, Cantor felt the blood rush into his face. "Come in," he stuttered, "I hadn't expected anyone yet." Pallas Athene with her spear was all he could think of as she floated by him; or perhaps Brünnhilde in *Walküre?* Her blond hair, cascading in waves down to her shoulders, made him think she was lucky not to be a violinist, in case it tangled with the strings.

"Come in," he repeated, "and let me help you with your coat." This ritual produced her first peal of laughter as she moved the cello from one hand to the other, while Cantor pulled each time on the occupied arm. When Cantor finally held the fur coat in his arms he decided she was Pallas Athene after all: her sleeveless, champagne-colored dress could easily have passed for whatever toga-like garments the Greeks wore. Carefully, she put her cello case on the floor and stepped into the living room. "What a view!" She strode to the low sofa against the wide window and leaned across to look at Lake Michigan, the water etched velvety black against the snow-covered shore. "Do you ever get tired of this?"

"No, I don't. But then I don't spend that much time here—generally just weekends."

"Why is that?" Without prompting, Paula Curry had sat down on the sofa, her bare arms, brushed by strands of blond hair, stretched out along the backrest. The narrowed eyes holding mischief, the slightly open mouth, the wide lips painted red, the high Slavic cheekbones, her full breasts, that made her otherwise svelte body seem almost *zaftig*—the combination was a striking sight as Cantor stood in front of her. "Do you travel a lot?" she inquired.

"Not too much. But the place where I work is too far for commuting." Cantor wanted to change the subject.

"Where is that?" she pressed.

He mentioned the university briefly, assuming that, like a graduate student, she would recognize his reserve and respect it. But to his surprise he found that he had only succeeded in whetting her curiosity.

"So you teach?"

Cantor nodded. "And do research. In fact, that's what I do mostly."

"In what field?"

"Cell biology."

"Now isn't that a coincidence!" she exclaimed. "I have a niece doing chemistry there. She's a graduate student, working on her Ph.D. I wonder whether you know her. Celestine Price. She's the daughter of my stepsister."

"The name doesn't ring a bell," replied Cantor after some reflection. "Unless she took a course with me, it's unlikely that I would've met your niece. Our school is huge—nearly thirty thousand students—and the Chemistry Building is quite far from Life Sciences." He decided to go on the offensive before she could ask another question. "Miss Curry . . ."

"You can call me Paula. After all, we'll be in the same quartet. What's your first name?"

Cantor reddened. He was never comfortable when familiarity was thrust upon him. That was one reason he only published under his initials. The same was true of his visiting card. "People just call me 'I.C.,' " he muttered.

"Icy? Even on this cold December night, you don't seem icy to me. How did you end up with that nickname?"

Cantor refused to see the humor in the situation. "Not icy. Eye cee," he enunciated the letters carefully.

"Oh, I see," she said, teasing him, "I.C. And what does—"

Cantor knew what was coming. He decided to put a firm stop to it. "Miss Curry . . . I mean Paula . . . I understand you just moved here from Portland. What brought you to Chicago?"

"Come, sit down here." She patted the cushion next to her. "I'm not accustomed to having people tower over me. Besides, you don't look very comfortable standing there." She turned sideways to face him. "What was the reason for my coming to Chicago? The usual, mundane reason: a man."

"And what does your . . ." Cantor's question had slipped out before he even realized the problem. What do I call the man, he thought frantically: husband, lover, friend? ". . . man do?" he continued lamely. "Why did he move here?"

Another laugh rang in his ears. "I didn't mean to imply I moved here *with* a man. In fact, I came to Chicago to get *away* from a man. He's still in Portland. Thank God," she added and sank back into the pillows. "What about you, I.C.? Is there a lady of the house?"

Cantor blushed for the third time this evening. "I'm single."

"Are you gay?" she asked. Cantor's shocked expression made her put her hand over her mouth. "I'm sorry, I was just kidding. Out West, where I come from, that's a perfectly friendly question. But I guess it's really none of my business."

"That's all right," he said stiffly. "I'm divorced. Have been for a long time." Is eleven years merely a long time? He hadn't thought of his former wife for months. He would be hard put now to describe Eva's face, it had receded so far into the dead files of his memory. But what he still remembered was the evening she'd stepped into his dimly lit study, where he'd been sitting by his desk, reading *PNAS* or whatever journal it was. He didn't know how long she'd been observing him as she stood by the door. It was her "I.C.!" enunciated with a coldness that indeed had made him think of ice, that had brought his head up, his finger resting on the paragraph where he'd been interrupted. "Let's stop it, all of it," she'd said.

"Stop what?" Cantor asked, his mind still fogged by terms far longer than such pithy words.

"All of this," Eva replied, vaguely waving her hand around the room. "Let's get divorced."

Paula Curry stepped over to inspect the four chairs lined up behind each of the music stands. "I've never played sitting on a Hepplewhite. And this sideboard: it's Queen Anne, isn't it?"

Cantor nodded without uttering a word.

"But what about that chair?" asked Paula. "Why are the candle sconces mounted like that on the armrests? You'd burn your elbows if you had real candles."

"Not if you sit the right way. They'd be in front of you, not behind." Cantor became animated. "It's a 'smoker's chair,' which you straddle. Like sitting on a horse," he added.

"Of course! How stupid of me to ask."

He walked over and swung out two hinged boxes on either side of the armrests. "A man would store his smoking paraphernalia in them and use the wide back surface as a reading desk. I don't smoke, so I keep some paper and pencils there. The chair isn't bad for reading journals. You can take notes quite easily."

Paula Curry looked impressed. "May I ask where you found it? Here in Chicago?"

"No. In London."

"Not by any chance at Mallet on Bond Street?"

"No. At an auction."

"Sotheby's or Christie's?"

"Why are you so interested?"

"Just professional curiosity."

Now that was clever, conceded Cantor. She wants me to ask about her profession. "I'm sorry," he countered, changing the subject abruptly. "I'm not a very good host. Can I bring you something to drink? I've got—"

"No, thank you, nothing." She placed her hand on his arm to restrain him from rising. "Come to think of it, you can bring me something. Your view"—she pointed out the window overlooking the lake—"and your furniture made me forget why I came early. May I take a look at the Boccherini score? I've never played that piece and I didn't have time to get hold of the music."

"Only if you don't tell Sol Minskoff that I've shown it to you. He doesn't believe in advance practice."

"So I gather. I won't breathe a word."

Cantor felt they had returned to neutral territory. "How did Sol hear about you?" he asked.

"Through an attorney in Portland I used to play with." Cantor realized that she had caught his look of inquiry before he knew he had given one.

"Just a second fiddle," she added, smiling.

For a first run with a new member, the Boccherini quartet turned out to be a solid success. At the end of the third movement, the allegro, the pleasure shone on their faces. "Not bad, eh?" crowed Minskoff. "And we didn't even practice. Let's see how the last movement goes."

He wiped his forehead with his handkerchief before placing it back on his neck. He turned to the cellist, who sat directly across from him. "Paula, what do you suggest for an encore?"

Cantor raised his eyebrows and caught Ralph Draper, the second violinist, doing the same. They knew what the signal meant: Sol Minskoff almost never consulted his colleagues about music choices. He either proposed or vetoed.

"Let's do Opus 59, No. 1," she replied without a moment's hesitation. "At least the first movement."

Again, Cantor and Draper exchanged glances. Was he going to

let her get away with that? The first movement of this particular Beethoven quartet, the first of the three Razumovskys, was famous for the cello part with which the piece opens. The first violin certainly ended up as second fiddle in this selection. "Let's," Minskoff said.

Another unsought memory checked into focus in Cantor's mind. By God, he thought, I'll have to ask Sol whether he'd recalled the same scene. During their senior year at City College, Minskoff and Cantor had walked through Washington Square. An outdoor painting exhibition was on. Idly, they had inspected the many landscapes, violent abstractions, and kitschy subjects which are the common fare among such events. That was when Sol pointed to a large oil hung on a tree. "Look at her tits. How would you like to play with her?" he had asked, a salacious grin all over his face. The painting showed a naked woman, cello clasped between her thighs, the bow in her raised right hand as if she were about to start. This evening's picture was much more subtle and refined: the blond Paula Curry embracing the polished cello, her head nuzzling the neck of the instrument, eyes half closed with a dreamy expression on her face.

"I.C.!" Minskoff's sharp command brought him back to reality. "We're playing a quartet, not a trio. Let's start again."

Cantor jumped up the moment the last note sounded, before Minskoff had even lowered his bow. "You people can put away your instruments and move the music stands out of the way. I'll be back in a few minutes. Tonight, we have a small celebration." Cantor closed the kitchen door behind him. Everything had been laid out ahead of time: the caviar in its glass bowl ready to be set into a silver container with crushed ice up to the brim; the thinly sliced brown bread arranged meticulously and covered tightly with plastic; the smoked trout; and the crystal decanter filled with dark red wine. All that remained was to beat the egg white. Cantor was about to fold it into the soufflé base, which he'd prepared earlier that afternoon, when the door behind him opened. "May I help?" asked Paula Curry. "And what are you doing there?"

"I'm just finishing the dessert. It's a surprise. Why don't you take the caviar and trout?" He motioned with his head. "I'll just put this in the oven. I'll be with you in a moment."

Back in the living room, Cantor lit some candles, dimmed the lights, drew himself up, a bit stiffly, and announced, "This week, we've finished a very important experiment. It calls for a celebration: caviar, smoked trout and"—he looked at his gold Patek Philippe—"a surprise dessert in exactly twenty-nine minutes."

"Tell us about the experiment," prompted Paula.

"Before you do," interrupted Minskoff, "where's the vodka? Who's heard of caviar without vodka?"

"You're about to. I don't have any in the house." Cantor turned to Paula Curry. "I hope you don't mind. I do very little entertaining. I could have had some white wine, but this"—he lifted the decanter against one of the candles to show off the clear red color—"is a very special bottle—a '61 Château Margaux. And if our lawyer here needs a justification for red wine, the dessert will provide it."

"Okay." Minskoff appeared satisfied as he scooped a generous portion of the glistening black pearls onto his plate. "But where's the egg white, the onion, the lemon?"

"Sol, this isn't some Caspian reject eaten in the *shtetl* of your forefathers, this is Beluga. I'm not going to have you smother its taste with eggs or onion. Lemon, perhaps—if you insist."

Paula Curry had been spreading some caviar on the bread. "Why don't you two drop this stag baloney and enjoy the Beluga?"

"*Brava!*" exclaimed Draper, and raised his glass.

The chocolate soufflé was a real coup. Even Minskoff said so. "I.C., *maestoso!*" He raised his glass. "If your laboratory experiment was half as successful as this, you'll become famous." He smacked his lips and looked at his companions. "Time to go. Paula, can I give you a ride?"

"No, thanks," she replied. "I drove here myself. I'll stay for a little while and help I.C. clean up. He shouldn't be left to do it alone—not after this display of virtuosity."

As the front door closed, she continued. "Now that the violinists are gone, we're left with a rare duo: cello and viola. What's there to play?"

The comment caught Cantor unprepared. He stalled while he tried to read her face. The expression in her eyes, her satisfaction in her wit masked by their sparkle, could mean almost anything. He decided to play it safe. "Well, there is the Beethoven Duet in E-flat major and also the Hindemith—"

"Never mind," she interrupted and took him by the arm. "Let's go into the kitchen and clean up. Do you have an apron?"

Together, it took them only a few minutes to load the dishwasher. Cantor was just drying the last wineglass, which he'd washed by hand, when his guest again took him by surprise.

"I like you, I.C. You're an outstanding cook; a connoisseur of antiques; I presume you're a good cell biologist . . ."

"In all modesty, among the foremost," he retorted with mock smugness.

"A passable violist . . ."

"I knew there was a 'but.' "

"No, no 'but.' You wouldn't make it into the viola section of the Philharmonic, but I like the way you play. You don't tap your foot all the time. You clearly enjoy the music; your face shows it. And, unless you were cheating about this business of no advance practice, you did quite well with the Boccherini. A real Renaissance man. I think I'll call you Leonardo, rather than 'Icy'—it's much warmer. Tell me, Leonardo, before I leave, what else do you do?"

Already on his guard, Cantor had his response prepared. "Paula, I've only seen you in action for a few hours. But I'd bet that, if you really wanted to know, you'd find out by yourself. Right?"

"Right you are. By the way, how old are you, Leonardo?"

"Is that related to the preceding question?"

"It could be," she admitted. "So how old are you?"

"Nearly sixty."

"Really? I would've guessed you were in your mid-fifties. You seem to be in pretty good shape. What do you do for exercise? Jog?"

"Jog?" Cantor tried to put as much disdain into that word as three letters could bear. "Paula"—he pretended to scowl—"when I feel like exercising, I lie down quickly until the feeling passes."

Paula regarded him dubiously. "That's a bit too clever. Did you just make that up? Confess, Leonardo."

"I just thought of it." He paused for a moment and then continued, a grin all over his face, "But I didn't make it up. As I recall, the first person to have said it was a former president of the University of Chicago."

"At least you're honest, if not original."

"Of course I'm honest," he replied. "Don't you know all scientists are honest? Some are even honest and original. Like this Leonardo."

"Since I have no basis for comparison, I'll change the subject. When are you leaving Chicago for the university?"

"Sunday night. Or maybe Monday morning. For once the pressure is off in the lab," he said with a satisfied sigh.

"In that case, come to my place on Sunday. I'll demonstrate my versatility. Lunch or dinner?"

"Let's make it lunch," he replied after a pause.

"Hm," she murmured, not looking up as she wrote her address on a slip of paper.

Two weeks had passed without a new snowfall. It was still cold but, according to Celestine, the old snow was too crusty for a total novice in cross-country skiing. "Let's take the train to Chicago," she suggested to Stafford, "and stay overnight with my aunt. You'll like her. She's quite special."

"Does she know that you're bringing someone along?"

"Not yet, but she won't mind. She's very hospitable. I'll warn her, though."

"About what?" He grinned at her.

"Your table manners, of course."

"So what does she do, this aunt of yours? Is there an uncle?"

"No. She used to live with a man in Portland, a lawyer. . . . Leave it to my aunt to be the maverick of the family. But she lives alone in Chicago."

"What does she do?" persisted Stafford.

"She was one of the best interior decorators in Portland: fancy offices, yuppie apartments, restoration of old houses—the lot."

"Why did she move to Chicago?"

"Why? Why? Why? Jerry, you ask too many questions. Ask her yourself next Saturday."

"Why did you move to the Midwest, Miss Curry?" Stafford asked, just minutes after he'd thanked Paula Curry for her hospitality.

"Why did you?" Paula had a way of turning questions into questions if she didn't wish to answer. "You don't sound like a Midwesterner."

"I'm from South Carolina."

"And a Baptist to boot," laughed Celestine.

"And what has this Western Unitarian maiden learned from her Baptist beau?"

Celestine took up her aunt's mockery. "Very little. I'm doing most of the teaching. Paula, do you know what they teach the young Baptists about the facts of life? They tell them—"

"Celly!" Stafford was visibly embarrassed.

"Don't mind her. I know how precocious my niece is. But tell me, Mr. Stafford—"

"Please call me Jerry," he interjected.

"In that case, call me Paula. Why did you move here from South Carolina, Jerry?"

"So I could get my Ph.D. with a certain professor."

"Are you also a chemist, like Celly?"

"No, I got it in cell biology with Professor Cantor."

"Let me get you two some coffee," she said, getting up abruptly.

When she returned with the cups and saucers, Paula had regained her composure. "He must be quite a star, your professor, to draw disciples from as far off as South Carolina. What did you say his name was?"

"Cantor. Usually known as 'I.C.'"

"Icy Cantor? Why do they call him that? Is he such a cold fish?"

"No," laughed Stafford, spelling the initials.

"So what's he like, your Professor Cantor?"

"He's a first-class scientist—"

"That's not what I meant," Paula broke in. "What's he like as a person?"

"As a person? That's a funny question. He's . . . he's precise. Careful. Pretty open-minded. And he has this uncanny ability to synthesize concepts from a few isolated observations. I guess that's how the great diagnosticians in medicine must have operated before the days of clinical labs and lots of instrumentation."

"No, no, as a *person. Outside* the lab."

"That's difficult to say. We hardly know anything about his life away from the lab."

"Come now, doesn't he invite you to his home? Doesn't his wife give a party for the students?"

"He's divorced. I've never heard him even mention any other woman's name. I've never been to his house, either, now that you mention it."

Stafford didn't notice the mischievous gleam in Paula Curry's eyes. "Surprising, isn't it, that you people know so little about him? He could be living a double life: he could be a real lady's man . . . or a musician . . . or an antique collector . . . or all these things and then some."

"Impossible."

"Why do you say that?"

"I.C. wouldn't have the time. You have no idea how many journals the man must read, the meetings he attends, the committees he's on. He even does a bit of lab work. And he teaches and writes papers."

"And pushes his students like a slave driver," added Celestine. "Jerry here worked day and night, seven days a week, for nearly three months. I hardly saw the guy."

Paula Curry looked with open curiosity at the young man. "How come?"

Celestine didn't let him answer. "Jerry's not only Cantor's favorite. He claims to be a real whiz in the lab. So the professor goes to Jerry and says: 'Jerry, I have this fantastic idea, but it needs experimental proof. I want you to go into the lab and not come out until you've finished it.' And what does my Baptist lover do?"

Stafford tried to put his hand over Celestine's mouth, but she fought him off. "He actually does what his professor tells him and ignores his lady love. If you don't call Cantor a slave driver, at least I'll call you, Dr. Jeremiah P. Stafford, his slave. So there you have the whole story, Paula."

"What were you working on? Was it really so important?"

He nodded. "It was, and Celly was right: the prof was so convinced the experiment had to work, he hardly left me alone. I really thought if I didn't get it, he'd . . ." Jerry trailed off abruptly.

"Let me pour you some more coffee," Paula said. "Earlier you referred to him as a first-class scientist. What's so first-class about him?"

Stafford gave her an amused look. "He may well win the Nobel Prize."

"Well, well," exclaimed Paula and set down the coffeepot. It had begun to shake in her hand.

11

When the tumorigenesis article appeared in *Nature*, even Cantor was surprised by the number of reprint requests. They came in waves. The first arrived from people who always head for the library as soon as the latest number of *Nature* hits the Current Periodicals shelf: the eager beavers who can't wait a day for the hot news in their field. After a temporary lull, when the table of contents of that particular *Nature* issue appeared in *Current Contents*, a second avalanche poured in. As journal subscription costs soar, *Current Contents*, which simply lists the titles of articles in other journals, along with the addresses of the authors, is God's gift to scientists from soft-currency countries. Cantor's secretary, whose brother was an avid stamp collector, was suddenly busy removing stamps from all the reprint request cards from Argentina, Bulgaria, India, and dozens of other countries.

But to Cantor the most gratifying response to their article was a single telephone call. The day after the journal appeared, Kurt Krauss called from Harvard to say that this paper could not possibly escape notice in Stockholm. "I.C., if I were an envious man, I'd be bright green. But you know I'm not." The words sounded almost convincing. "If I couldn't think of this experiment, then I'm at least glad you did." Cantor could feel a warm flush of pleasure rise to his face. But Krauss was not finished. "I.C., you know the Swedes canvass people all over the world for nominations. You must've gotten such forms yourself in the past. This year happens to be my turn—in fact, I have it right in front of me. Under the section 'Grounds for nomination,' they ask for a bibliography, biographical details, and other supporting documents. Why don't you simplify life for me and send me your stuff? I'll take care of the rest."

At such moments, scientific etiquette demands modesty. But the demure look toward the floor, the disclaimer with the hands often as not look faked when seen. The telephone is kinder.

Cantor rose to the occasion. "Kurt, I knew it was a good idea." *It was the greatest idea I've ever had!* "But I was also lucky. I've told you before about my postdoc Jeremiah Stafford? The man has golden hands—you've never seen such lab technique. I don't know if anyone else could've pulled this off."

"We all have people like that," Krauss chuckled. "It just takes talent to find them. Still, sooner or later, someone will have to repeat the experiment. You might as well have us do it—after all, you first announced your idea at my seminar."

"I haven't even started to write our detailed paper," replied Cantor. "I don't think there's any hurry."

"There isn't," Krauss said flatly. "As long as you don't publish the full details, nobody can start on any replication. Just send *us* the experimental details. This way, you'll know who's providing the *Good Housekeeping* seal. But tell me, I.C.," he continued, "how did you manage to get that article published in less than two weeks?" Cantor was pleased that Krauss had caught even that nuance of his triumph.

Climbers of Himalayan peaks count their glory in minutes. Hardly has the photograph been taken—flag in one hand, ice ax in the other—than the return to the last camp is already under way, lest the next storm approach or the oxygen supply give out. Not so with scientific Everests. For a couple of months, until the middle of February, Cantor basked on the summit, at lectures, seminars, and symposia where he presented the theory and outlined its experimental proof.

For Stafford, however, this period was itself an experimental demonstration of Leah's Bakhtinian analysis. At those events where

Stafford was in the audience, the professor's acknowledgment of his student's contribution was exemplary. "I'm not sure that *we* could've provided this proof so quickly—or at all—were it not for the laboratory skills of Dr. Stafford, who's here in this audience." The accompanying smile seemed genuine, and the nod in Stafford's direction hardly perfunctory. Yet Stafford counted and weighed each "we" and "I." Admittedly, there were many fewer "I's." But was their function perhaps to transform the rest of the "we's" into the royal form? "The word in language is half someone else's." Leah had pasted Bakhtin's dictum on the wall over their telephone. "I'm becoming paranoid," he swore under his breath. In fairness to his professor, Cantor had gone out of his way to let him answer most of the questions pertaining to the experiment. Cantor had even asked him to supply Krauss with the requested details so that the Harvard group could start on the replication of their experiment. But Stafford always wondered how the "we" rang in his absence, how his experimental skill was presented when he was not there.

Even more grating was Celestine's appearance at a symposium, "Recent Advances in Insect Hormones," held at Northwestern University, where she, rather than Jean Ardley, presented their allatostatin results. As he sat in the audience, Stafford recalled how Cantor had indicated that Stafford might serve as their spokesman at some future lecture. But it hadn't happened yet. "I know you won't repeat your first seminar fiasco," Cantor had said, without a trace of condescension in his voice, "but you do understand . . ." Stafford did understand: after all, cockroaches were not in the same class as tumors. And did it really matter? The permanent record of their work, the very first publication, which every other scientist in the field would have to cite, bore only two names: Cantor and Stafford. At least Stafford was spared that most ignominious fate of a scientific collaborator, the most anonymous of all appellations: *et al.* Avoiding that bibliographic equivalent of "John Doe" was something to be thankful for.

Although savoring the triumph of the summit is longer in the scientific Himalayas, it is not forever. Sooner or later even Cantor and his restive Sherpa had to look windward, where, one afternoon in February, the first small cloud appeared in the clear blue sky. Kurt Krauss telephoned from Harvard to say that one of his best associates, Yuzo Ohashi ("You remember him, I.C., don't you? He's my Stafford"), had been unable to replicate Stafford's experiment. Such failure was not uncommon in their field. Since Cantor and Stafford had published only a preliminary announcement without experimental detail—it was like one chef describing a marvelous dish to another without handing over the exact recipe—Krauss and Ohashi had at their disposal solely what Stafford had mailed to them. Most likely, he had missed some crucial detail.

"Jerry, I should've gone over that material with you before you sent it off," proclaimed the professor, "but I guess we were too busy basking in our glory. I want you to write up the entire experimental work in extreme detail. The next time around, Krauss's man must be able to repeat *your* experiment."

Leah Woodeson was at a stage of her dissertation in which much of the writing was done at home. It was after ten in the morning and she had just entered the kitchen to replenish her coffee mug. Stafford was standing barefoot by the sink, wearing blue jeans and a T-shirt.

"Jerry, do you know what time it is? I thought you'd left with Celly."

"I'm not going in today."

She scrutinized him with concern. "What's the matter? Sick?"

"In a way. But not the way you mean it. I've got to get a lot of material together for I.C. It'll take me days and I hate writing that stuff."

"Days?" She clucked her tongue. "I thought you people finished your masterpieces in hours. Isn't that all it took for that famous *Nature* paper of yours? Or haven't you learned yet from your professor how to write quickly?"

"It's not funny," he said morosely. "What I've got to write isn't some exquisitely concise letter to the editor. I've got to produce the equivalent of a cookbook: style doesn't count and brevity is frowned upon. And it has to be exact: not just 'add a few drops of

Tabasco, season to taste, and cook until done.' I.C. wants a description of everything I did those three months and in enough detail so they can repeat it at Harvard: the precise amount of Tabasco, was it added dropwise or in one portion, the temperature and the time the dish cooked . . ." He gave a snort. "And I've got to hand it all over by Friday."

"Cheer up, Jerry. I've a surprise for you and Celly. Has she ever told you about the Kronos Quartet?"

Stafford gave her a suspicious glance. "Never heard of them."

"Really? I'm surprised Celly never told you. Well, her business, I suppose. Anyway, I've got tickets for the three of us for a special performance they're giving in Chicago Saturday evening. We'll leave early enough to have dinner: there's a Greek restaurant in Hyde Park I've heard about."

"All the way to Chicago just for a concert and Greek food? We'll get home damn late."

"Don't you know what's special about this coming Saturday?" Leah started to get annoyed.

"No."

"It's Celly's twenty-fifth birthday. Don't tell me you forgot?"

"I didn't forget. I never knew. She never mentioned it."

Leah kept an embarrassed silence. Stafford looked crestfallen. "Thanks for telling me."

"Hey, buck up, Jerry. Now you've got a chance to surprise her with your thoughtfulness. And it'll do you good to get out after writing all week," she consoled him. "On the way back, you can always sleep in the car or whatever."

"Your car is too small for 'whatever.'" Stafford was rapidly snapping out of his dejection.

"You'll think of something."

Thursday morning, Stafford, who had not missed a day because of illness in six years, phoned in sick. He timed the call to catch the fifteen-minute interval between the arrival of Cantor's secretary and the professor himself.

The message annoyed Cantor. Stafford, whom Cantor needed

to prepare that report for Krauss; whom Cantor had always found in the laboratory; who pronounced the word "vacation" with a disdain that echoed Cantor's own scientific machismo—this Stafford had to pick *this* time to fall sick. On Monday morning, when he was told that Stafford had telephoned from South Carolina to say that his grandfather had suffered a heart attack, Cantor's annoyance escalated to real irritation. "Where's the man's loyalty," he grumbled, "to his grandfather or to the lab?"

Such gracelessness was completely atypical of Cantor, but one did not keep Krauss waiting. Cantor decided on a sloppy but simple shortcut; he would photocopy all the appropriate pages from Stafford's laboratory notebook and send these to Harvard with a brief explanatory letter.

There was nothing improper in copying Stafford's notebook. A scientist's laboratory journal is not a personal diary; its whole reason for existence is to be produced on demand for inspection by others. Invariably, such notebooks are the kind one can buy at larger stationers, solidly bound, with page numbers already stamped in the upper corners. Entries reflect this solid, orderly facade: all are written down chronologically, completely, conscientiously, as a guide for others to follow. Just as Everest expedition leaders insist in maddening detail on seemingly trivial discipline, Cantor behaved in such a manner when it came to laboratory notebooks. Everything had to be entered in indelible ink, not pencil; even trivial calculations had to be included rather than jotted down elsewhere on loose sheets. Every first-year graduate student got the same speech: "You can't put too much into your notebook, but you can write too little. You never know which details may turn out to be crucial." When the students departed from Cantor's laboratory, the notebooks had to stay behind. A locked bookcase in the professor's spacious office contained over two hundred such books, carefully catalogued—the evidence of more than a quarter of a century's experimental work.

What Cantor saw in Stafford's notebook bothered him. The experimental protocol was indeed there, but the actual details seemed surprisingly scant. Stafford had been such a star in Cantor's laboratory that the professor had never had reason to question any of his results, nor had he examined his notebook for a long time. After a morning spent stewing about it, he decided to telephone Stafford in South Carolina, at which point a second snag appeared. Stephanie did not have his number or address there. "Then get me his local phone number," he ordered brusquely.

The first two calls went unanswered. Only in the evening did a woman's voice say "Hello."

"Good evening," he said curtly, "is this Dr. Stafford's home?"

"Well, he lives here," replied Leah, "but he isn't here just now. He's out of town."

"Do you have a number where I can reach him?"

Cantor's impatience could be sensed over the phone, sufficiently so that it sparked Leah's curiosity. "Who's calling?" she asked.

"My name is Cantor."

"Oh," she said, startled, "just one moment." Leah had heard a great deal about the professor, but she'd never fully believed in his existence. She pressed her hand over the mouthpiece. "Celly, you better take this. It's Cantor, looking for Jerry. He sounds icy," she warned as she handed over the instrument.

"May I help you, Professor Cantor?" asked Celestine.

The use of the title mollified him, as it always did when he discovered that the other person had heard of him without prior introduction.

"I'm Celestine Price," she added, and stopped. Let's see whether Jerry has finally told his prof about me, she thought. But Cantor gave no response. Her first name sounded vaguely familiar, but he had more urgent matters on his mind. "I'm"—she hesitated for a moment and then continued—"one of Jerry's housemates."

"I'm wondering whether you could help me." Cantor brushed his assistant's personal life aside. "I'm very anxious to get hold of Jerry. Do you have a number where he can be reached? His grandfather is supposed to have had a heart attack in South Carolina."

Supposed? Celestine fastened on that word. She'd also used it last Friday evening when she found a vase of roses and an envelope from Jerry upon her return from the lab. It was only the second bunch of flowers he'd given her. The parsimonious contents of this envelope were very different from the first. It contained one of those corny birthday cards depicting a boat with a figure on the distant shore. "Sorry, I missed the boat. Happy birthday," the printed message read. Underneath, there were some handwritten sentences:

My grandfather had a heart attack (mild!). I am taking off for South Carolina for a few days. You can call me at (803)555-7182. Sorry I couldn't go to Chicago with you. We'll make up for it. Love, Jerry.

"Look at this crummy card," Celestine had complained. "If the heart attack was supposed to be so mild, why couldn't he wait until Sunday? He could've caught a plane in Chicago. I didn't even know he had a grandfather."

"Celly, everybody has a grandfather." Leah read the card over her shoulder. "Poor Jerry. But don't worry, Celly. We'll celebrate by ourselves. I won't have anybody spoil my chemist's birthday."

In the end, they had a memorable time: the Greek waiters danced; the Kronos Quartet played a restrainedly modern Viennese evening—Schönberg, Webern and Berg; and, as a bonus, Celestine got an extraordinary surprise. The concert was held in a large hall with a balcony, where the two women sat. Leah had thought of everything. She'd even brought a pair of opera glasses, through which they watched the musicians in almost unseemly detail. Leah had recalled Celestine's story about the far-out clothing the quartet was notorious for—as far out as some of the music Celestine had heard with Graham Lufkin.

"Hand me the binos," Celestine had said as the lights came up for intermission. "I adore people-watching." She swept slowly through the audience. Suddenly she stiffened. "I don't believe it," she whispered too low for Leah to hear, "there's Paula."

Her surprise had not been prompted by Paula's presence; after all, Celestine knew her aunt's musical interests. She'd even mentioned them to Lufkin at the first Kronos concert when the quartet's cellist, Joan Jeanrenaud, appeared on the stage. What startled her was Paula Curry's companion: I. Cantor. She'd never met him personally, but she'd gone to one of his lectures with Jerry.

And now, two days later, she was actually talking to Cantor. Who would have thought that he was leading a double life? But what about Jerry himself? His departure for South Carolina was simply too sudden.

"Yes," she told Cantor, "his grandfather is supposed to have had a heart attack. A mild one, he told me. I'll get you the number."

"I hope your grandfather is getting better." Cantor left no opening for a reply; he hadn't meant it as a question. "Jerry, you know that Krauss is having one of his postdocs repeat *your* experiment. You know they're having trouble with it and I can't let Krauss wait much longer for the details. Thank God there are no other people trying to do the same; they might not be so polite as to tell us about their difficulties. They might just publish their failure. I thought I'd simply send Krauss Xeroxes of your lab notebook."

All Cantor heard was a low "Yes?"

"I hadn't looked at your notebook for months—"

Before Cantor could continue, Stafford moved promptly to the offensive. "Well, you had no reason to, did you? Except for our *Nature* article"—there was no ambiguity about "our" in this instance—"you'd asked me to write the initial draft of our last two manuscripts. All you've wanted to see were my drafts."

"Yes, I know." Whatever accusatory undertone Cantor's earlier words had held had now been muted. Unlike some people he could mention, who hardly ever wrote drafts of manuscripts that eventually bore their names, Cantor almost always prepared the first versions of his articles. On more than one occasion, he had pointed with pride to the difference between his practice and that of the professorial nonauthors who nevertheless appeared as authors. Cantor was unforgiving in his condemnation of such conduct. He felt that, if one's name was on a paper, one was responsible for everything in it. The best way to exercise that responsibility was to write the actual article. But even he, Cantor—the conscientious superstar, who had resisted the temptation of huge research groups in order to maintain his scrupulous standards, both in the lab and in his writing —had made an exception in recent years with Jeremiah Stafford.

Cantor's tone had turned apologetic. "Jerry, I can't send just Xerox copies of your notebook pages to Krauss. There are too many missing details. You don't even indicate which buffer you used in the original extraction; you don't give the column support for your high-pressure liquid chromatography separation; you don't say where the arginase came from—"

Stafford's interruption was peremptory. "But, I.C., those are trivial—routine stuff, and you know what time pressure I was working under. Finishing what *I* did"—the first person singular was audibly underlined—"in less than three months took some doing. I guess I was just rushed with my notebook entries. I'll do a better job with the missing details when I get back on Wednesday. You'll have them in your office first thing Friday morning."

This was what Cantor had wanted to hear. The letter to Krauss was mailed the following week.

For most of March, the single cloud on Cantor's glorious horizon had not grown bigger, nor had it darkened. But, like the weather on Mount Everest, the scientific sky can change with dramatic speed: in this instance, through one phone call.

"I.C., I wouldn't worry," Krauss started innocently enough. "That is, not yet," he added after a pause, so small that only a listener's ear calibrated to the most careful nuances of Krauss's speech would have read meaning into it.

Cantor had hardly replied, "What do you mean, Kurt?" when he knew what was coming.

"My postdoc, Ohashi—you know, the one I have working on your experiment? He's an experienced enzymologist. There's simply no question about his ability. And this is now his second try. He's still unable to observe any arginine rise at the end. And if there isn't any increase in that amino acid, where does this leave your—"

Cantor cut him off in mid-sentence. "I know perfectly well what it means. What it *would* mean. Kurt, I'll repeat the experiment myself with Stafford. Then I'll invite your Ohashi to come to my lab and do it with us."

"I thought you'd say something like that." Krauss sounded reassured and reassuring. "Don't worry about us, I.C. We certainly aren't going to publish anything about it at this stage. But you're lucky: so far, nobody else is in a position to repeat your work. You haven't sent the experimental details to anyone else, have you?"

Cantor wondered why he sounded so proprietary. "Of course not."

"In that case, don't worry about it."

They both knew what "it" meant. In a little over a quarter of a year, "it" had become known as the Cantor-Stafford Experiment. Naming an experiment or theory after the original authors is the ultimate historical accolade in science: Boyle's Law, Avogadro's Number, or even Millikan's Falling Drop Experiment, which had won him the Nobel Prize in 1923 in spite of some shady data manipulation, are just a few examples. However, such an accolade is only rarely bestowed without independent verification, which Krauss had intended to provide. "It" could also come to mean the Cantor-Stafford Fiasco. For a month or two, anyway, until the experiment was forgotten along with dozens of other failures in the field. "You better hurry," Krauss repeated the warning, "because, once you've written up your full paper and it's out in print, you don't know who else will take a look at it in their lab."

Cantor needed no reminder about the value of time, even though he hadn't even started on the detailed manuscript. In just a few minutes, Stafford was summoned to the professor's office, the door closed as usual. "Jerry, you know how Krauss put it? 'Don't worry . . . not yet.' Well, I'm starting to get worried." Cantor stared at his young collaborator—but Stafford's eyes held steady.

"What do you plan to do?" The younger man's voice was subdued.

Cantor felt sorry for Stafford. He wanted to impress upon him the urgency of the situation, not discourage him. "We'll repeat *your* experiment together. Not out in the main lab. In my private lab. I'm taking no chances this time. Everything will be under control. It's got to be another instance of what happens so frequently: a minor but crucial experimental variable, not recognized by us, must be responsible. This time, you'll do every step in my presence. That's how we'll find what was missing in your report. I'm not going to allow something like that to cast the entire theory into question. *Allons, enfants de la patrie,* right into the lab and start."

Cantor's year at the Pasteur Institute in Paris still led him into occasional, somewhat forced bons mots. In this instance, Stafford, who had passed his Ph.D. foreign language proficiency in FORTRAN, didn't look up.

Stafford's temporary move into the professor's private laboratory caused considerable comment and even gloating among some members of the research group. Krauss's initial failure to repeat the work outlined in their *Nature* article had not been discussed at the weekly group seminars, but it hadn't been kept a secret either. While none of the students and research fellows had ever been asked to work in Cantor's own laboratory, it was hardly a promotion that the professor's fair-haired boy had now been ordered to repeat his spectacular experiment under the watchful eyes of the master.

The weeks in the lab slid by without difficulty. Of course everything depended on the final amino acid analysis due on Monday. When Cantor arrived that morning, nervous and concerned, he encountered an impressively confident and self-assured Stafford. Within a few hours, Cantor was in a joyous mood. The assay had come out as expected: the arginine level was six times that of the control.

"I'm using this opportunity," Cantor declared in a somewhat pompous manner during the special group meeting he had called together that lunchtime, "to once more pay tribute to Jerry's green thumb." Several pairs of eyes went up to the ceiling, a few grimaces appeared. The eyes all leveled, the grimaces vanished as soon as Cantor continued. "But I shall also castigate him so that everybody learns from this lesson." And then Cantor announced officially what until then had only been intimated: that Krauss's group at Harvard had been unable to repeat the Cantor-Stafford Experiment. "But"

—the right index finger shot up triumphantly—*"we* have done so now." After detailing their work and speculating on reasons for the failure at Harvard, Cantor concluded. "Let this be a lesson to everyone about notebooks." At least half the audience anticipated the next sentence. "You can't put too much into your notebook, but . . ."

When Cantor returned to his office, he stepped on an envelope, marked CONFIDENTIAL, that had been slipped under the door. The message, unsigned and typed, was only one line long:

Why was Dr. Stafford in your private laboratory Sunday evening?

12

For Cantor, the dilemma was enormous. It hardly mattered whether unfounded suspicion, bred by professional jealousy, or something more serious had prompted this anonymous note. Any one of eight or nine men who were always in the lab on Sundays could have written it. The proper steps would have been to call Stafford in, confront him with the accusation, repeat the experiment without him and, if it failed, to inform Kurt Krauss. If that were not traumatic enough, he would then have to undergo the expected public penance: a letter published in *Nature* in which he would withdraw the Cantor-Stafford Experiment. The standard ending would be "pending experimental verification." Depending upon the authorship of such a retraction, different conclusions would be reached: if it were issued only under Cantor's name, everybody would suspect fraud; if both their names were included, sloppiness or simple irreproducibility. Under any circumstance, an official retraction is a terrible hair shirt. If Cantor decided to wear it, his tumorigenesis theory would become just another discarded conjecture in the cancer field.

Until now, Cantor had never withdrawn a published paper; he had never reported in public an experiment that could not be duplicated elsewhere. An error of this magnitude—even though committed by a younger collaborator—would never be forgotten. After all,

Cantor was coauthor of the paper; it wouldn't have made any difference if his name had been last; it was still the senior's responsibility. Cantor recalled—now with a shudder—the barely repressed glee with which he'd first heard of a distinguished colleague's humiliation. The man was a scrupulously honest professor at Cornell who had withdrawn a widely publicized paper when he realized that his collaborator's data were tainted. Only after Cantor read the official retraction had he felt some compassion for the man, and some remorse for his own pride that such an event couldn't possibly occur in his own laboratory.

Given what was at stake, Cantor decided to say nothing—neither to Stafford nor to Krauss. By saying nothing, he considered himself still unbesmirched by any possible scandal. But silence could only buy him so much time, in which he must either verify his theory or abandon it. Expending precious weeks on another attempted repetition of Stafford's Experiment was out of the question: the price of another failure would be too high. But the alternative was also intolerable: his theory was too sweet. He sensed—"down to my quarks," he was fond of saying—that it had to be right. Even before he had found the anonymous accusation at his feet, Cantor had conceived of a second experiment that might provide independent verification. It was a risky one, by no means as straightforward as the Cantor-Stafford Experiment, but Cantor concluded that there was now too much at stake—not the least of which was the Nobel Prize. Instead of looking for changes in the amino acid content, notably that of arginine, Cantor now focused on the nature of the ribonucleic acid—the template responsible for the synthesis of his arginine-containing protein. With the Prize before him and the specter of withdrawal behind, he disappeared into his private lab, taking care now to lock it whenever he left, even for a trip to the bathroom.

Cantor's sudden unavailability surprised and troubled his collaborators, none more than Stafford. In the past, most students, and certainly Stafford, were privy to what the professor was doing in his own laboratory. He'd never said so in public, but deep down Stafford had long ago categorized Cantor's occasional forays into his private lab as puttering, if not outright dilettantism. After all, it was the professor himself who'd taught him that only perfect dedication produced real results. But now, every request by Stafford to see Cantor in his laboratory was met by an unprecedented response from Stephanie, who usually just waved the young man in: "I'm sorry, Jerry, but Professor Cantor is working on a very important experiment. All I can do is take a message." Stafford found his former condescension giving way. He was not quite sure with what he should replace it.

Stafford had been listlessly turning the pages of the most recent issue of the *Journal of Biological Chemistry*. It was obvious to Celestine that he was thinking of something else. She leaned across the sofa and ruffled his hair. "What's the matter, Jerry?" The look Stafford gave her mixed guilt and misery in quantities that startled her.

She'd asked similar questions during the past couple of weeks, but he'd always stalled or talked around them. He was not the sort of person who found it easy or comfortable to open up about personal feelings. But tonight, just as the realization dawned on her that something really was the matter, something clicked: perhaps just the way she'd touched him.

"Celly," he began in a muffled voice and stopped. Tears appeared in his eyes.

"Don't worry, Jerry," she whispered, wiping his tears away with her bare hand. She stifled the urge to ask questions. "Everybody has to cry sometimes. Just talk when you're ready." Celestine put her arm around him and drew his head to her shoulder, slowly stroking his hair.

"Celly," he said in a low voice, "I've got to admit something: my grandfather never had a heart attack."

Her hand did not miss a beat in its rhythmic stroking. "I thought so all along," she replied quietly.

"You did?" Stafford tried to raise his head, but Celestine drew him back to her shoulder. "How come?"

"It was so unlike you: the way you took off, the flowers, the card you left. It was so unlike the only other flowers you ever sent me. I've never forgotten my 'cardinal constancy,' my 'royal excellence' . . . my 'well-favored flanks.' . . ."

Stafford seemed not to hear. "Why didn't you say something when I got back?"

"What was there to say? Ask why you fibbed? I figured you had a reason. I knew that, sooner or later, you'd tell me."

He raised his head to look her in the face. "Celly, you're something." He caressed her cheek. "I would've acted differently if our roles had been reversed."

His look of guilty misery returned. "I told you how Krauss, at Harvard—the man whom I.C. respects more than any other—couldn't repeat our experiment? Or at least one of his postdocs couldn't."

"Yes, but—"

"Wait, Celly. Let me finish. This is big. Easily the biggest thing that ever happened in I.C.'s lab. I was sloppy in my notebook. . . ."

"You worked too hard, Jerry. We hardly did it once during that time."

"I know." He seemed oblivious to her teasing, her use of his "it." "I.C. was damned decent about it, but I knew that, underneath it all, it bothered him a lot that, of all places, Krauss's lab should have problems with my work. Remember all the trouble he took to impress Krauss, publishing in *Nature* rather than *Science?* He even blamed himself for not having selected *PNAS.* 'At least then we'd have been required to include the experimental details,' he said. I knew what he meant, because he drums it into everybody's head in the lab: 'Write up your experimental work in sufficient detail so that anybody can duplicate it.' It was up to me to do so. I was worried that I wouldn't recapture all the details and that the Harvard group would fail again. Instead, I chickened out and took off for South Carolina. You know what brought me around?"

"You told me when you came back: Cantor's phone call. Frankly, I was pretty pissed off."

"You shouldn't have been. The whole affair had nothing to do with us. But it wasn't the phone call, it was what I.C. said he was going to do: send Xeroxes of my notebook pages to Harvard."

"So? What's the big deal? I would've thought that was the simplest solution."

"No!" The vehemence of his reply startled her. "I told you, my notes were sloppy. It would've been very embarrassing if Krauss had had to call again for some detail."

"Well, in the end Krauss did call again," she said quietly.

"Yeah. I can't tell you how I felt when I.C. called me into his office. The words are etched in my brain: 'Don't worry . . . not yet.' I've never seen Cantor lose his temper with a student or postdoc, but I wouldn't have blamed him if he had at that moment. Still he didn't. He just said it must be some missing detail and we'd repeat it together in his lab. Do you see why people want to work with him?"

"I wonder what he was really thinking," Celestine mused.

Stafford seemed not to hear. "I never told you how I felt during those weeks."

"You didn't have to, Jerry. I could sense it. But so what? It all ended well. Hasn't it?"

Stafford just shook his head. "I thought it would end well, but it didn't. I haven't told you but, for the last three weeks, I.C. has been a changed man. He liked to dabble in the lab: he'll take a little experiment, here or there, that one of us is doing, and repeat it; or try something new for a couple of days and then hand it over to someone. Sure, it's remarkable that he does even that—I bet that Krauss and most other people in that league haven't dirtied their hands for years."

"So what happened?" Curiosity and concern showed in her voice.

"He's locked himself in his lab. He hasn't told anyone what he's working on and he's been at it for several weeks. He's ignored almost everybody, and especially me. I.C. used to walk through the group's labs almost daily. He always asks people what they're doing —I often wished he wouldn't breathe down our necks so much. And now—" His voice trailed off.

"Why don't you ask him, Jerry? You always told me how open the man is. Walk into his lab."

"It's locked."

"No kidding?" Her cheery tone sounded forced. "So knock on his door until it opens," she offered lamely.

"I can't, Celly. I'm afraid to."

"Jerry!" She reached out to stroke his head, but he shook her hand aside.

"I'll tell you why," he whispered. "I think he's repeating my work. And he doesn't want me around."

"Leonardo, you're the only person I know who doesn't own an answering machine. I hope I'm not phoning too late. You're becoming a stranger." Paula Curry was good at hiding discomfort behind easy patter, but the strain was starting to tell. So far, she had invited Cantor for lunch; she had proposed the Kronos Concert and then had bought the tickets; when the chamber music group played at her apartment, she had suggested, subtly to be sure, that he stay behind to help with the cleanup. For once she'd encountered a male who wasn't continually on the make. But he seemed to be overdoing it—it was time for him to make a move. When she didn't hear from him for three weeks, she decided to try once more. "Do you know how difficult it is to find a violist on short notice? Even more difficult than a cellist. If it weren't for your favorite Boccherini . . ."

"Don't tell me: Sol announced how many trios for two violins and cello he'd written," Cantor beat her to the draw.

"*Mais oui, monsieur.*" She'd caught on quickly to Cantor's fondness for French phrases. "Forty-six, to be precise. Isn't Sol remarkable? Now it's your turn, Leonardo. How many did Haydn compose?"

"Twenty-one," he said quickly.

"Correct! But how did you know that?"

Cantor chuckled with pleasure. "If I weren't such an honest man, I'd reply, 'Doesn't everybody know that?'"

"But since you are honest . . ."

". . . and original," he completed the phrase, "I'll admit that I also learned that piece of musical trivia from our first violinist. The last time I had to back out of playing, he complained that, except for the Mozart divertimenti, the only other scores he had at home for two violins and cello were a couple of Haydn trios. 'And did you know he'd composed twenty-one, although three were lost?' he announced without any prompting on my part. But tell me, Paula, how have you been?"

"I missed you, Leonardo. I'd hoped you'd call."

After a longish pause, he said, "I did also."

Is he totally noncommittal, she wondered, or just shy? Oh, what the hell, she decided: I might as well be hung for a sheep as a lamb. "Also what?" she asked out loud. "You also missed me or you also hoped I'd call?"

"Both."

"Then why didn't you pick up the telephone? I thought you come to Chicago most weekends."

"I would have called, but the last few weeks have been frantic. I've been working every day, and most evenings, in the lab. . . ."

"I thought that you had a whole group of devoted slaves at your beck and call."

"Paula, we call them collaborators, colleagues, coworkers . . ."

"Excuse me, Professor."

"I'm doing this work completely alone. It may be the most important experiment of my life." *I finally announced it, and look whom I picked as my confidante.* "Please don't tell anyone," he hastened, "it may turn out to be nothing if it doesn't work. In fact, less than nothing."

Paula Curry was struck. How many men will tell you on the spur of the moment that they're working on the most important thing in their lives? "I wonder whether Leonardo said that when some silly woman interrupted him while he was painting the Mona Lisa? Listen, my Leonardo, of course I'll keep quiet. But, someday, will you tell me more about it?"

"Yes."

Paula was surprised by his quick, almost explosive reply. "When?"

"Could you drive down here this Sunday? It will probably do me some good to take a break. Can you come for lunch?"

"Oh, of course I can come. Yes, I will." For a moment this forty-four-year-old felt like a teenager who'd finally been invited to the senior prom.

Sunday, May 24, was one of those Midwestern days when it was spring in the morning but sultry summer by noon. On this first visit to Cantor's home ground, the weather offered Paula an opportunity to array herself in a manner distinctly different from any he'd seen earlier. She felt she had nothing to lose by being a bit more daring, and had chosen her wardrobe accordingly: the sheerest of stockings; a mauve-colored skirt ending just above her knees, with a discreet slit on the left side; and a pair of spike heels, Charles Jourdans, which accentuated her jogger's calf muscles. That the high heels made her appear even taller seemed of no consequence. What difference would it make whether she was three or four inches taller than Cantor? She'd long ago resigned herself to towering over most men of her acquaintance; if Cantor minded, he hadn't shown it so far. In front of the mirror, she undid first two, then three buttons of her light gray silk blouse. No, she concluded, two is better: no sense overdoing it.

Paula arrived nearly twenty minutes early and decided to drive around town, circling the sprawling campus that dominated it physically and economically. She made one pass along the tree-lined street where Cantor lived, observing the comfortable houses, the carefully tended lawns, the absence of fences, the sameness of the architecture. She was surprised. She had expected something else of Cantor, not this large, white, two-story house from the twenties or thirties. Hamper in hand, she walked along the juniper-bordered path up the steps and to the door, where she found an envelope with her name on it. The note inside read:

Paula, I had to check something in the lab. The key is under the doormat. I will be back shortly. L.

It was the first note she'd ever received from Cantor. The signature, for all its conciseness, especially pleased her.

As an interior decorator, Paula Curry was a real professional. When she first visited the home of a potential client, or anybody else's for that matter, she never inspected. At least not visibly so. Her eyes, however, were like a wide-angle lens attached to a motor-driven camera; she instantaneously captured, compared and filed the resulting images in her enormous memory bank. Alone in Cantor's house, for once she could afford luxuriously slow reconnaissance without the usual mask of indifference. Now that she found herself there, she wasn't sure what she'd expected to see. Cantor's Chicago pied-à-terre had prepared her for a connoisseur of English furniture, a reasonably affluent man of excellent taste. The one omission she had commented upon after the Boccherini-Beethoven evening—the virtual absence of any pictures on the walls—he had explained with no hesitation. "I don't care for, nor do I know anything about, English hunting scenes. The English painters I like and who would go with this type of eighteenth-century setting are Hogarth or Romney. A Romney portrait would be particularly appropriate, because his father was a cabinetmaker." Cantor had shrugged his shoulders. "They're hardly available, and if they were, I couldn't possibly afford them. I wouldn't mind a small Reynolds or Gainsborough, but it's the same story. So I'd rather just have my books and, of course"—he had pointed to the window—"that view." Was it that a view like that could not be found here? wondered Paula Curry when she saw the art on the walls of the living room. Fascinated, she drew open the curtains to let in more light.

So Cantor found her when he crossed the threshold of the living room; he'd entered the house through the garage side door. Paula was kneeling with one knee on the cane seat of an unusual beechwood settee, her hands against the high backrest, her skirt stretched tight as she leaned forward to inspect the watercolor on the wall. Cantor was startled. It wasn't only Paula's pose; he was equally taken aback by the bright sunlight, which to him, out of concern for his rare watercolors, was usually anathema. *"Bon jour,* Paula," he said finally, "welcome to the provinces."

Paula jumped in surprise. "Oh, I.C. . . . I didn't hear you." She extended her hand. Handshakes, and holding her by the elbow as they crossed a street: these were the only forms of physical contact that had occurred so far between them. "Leonardo," she blurted out, "why didn't you ever mention this?" She waved her hand around the room. "It's mind-boggling. And in this house!"

"What does that mean? 'This house!' "

"Oh, I'm sorry, but you know what I mean. It's a perfectly respectable house on the outside, but . . ."

"Go on, go on." Cantor was beaming.

"Who'd expect to find such a chair? I'm trying to remember what it's called . . . some kind of seating machine . . ."

"Sitzmaschine," he said proudly.

"Why, this room is pure turn-of-the-century Vienna: Josef Hoffmann! Kolo Moser! Just look at that marvelous Moser desk: those brass inlaid figures! What's going on, Leonardo? Eighteenth-century English antiques in the city, Viennese *Jugendstil* in the hinterland? But this"—she grinned, and pointed again to the walls —"this takes the cake. And you had the nerve to tell me in Chicago that you didn't have any art on the walls. That you couldn't afford the matching Romneys. And what do I see here? Matching Schieles."

"Well?" He pretended innocence. "Egon Schiele died in Vienna in 1918. As far as this room goes, he worked in the right place and lived at the right time. Besides, I like his work better than that of any other modern painter. Does that answer the question?"

" 'Does that answer the question?' " she echoed. "And to think you let me lecture you on Viennese chamber music all through that program last month—music that could have been written in this room—and you didn't breathe a word!"

"Paula, be reasonable," he protested, his delight plain to see. "What did you want me to say? 'This program reminds me of home, where I recline on a *Sitzmaschine* scrutinizing my Schieles and sampling some Schönberg on my stereo'?"

"There are times when you try too hard to be clever." She wagged her finger in mock admonishment. "Of course, it's none of my business. But how can you afford"—she started to count—"at least seven Schieles."

"They aren't oils," he said in mock deprecation, "they're only watercolors and drawings."

"Only!"

"I bought them in the sixties. I couldn't buy them now."

"But aren't you afraid somebody might steal them?"

"Hardly." He took that opportunity to draw the curtains. "They're insured. Furthermore, I have very few people over. And those that come have never heard of Schiele. Until today, that is. I saw you studying this one." Cantor pointed to the wall. "Any particular reason?"

She looked him straight in the eye. She felt it was time to reestablish equality between them. "Yes. It's the most erotic of them all. Even though the couple is almost completely dressed. Those eyes: they look haunted. There's a shock of recognition—as if someone had just caught them . . ." She hesitated. Should she say "fucking" or "making love"?

Cantor solved the problem for her. He walked to the wall and removed the drawing. "Here," he suggested, "look at it this way." He held it in a vertical position, the woman standing with the man clasping her by the waist, his head by her belly. Then Cantor turned it sideways. Now the woman appeared to be on her back, the man above her as if he'd just withdrawn. He might even be buttoning his pants.

"Amazing!" She took the picture out of his hands and tried it herself—first one way and then the other.

"Which do you find . . . more . . ."

"Exciting?" she broke in. "Oh, the vertical. No question."

Cantor looked at her quizzically. "You seem so sure. Why?"

"First, they're standing. Making love standing up has something trystlike about it. And this couple certainly looks as if they'd been surprised doing something forbidden. Second, if you look at their relative positions, they weren't . . . copulating, it looks more like cunnilingus. And," she hurried on, still looking at the picture, as if she were addressing it rather than Cantor, "since she's standing and he's sort of crouching, you can't even tell whether she's really so much taller."

"I see," he said after a long pause, and hung the picture back on its hook. "Let's have lunch out in the garden. I already set the table. What kind of wine should I open?"

Paula had her agenda, Cantor had his. Originally, Paula had wanted only to learn more about Cantor and see his university home. Now she was even more curious about his tastes, his means, his life alone. An ostensibly celibate man surrounded by erotic art? Cantor's purpose, on the other hand, was much more specific, his focus almost totally egocentric: he needed someone to talk to. During the past few weeks, he'd been a virtual hermit. Picking for his confidante a person like Paula Curry, who knew no science, but was clever, discreet and perhaps on the way to becoming a friend: as the lunch proceeded, Cantor felt his choice had been just right.

As soon as they sat down, he realized that he'd first have to satisfy Paula's curiosity. When he asked her to come—or had she invited herself?—the invitation had been so spontaneous that he hadn't given any thought to the questions his domestic setting might raise in her mind. She was the first interior decorator he'd ever met, with credentials in art history to boot. He decided to get it over with—quickly and succinctly. Even the absurdly low prices of the Schieles—at least by contemporary art auction standards—still seemed to her to be outside the range of a young professor's income in the early 1960s. Of course, she was right. Since she was also persistent, over the course of lunch she elicited an explanation for his comparative affluence and the transplanted Viennese setting.

The explanation was simple, or so it seemed to Cantor in his impatience to get past the biographical details. His father-in-law—a wealthy Jewish industrialist from Vienna, whose only daughter Cantor had married when she was thirty-six—had made him heir to half his fortune. The old man had had the foresight, unlike most other Viennese Jews, to predict that Hitler's virus would not stop at the Austrian border. Two years before the *Anschluss*, he'd left Vienna for America with all his family, money, furniture, and art intact. "Now do you understand why I own a *Sitzmaschine*, and the Schieles?" Cantor had asked, expecting an understanding nod.

"No," Paula said with a dazzling display of teeth, "not so fast. Why did he make you one of his heirs? And what about your wife: what did she get? And why did you get divorced?"

In the end, Paula extracted it all. Papa Löwenstein, a grand old man, had been delighted that his only child, Eva, had not only found a husband—just after he'd given up all hope that she'd marry —but a real *Herr Professor Doktor*. Why not leave the son-in-law half the estate? Fortunately, the old man had been spared the pain of their divorce: he had died four years earlier in a car accident with his wife. When Eva and I.C. broke up, the property settlement presented no problem because Eva's father had already taken care of that in his will. Both ended up with ample money. Eva was through being Mrs. Cantor, the faculty wife. Nothing was going to remind her of that status—least of all the house and furniture.

"But that's not what I invited you here to talk about." Cantor couldn't restrain himself any longer.

"It wasn't?" Paula's eyes widened in a mocking smile. "Oh well. I suppose you've satisfied my curiosity enough. For now, anyway. What was it you wanted to tell me about, Leonardo? The most important experiment in your life? Or the most successful?"

"Successful?" Cantor was momentarily piqued. "Ah, Paula, that's just what I need to talk to someone about. I'll try to keep it short and simple—"

"Simple?" A smile played again about her lips.

Cantor caught himself looking into her face rather longer than seemed appropriate. "I mean nontechnical. You see, for years, my research group has been focusing on tumorigenesis."

"I know you'll hate me for interrupting right in the beginning, but what, precisely, does that mean?"

"Tumorigenesis? The formation of tumors."

"Are you trying to produce cancer or to cure it?" She meant it in jest, but by now Cantor had mentally entered the lecture hall.

"Neither. We're just trying to understand the process. Last year, I had what in all due modesty I shall call a brilliant idea. It seemed to account for most observations dealing with the onset of malignancies and explained tumor production in a very generally applicable way." Cantor picked up his paper napkin and drew a rough sketch of a cell membrane. Quickly, and with a minimum of scientific jargon, he outlined to Paula the basis of his tumorigenesis theory. "Now there've been plenty of hypotheses in the cancer field —many of them since discarded—but none of such all-encompassing scope as mine. If I may say so, it caused quite a stir. I was absolutely sure it was right. But it was only a hypothesis and it was bound to remain one, unless"—he paused for effect—"we could provide some experimental proof. Late in the fall, I thought of an experiment that could do so, and I put my best young collaborator, a Dr. Stafford, on the project."

"One of your slaves."

"No, one of my collaborators. Perhaps the most promising I've ever had. But I drove him very hard, I'll admit that. I was so convinced that the theory was right, I did something that under ordinary circumstances I would never have dreamed of doing: I basically told the man that he had to finish the work in three months."

"And did he?"

"He did. We published the work—"

"We?"

Cantor looked puzzled. "Yes, we. Why do you ask?"

"Well, if he did the work, why did you publish it with him?"

"God, Paula"—he sounded annoyed—"we do have a cultural gulf to bridge. I don't want to spend the time on it now. Let me just assure you that in science it's *de rigueur*. *I* thought of the problem and the solution, *he* did the actual work, and *we* published it together. That's how it's always done."

"Go ahead, Leonardo." Paula set her voice to soothe. "It's not important. Then what happened?"

"Well, after we published it, literally all hell broke loose. I mean in a nice way." He grinned self-consciously. "Phone calls, congratulations, invitations to lectures, all that stuff. But"—he wagged his index finger for emphasis—"there was also a problem. An important colleague—or maybe I should call him the mentor I never had—at Harvard assigned one of his postdoctorate fellows the task of repeating our work."

"Now why would he want to do that? Dr. Stafford—I mean, you people had already done it. Didn't he trust you?"

"Paula, in science, we have something that could be called a 'social contract.' We must be able to depend on the reliability of other scientists' work. If you ever look at a scientific paper—wait a moment: I'll just run in and bring you one."

Paula was touched by his boyish enthusiasm, the manner in which he jumped up and took the garden steps two at a time.

"Here, look at the end of this article." He had opened the reprint of their *Nature* paper. "There are eleven references to the work of other people—work and results that we used to complete our own research. If their work isn't reliable, our work can't be. Science is an edifice founded absolutely on good faith. If that weren't so, it'd be sitting on a swamp."

"I still don't see how your social contracts relate to that man at Harvard repeating your work," she persisted.

"Aha, that's precisely it. An experiment should be replicated independently, to demonstrate its reliability. Just to make sure we didn't make some mistake. Of course, one doesn't do that with every experiment. But all *important* ones must pass through that process, and ours certainly falls into that class. That's why Kurt Krauss decided to check it. He's one of the most prominent men in the cancer field. A sarcoma has even been named after him."

"So he repeated your work out of friendship for you?"

Cantor hesitated. "No, not just friendship. Although we are collegial friends," he hastened to add. "I would also attribute it to some skepticism."

"But I thought you said this was built on trust."

"Krauss never takes anything on blind trust. Especially if it's important. But irrespective of the personal motive, skepticism in science is healthy."

"So now that he has verified your work, what comes next? Will you win the Nobel Prize?"

Cantor flushed. "What made you ask that?"

"Oh, coming up with a theory that explains cancer seems to me important enough for a Nobel. Don't you think so?" She pretended naiveté. "Leonardo Cantor, the Nobel laureate. It sounds great."

He pretended humility, as every serious contender does when the subject comes up, whether it is broached in public or in his own home. " 'The world is full of people who should get the Nobel Prize but haven't got it and won't get it.' Arne Tiselius, who said that, knew what he was speaking about. He won the Prize in Chemistry and was president of the Nobel Foundation."

That only shows he thinks he should get it. Paula Curry considered for a moment giving voice to the thought but decided that, on this subject, Cantor's sense of humor might have its limits. She returned to her earlier question. "So now that your friend Krauss has satisfied his healthy skepticism, what happens next?"

Cantor leaned back in his chair, his eyes scanning the garden. The interval seemed so long that Paula was almost prompted to repeat the question. Finally, his gaze settled on her. "His skepticism was not satisfied. They couldn't repeat Stafford's results."

"What? Why not? Surely he's not calling you a—" Paula stopped short, surprised to find herself bristling so strongly at this imaginary slight to I.C.

Cantor waved her airily to silence. "Tut-tut, Paula, nothing of the sort. You still don't understand the terms of the contract. It has nothing to do with name-calling. It's just science: we have to establish the validity of results. And in any case, initially at least, Krauss's failure was not too surprising. We'd only published a brief communication in *Nature*—the one you see here." He pointed to the reprint on the table. "It's very sketchy, really: merely a basic description of the theory, and that the experiment had succeeded. It didn't give sufficient detail to be reproducible in another laboratory. But when Stafford wrote up the experimental details in full, and we sent them to Harvard, they still couldn't duplicate his results."

"You mean what Stafford did was wrong?"

"No!" Cantor said sharply. "It doesn't mean that at all. You put it too black and white. It could mean that, unknowingly, he has neglected to mention some crucial detail. Or Krauss's man neglected to follow one. I had that experience in my own graduate work as a chemist. I carried out a reaction, called a 'decarbonylation,' which involved heating a substance in a glass tube above its melting point. The first time, it worked beautifully, but later I had very erratic results. It took me a long time to figure out the explanation: initially, I'd used soft glass, which is slightly alkaline, while later I'd picked Pyrex. It turned out that the reaction was promoted by traces of alkali."

"But does that happen very often?" Paula was intrigued. She'd always assumed scientific experiments to be unambiguous.

"Absolutely!" Cantor was anxious to make that point. "I'll tell you another true story that will surprise you. Carroll Williams, a distinguished insect biologist at Harvard, once had a Czech postdoctorate fellow, Karel Sláma, come to his laboratory to continue some research he'd started in Prague. He brought with him the bug that he'd studied at home for years, but, lo and behold, Sláma couldn't get the insects to mature and reproduce in Massachusetts, even though he fed them the same diet. You know what it finally came down to?

"The crushed paper on the bottom of the jars in which they kept the insects!" Cantor looked triumphant. "The paper was only supposed to play the role of inert support material—they'd always done that in Prague—but once they eliminated the paper, the insects grew happily in Cambridge." Cantor enjoyed drawing out the story; it made him forget his real problem. "European paper is made from different trees than North American, which is derived from balsam fir. From balsam pulp they isolated what has since been called the 'paper factor,' which causes abnormal growth and premature death of the insects. I still remember the conclusion to their otherwise very serious article: the *Boston Globe* and the *Wall Street Journal* were inhibitory, whereas *Nature* and *The Times* of London were harmless."

"Leonardo, I'm amazed at the scope of your field: we started with tumors and ended up with the inhibitory effect of the *Wall Street Journal.*" She lifted her glass of wine. "Let's drink to something similarly amusing in Dr. Stafford's experiment."

"That would be nice," he answered somberly, "but we may never know. When Krauss failed the second time, I had Stafford do the experiment with me in my own laboratory next to my office."

"And?"

"And it worked."

"That's wonderful," she beamed, "you must've been pleased. What did the Harvard man say to that?"

Cantor continued as if he'd not heard her last question. "A couple of months ago, I thought of another test of my theory. Conceptually more complicated, but experimentally simpler. I decided to work on it myself." He looked up at her, half apologetically. "That's why I haven't been to Chicago, or anywhere else. You're the first one to know what I'm working on. All I need is another week or two to find out . . ." He didn't finish the sentence. What could he say? That he would then know whether he'd have to flagellate himself in public?

"But I don't understand. Why are you starting a new experiment? Since Stafford had no difficulty with the work in your presence, why not let the Harvard people repeat it once more? Or even simpler: ask someone from Harvard to come to your lab and do the experiment with Stafford. The way you did."

Paula is nobody's fool, he thought with admiration: let's go closer to the truth. "Suppose, the next time, it doesn't work again? Remember, this isn't an experiment that takes just a couple of days: it requires weeks to complete. If we can only succeed in the presence of Stafford, then it's not a real experiment. Not in the context of the social contract I spoke about. Do you know what I would then have to do? Publish a retraction in the same journal saying that the Experiment, for some unknown reason, is not duplicable. As far as Krauss and others like him are concerned, that'll be the end of my generalized tumorigenesis concept. It's not the question of a Nobel Prize but of my credibility. Do you know the word *Schadenfreude?*"

"No."

"It's one of those German words, like *Gestalt* or *Weltschmerz,* that has a special flavor that doesn't come across in the English equivalent—'gloating.' *Schadenfreude* is more subtle and yet meaner. The more impeccable your reputation, and the more significant the work you retract, the greater the *Schadenfreude* among your peers."

"I can't believe what you're saying," exclaimed Paula. "You scientists, you upholders of the social contract, gloat like other mortals when somebody makes a mistake? Even when he confesses the mistake?"

Cantor let out a sigh. "I'm afraid the answer is yes. I've been guilty of that. I mean gloating," he added quickly. "I've never had to retract any of my published work and I hope to God I won't need to do it this time. Because of the rareness of such events, innocent or otherwise—"

"What does 'otherwise' mean?" interjected Paula.

"Data manipulation, even outright fraud . . ."

"Does that happen?"

"Not often," he responded firmly. "But just as I said, precisely because of the rarity of such retractions, people's memory is unbelievably long: I'd guess a lifetime. Because of our mutual dependence and our need for absolute trust, once somebody's credibility in science is damaged, it can never be totally repaired. Most often, it's gone for good."

"What do you people expect from each other? Absolute perfection?" exclaimed Paula.

"Of course not. But if the work is important, if it influences the thoughts or research direction of many others, the accusation would be: 'Why did you publish in such a hurry? Why didn't you wait until your results were validated?' "

"And what would your answer be, Leonardo, if you were asked? Why *did* you publish in such a hurry?"

"To be quite honest, most scientists suffer from some sort of dissociative personality: on one side, the rigorous believer in the experimental method, with its set of rules and its ultimate objective of advancing knowledge; on the other, the fallible human being with all the accompanying emotional foibles. I'm now talking about the foibles. We all know that in contemporary science the greatest occupational hazard is simultaneous discovery. If my theory is right, then I'm absolutely certain that, sooner or later—and in a highly competitive field like mine, it's likely to be sooner—somebody will have the same idea. A scientist's drive, his self-esteem, are really based on a very simple desire: recognition by one's peers, the Krausses of this world. That recognition is bestowed only for originality, which, quite crassly, means that you must be first. No wonder that the push for priority is enormous. And the only way we—including me—establish priority is to ask who published first. Suddenly you seem very pensive, Paula. Did I disappoint you?"

She hesitated for a long while before replying. "Not so much disappoint as disillusion me. Is that why you haven't told anyone about your most recent idea, which might offer independent confirmation of your theory? So nobody publishes it first?"

He nodded. "I suppose so."

"Leonardo, one last question." She leaned forward across the table. "Why are you doing this work yourself, burying yourself in your laboratory, not seeing anybody? Why didn't you ask your man Stafford to do the work for you as he did the first time around? Isn't he the best person in your group? What's different this time?"

"A good scientist changes only one variable at a time."

Paula Curry looked puzzled. "What's that supposed to mean?"

"I don't trust Stafford anymore."

13

In the end, the second experiment—Cantor's independent test of his tumorigenesis theory—came out precisely as the professor had hoped: the changes in the structure of the incriminating protein were mirrored perfectly in the composition of the protein's template, the ribonucleic acid. He had vindicated his earlier optimism: first a sweet theory, and now an even sweeter experiment!

Rather than rushing into print in *Nature,* however, Cantor played it cool and cautious. He telephoned Krauss: it was now unnecessary for the Harvard group to examine further the verification of the Cantor-Stafford Experiment, because he'd just completed a second and experimentally much simpler one.

"Kurt, just wait till you see the details: it's a beauty. And contrary to what I'd expected, it turned out to be easier to look at the RNA than the protein. But I won't write it up for a while—not till someone in your lab has time to take a look at it. I'll send you Xeroxes of my own lab notebook by Federal Express. You'll get them tomorrow." In a subtle way, Cantor had forced Krauss to center his attention on his own experiment and away from Stafford's. Krauss couldn't help but agree to become the irreproachable witness of Cantor's scientific veracity.

Since Cantor was certain that his latest work would be confirmed at Harvard, he had no reason to delay announcing his success through the grapevine—another time-tested way of nailing down questions of priority. He called a special departmental seminar and announced that he would be speaking, without listing a title. Only superstars can use such a ploy. When the notice reads "Topic to Be Announced," lesser lights run the risk of an empty room.

In Cantor's case, even without the mystery of an untitled talk, rumors had been flying: his virtual disappearance for weeks from public view guaranteed an overflow. The lecture hall was jammed when Stafford deliberately arrived at the very last moment. As he sat in the back, he was convinced he was about to witness his own public crucifixion—or perhaps only humiliation, he told himself wryly as he scanned the restless crowd, counting the familiar heads. Shortly after Cantor's start, however, Stafford realized he was not even a bit player in the drama unfolding before the abruptly hushed audience. Without once referring to Krauss's inability to validate Stafford's work, Cantor described his *second* experimental test of the generalized tumorigenesis theory.

In the excitement as the applause commenced, nobody had noticed Stafford slipping out of the lecture hall. He headed straight for the professor's office.

Stafford's voice was composed as he sank into a chair in the secretary's office. "Stephanie, I.C. just gave the most fabulous talk you could imagine. I'd like to wait for him here. I want to tell him what I thought of the presentation."

Stafford had to wait for a long time; he didn't mind. It gave him time to rehearse his little speech.

He was silently debating whether to offer detached congratulations or bubbling enthusiasm—matters of style—when Cantor appeared. The young man jumped up. "Prof"—he didn't consider "I.C." appropriate under the circumstances, and "Professor Cantor" was clearly too formal—"could I see you for a moment?"

Cantor merely glanced at his student and then motioned him into his office. As soon as the door was closed, Stafford switched into high gear. "I.C., I was sure that downstairs you'd be surrounded by everyone. I just wanted to tell you this was the most fantastic lecture I've ever heard you give. I'd been concerned when I didn't see you for all these weeks, but now I'm relieved."

The older man's expression did not change. "You damn well ought to be," was all he said.

Stafford's face turned crimson. "What do you mean?" he stuttered.

Climbing Everest by two different routes is sensational; almost nobody has been photographed twice on top. This time, however, Cantor's basking on the summit ended much sooner than the first time around. Again, the message was from Harvard, the bearer Kurt Krauss. He informed his friend that the verification of the second experiment was well on its way, that no hitches of any kind had developed. Cantor was elated; a potentially devastating situation was about to be defused.

But then Krauss continued. "By the way, I.C., your man Stafford called the other day. He asked whether I'd offer him a postdoctoral fellowship in my lab. He said he'd spent his entire career in your department and wanted to work on some other problems before looking for an assistant professorship.

"With anyone else, I wouldn't even have called. But since he's working with you, I wanted to check whether you'd mind if he joined my group. I know your fabulous opinion of the man. But you're familiar with institutional red tape. We need some letters of recommendation in the files, and, clearly, one must come from you. You're his scientific father. But Stafford didn't even list you as a reference; I was surprised, but when I asked him, he said he didn't want to bother you with such a trivial request. Frankly, I think he thought you'd be annoyed that he wants to work in another lab."

For once, Cantor was speechless. Krauss mistook the silence for disapproval. He hastened on. "I.C., you've got to admit almost anything the man would do now in your place would be an anticlimax. After the spectacular work the two of you published in *Nature*, it's only natural he should want new worlds to conquer. Could you send me a letter about him? It can be quite short. Just write what you told me earlier: that he's the best man you've ever had in your lab."

Leah had just turned the corner when in the distance she saw Stafford carrying a suitcase to the car parked in front of their house. She caught up with him as he was pulling away from the curb.

"Jerry," she called, "what's going on?" She pointed to the back seat, which was stacked with cartons of books and clothing.

"Didn't Celly tell you last night?" he countered sullenly.

"I wasn't here last night," she grinned, "I'm only coming home to take a shower and change before I go to the library."

"Well, ask her then," he said, jerking his head in the direction of the house, "she's up there. I've got to take off."

Leah cautiously unlocked the door. "Are you home, Celly?" she called out. She stopped as she saw her roommate's face swollen from crying.

"Leave me alone, Leah. I'm livid."

"Okay, so you're livid." She tried to embrace Celestine, who shrugged her away. "Tell me what happened."

"That bastard. And after what he promised me only a few weeks ago." She scrubbed at her eyes with a fist. "Remember when you asked me what I really saw in Jerry? Why I put up with him after he didn't show up for that dinner with Jean Ardley?"

"Of course I remember. You said I wouldn't understand."

Celestine had calmed down. "*This* I think you'll understand."

Leah nodded and sat down, always the good listener.

"When I first met Jerry, he seemed so young. In certain respects, I felt the way Graham must have: the excitement of teaching someone younger about sexual pleasure. Jerry seemed so inexperienced and fresh and . . . needy, I guess is the word. He didn't need just a lover, in some fundamental way he also needed a mother. Remember how we once talked about the ideal relationship: the combined lover-friend-companion? Soon after we became lovers, Jerry started to open up—like a flower, petal by petal. And then he poured out his entire life story. Do you know that his father is a convinced Pentecostal? He speaks in tongues, he's a creationist, he won't even permit the word 'evolution' to be used in the house. I became his confidante; not a bad beginning to companionship. And when Jerry started on his personal desires and ambitions—what scientific research meant to him, what he planned to do professionally, even on what basis he'd selected a mentor—I realized that we had a great deal in common. Friends need that."

Leah looked wistful. "You never told me that."

"Why should I have? It didn't affect our friendship." She reached over and ruffled Leah's hair. "Jerry and I have very similar priorities: we both want academic jobs, and we both want to establish a scientific reputation. So we struck a bargain, or at least I thought we had. Jerry agreed to continue with his postdoc work in Cantor's lab until I got my Ph.D.—it'll only take another year at the most—and then we'd be able to look for jobs not too far apart. For example, if he got a position at Berkeley, I could find something at Stanford. At least that's what we had in mind."

Celestine's tone took on an angry edge. "Last night, Jerry walks in like a dog with his tail between his legs and announces that an opportunity has arisen he can't turn down. Remember Krauss, the cancer man at Harvard Jerry told us about? The one even Cantor wants to impress? Jerry says he offered him a postdoc starting next month and that he's decided to take it. It would plug him into the Krauss network for subsequent jobs. That's exactly what he said: 'plug.' And you know what I told him? 'You can plug *into* a network, and at the same time plug *up* a connection.' 'But, Celly,' he said, 'we'll get together weekends. I'll fly in from Boston, and you can visit me at Harvard.' 'But will I?' I asked. 'What if I'm too busy to go to Harvard? What if I crave a bit of companionship on a Tuesday or Thursday?' "

"What did he say to that?"

"I don't remember," Celestine muttered. "But he did look guilty. He even shed a few tears. He asked me to believe him. . . . I told him to pack up his stuff and get out now. He'd made a commitment, but underneath it, he'd kept his options open. Well, I told him, 'Now I'll keep my options open.'

" 'You mean you won't see me anymore?' Jerry asked. I told him that if he wanted an immediate answer it'd be yes. He begged me to think it over."

"And are you thinking it over?"

"Yes."

"A small dose of psychoanalysis wouldn't hurt you before you make up your mind," advised Leah good-naturedly. "You say that you and Jerry have so much in common in terms of your scientific culture. Maybe your access to Jerry's knowledge is through your sexuality. . . ."

"Oh, come on, Leah, get real: you don't think people really act that way, do you?"

"Oh yes, Celly, they do. Take your affair with Lufkin, for instance. Obviously your investment in it was pure transference: projection of desire for your father onto a convenient, older man."

"Now wait a minute," protested Celestine, her tone a mixture of annoyance and amusement. " 'Transference,' 'projection'—is that psychobabble from one of your classes?"

"All right." Leah waved the objection away. "Forget about Lufkin—"

"You said, 'Forget about Lufkin.' " Celestine let out a snort. "I've got news for you. He'll be here next week. And even if he doesn't show up," she added, "I doubt whether I'll ever forget my first dinner with him."

Celestine had been leaning against the refrigerator in Lufkin's airy white kitchen, sipping wine and watching him add some final touches to the main dish. "There we are," he said in a pleased tone as he stepped back to admire the quiche, "half an hour in the oven and it'll be ready. I'll just toss the salad and then we can start. By the way," he added without looking at her, "how many men have noticed your unsymmetrical earlobes?"

Celestine broke out laughing. "None, except my father."

"I thought so." He put the salad utensils down and walked over to face Celestine, who was holding the stem of the wineglass in both her hands against her chest. Just a suspicion of a smile showed in his eyes as he took each earlobe and commenced to squeeze them between index fingers and thumbs, every once in a while running his index fingers around the inside rims of her ears. Celestine was shivering with pleasure; the man had found her second most sensitive erogenous zone and he didn't let go. Slowly he pulled her by the ears toward him. "I'd like to taste you before we sit down," he whispered. His tongue traveled gently over her lips until gradually her mouth opened slightly, just wide enough for his tongue to enter. It continued its exploration. Suddenly, he withdrew his tongue from her mouth and ran it slowly, very slowly, along her neck, to precisely the spot she desired. As the tip of his tongue entered her ear, she let go of the glass and grabbed his head in her hands—whether to hold him there with his wicked tongue or push him away she was never sure. As the glass shattered at their feet, she broke loose. "I'm sorry," she gasped.

"I'm not," he laughed and resumed tossing the salad, while she bent down to pick up the shards.

"You're already twenty-one years old, aren't you?" he asked as they sat down for dinner at the round breakfast table in the kitchen.

"Yes, but why do you ask?"

Lufkin gave her a mocking look. "I just wanted to be sure I'm not breaking any law." He pointed to the bottle of wine.

They had dessert—cassis sorbet with fresh raspberries and whipped cream—in the living room. Celestine was scraping the last traces from her bowl when Lufkin walked over to the cabinet holding his record collection. He bent down and ran his index finger along the spines of the covers. "How familiar are you with Carl Orff's music?" he asked.

Celestine shrugged her shoulders. "*Carmina Burana* is about all I've ever heard."

"Already a legal adult and she's still not heard his *Catulli Carmina*! We better do something about this deficiency right now." Lufkin's choice was clever. He'd remembered Celestine telling him about her extensive Latin background in high school. A few minutes later, Celestine was reclining on the sofa, shoes on the floor, Orff's music resounding all around them. "Listen," he called to her, translating from the Latin words he had memorized. "The young men are singing, 'Oh, your tongue that always moves, your snake's tongue'; the women reply, 'Watch out for this tongue or it will sting you'; the men challenge them with 'Bite me'; the women reply, 'Kiss me, kiss me,' and then you hear their 'Ah.' But this is just the introduction. Wait till the chorus of old men starts announcing the entry of Catullus."

Lufkin sat by Celestine's bare feet. He'd taken her left foot into his strong hands and was alternating between massaging each individual toe and pressing his thumb hard against the arch of her foot. He couldn't see her face: it was hidden behind Orff's text, which she was holding up in both her hands. However, it was clear from the way she spread the toes of her other foot that it desired equal treatment. The music had reached the dialogue between Catullus and Lesbia. Lufkin slid to the floor and took Celestine's small toe into his mouth. With excruciating slowness and delicacy he sucked it before running his tongue in the space between the last two toes. And then the next one. No one had ever caressed Celestine that way. By the time he'd reached the big toe of her left foot, she lay at length on the floor; were it not for the loud music, her breathing would have been audible. "Don't worry," he murmured, "I've had a vasectomy."

At breakfast, wrapped in Lufkin's bathrobe, Celestine heard Lufkin refer to her skin as satin Teflon.

"Now what kind of a compliment is that?" she asked with a mock pout.

"The ultimate," he said, getting up and then returning with a frying pan. "Here, touch this surface while running your other hand up the inside of your thigh. Can you think of anything more appropriate than satin Teflon? It reminds one of sex and the lab at the same time."

Mentioning the lab caused Celestine to recall the almost subliminal manner in which Lufkin had introduced in his lectures topics which women college students often find offensive coming from male professors, but which he had somehow managed to make acceptable by relating them to his amorous insects.

"Take, for instance, some female mosquito species," he'd said in one of his lectures. "She's absolutely sterile after the first sexual contact, regardless of subsequent matings with different males. As sterile as a vasectomized man, who never fathers any children irrespective of the number of sexual partners and coital frequency," he'd added in an offhand sort of way.

"Professor." Celestine ogled her fifty-six-year-old lover across the breakfast table; in spite of his urging, she absolutely refused to call him Graham. "You were so smooth, it didn't even occur to me to wonder why you compared the female mosquito to a vasectomized man rather than to a woman with a tubal ligation."

"Did you know that some insects, like the male scorpion fly, can act as transvestites?" he replied.

"What's that got to do with my question?"

"Nothing."

"Nothing?"

"Nothing. I was changing the subject."

"Okay, Professor," laughed Celestine, "you win. Tell me about male scorpion fly transvestites."

"Not until you've kissed me. I love that tongue of yours."

"Blackmailer."

When she finally withdrew from his mouth, he ran his fingers up the nape of her neck and through her closely cropped light brown hair. She'd started wearing it that way during her swimming days at Branner; Lufkin had noticed it the very first time she came up to him after class to ask for a journal reference. The hairdo displayed her ears, which were almost perfectly formed except for the one minor asymmetry that hardly anyone noticed. Now he moved her head so close to his own face that she appeared to have three eyes— three hooded eyes, almost oriental in appearance, which became the narrowest of slits but never quite closed, even during the heights of her sexual passion.

"All right," he continued, "let me tell you about the transvestite scorpion fly. Before the female permits a male to mate with her, he must bring some morsel—a nuptial prey. She tastes it and only if she likes it will she present herself to the male. Now you realize that the male takes risks while hunting for such treats. He may get caught by predators, like spiders, and never return. But there are a few smarter males, the transvestites, who behave like females. They accept the offering of some hunter Lothario and make off with it to present it to an authentic female. She then mates with the transvestite who never risked his life. Clever, isn't it?"

"Professor, why do you tell so many sexy stories about insects?"

"Because, my lovely ignoramus, I wouldn't mind if *Callosobruchus* had a human counterpart."

"*Callosobruchus?*"

"A Japanese beetle. The female of that species secretes a substance called 'erectin,' which—you might guess—causes sexual tumescence in the male. Got it?"

"Got it." Celestine's head moved back slightly until two dancing eyes were focused on Lufkin. "I think I'll call you *Callosobruchus*. It sounds learned and naughty—like you. I think I'll come again—if you should invite me."

"Just so you can hear more stories?"

"No. There must be more to you than that."

14

"Seminar" is not yet officially a transitive verb. Still, most graduate students in any large research-oriented university have at times felt themselves more the helpless objects of a seminar than its active participants. "Seminared into numbness" describes that feeling of oversaturation. In Celestine Price's case, her seminaring began each week with the Monday chemistry departmental seminars at 4 P.M.; Professor Ardley's group seminars blanketed a two-hour lunch period on Tuesdays, while the organic chemistry seminars met Thursdays again at four. And then there were the visiting firemen, any one of whose talks might be related to her thesis work and thus must be attended: the biochemists in the medical school, the developmental biologists in the adjacent biology complex, and even some of the visitors to the ag school, which was a good ten-minute bike ride from the Chemistry Building. Under such pressure, no wonder the graduate students and postdoctoral fellows had set their selection threshold for those talks they actually did attend fairly high. Unless a seminar topic was of real interest or the student's absence was frowned upon—the weekly departmental seminar was one such event—it took a real star speaker or a very catchy title to drag Celestine or her lab mates to still another talk outside their specific area of interest.

Professor Graham Lufkin was more sensitive to the seminar saturation syndrome than most of the visiting speakers because he did not fall into the superstar category. He was realistic enough not even to place himself among the lesser stars. At Johns Hopkins, his home institution for the last quarter of a century, he was known and respected as a superb lecturer. His colleagues in the biology department were aware of his research accomplishments in the pheromone field: they characterized them as "sound" (an adjective almost pejorative in its faintness), "reasonably productive," but "nothing spectacular." His present research group consisted only of two masters students and one Ph.D. candidate. When he gave a research talk at Hopkins, people came because they wanted to hear Graham Lufkin, the pedagogic showman; they were not expecting a scientific tour de force. But now he was facing the prospect of having to present a seminar some seven hundred miles west of Baltimore at the chemistry department to which Jean Ardley had moved with her research group.

Lufkin knew why he'd been invited. At Hopkins, Jean Ardley and he had had the type of professional relationship that was good for his ego: he playing the role of detached adviser and scientific confidant, she that of a very bright but distinctly junior woman. As far as he was concerned, sex—or even sexual innuendo—had never entered into their personal intercourse. Although some twenty years younger than he, Ardley was not his type. When she moved to the Midwest, their contact had been reduced to regular Christmas greetings, occasional exchanges of journal reprints with messages scribbled across the top, and not much more. But a few weeks ago they'd bumped into each other at a scientific meeting. Lufkin had assumed that Ardley's parting remark—"Graham, you've got to visit us sometime"—was a polite conversational gambit requiring no response other than a noncommittal smile. To his surprise, a few days later he found himself choosing among three alternative seminar dates listed in Ardley's written invitation. He proceeded immediately to plot how to fill the lecture hall. The name Graham Lufkin and his provenance as a biologist were unlikely to represent much of a drawing card in a distant chemistry department. But Lufkin, the realist, knew what would do the trick: his latest research on the sweat bee dressed up in sexy language.

"You haven't changed, Celly," Lufkin murmured as he put his arms around Celestine, ready to kiss her on the mouth. "How nice of you to pick me up."

"Graham, you haven't changed either," laughed Celestine as she pecked him on the cheek, simultaneously pushing his hands discreetly but firmly away from her.

"What's the matter?" he countered with mock surprise. "What's wrong with kissing a former lover in a busy airport after two years? People kiss each other all the time in such places."

"Some people, yes. Maybe even some ex-lovers, but not this one. Don't you remember how we became ex . . . ?"

"Celly, that was more than two years ago."

"Which makes me more than two years older."

"So?"

"And many years wiser."

"I see." Lufkin's tone had switched from the intimate to the pragmatic. "Then why did you come to pick me up? Do you provide this service to all distinguished visitors?"

"Distinguished? You?" Celestine felt that a touch of sarcasm would help her get to the point. "No, that's not why I'm here."

"All right then, your professor told you to pick me up." He was now unmistakably annoyed.

"Relax, Graham. Jean wanted to pick you up herself, but she had to attend a faculty meeting. She's taking you out to dinner tonight. Jean didn't really have to ask me—I volunteered because I wanted to see you. Alone," she added. "Let's stop here at the coffee shop."

Celestine added a third spoonful of sugar. "You really haven't changed," Lufkin remarked, pointing with his spoon toward her coffee cup. "You're still a sugar junkie."

"True," she replied while slowly stirring her coffee. "I'm still the same as far as sugar is concerned. What about you? Your hair seems grayer but, judging from the title of your talk, you're still the same old Graham Lufkin."

"Don't you like my title? Isn't it prurient enough? Don't you think it'll tempt the chemists to come to listen to a biologist?"

"No. . . . Yes. . . . Yes." Celestine pronounced the words slowly, without any inflection.

"What's that supposed to mean?" Lufkin asked suspiciously.

"No, I don't like the title 'One-Night Stands Among Insects. Evidence for an Antiaphrodisiac in *Lasioglossum zephyrum.'* Yes, it's prurient enough. Yes, it'll bring in the chemists. After all, I'll probably be the only chemist in the audience who knows you."

"Only one? What about Jean Ardley?"

Celestine reached across the table and put her hand on Lufkin's. "Graham, I'm assuming that Jean doesn't know you in the biblical sense." Her voice had turned serious. "That's what I want to talk to you about."

"That?" Lufkin sounded wary.

"Graham." Celestine leaned backward as if suddenly wanting to put the maximum distance between the two of them. "Why did you, a fifty-six-year-old professor, seduce a student barely past the age of consent? What made you do such a thing?"

"What's come over you, Celly?" he whispered. "How come you didn't ask that three years ago? If I seduced you, why did you come to my place for almost a year? How come—"

"I went with you to New York, to hear my first opera?" she completed the sentence. "But didn't you see we weren't equals? And I'm not just talking about our age difference."

"Celly, you have some gall to hold that against me. Wasn't I the one who finally brought that up?"

"Sure," she replied, "but the operative word is 'finally.' It only took you twelve months."

Lufkin decided that the time had come to drop his defensive posture. "Tell me, why did *you* make love to a man some thirty years older than you, who, incidentally, was your ex-teacher." The emphasis on "ex" gave it an audible hiss. "We didn't become lovers while you were in my class."

"Graham, don't be legalistic. I'm not accusing you of sexual harassment at a tenure hearing. I just wanted to get something clear between the two of us. It took me a long time to face the real facts. . . ." She stopped and slowly stirred a bit more sugar into her coffee. "I'm sorry, Graham, I shouldn't get so angry."

"I shouldn't either, Celly." He reached over and covered the sugar bowl. "So what were the facts?"

"You were a superb teacher, and not just in class. But when you seduced me, you broke a confidence."

"There *you* go again," he broke in. "Just think back to the time we"—he hesitated before continuing—"became sexually intimate. You were listening to the Orff music—"

It was her turn to interrupt. "And reading an extremely lascivious dialogue you just happened to have there. Now you'll tell me that was just a coincidence, you were just testing my competence in Latin."

"No, I won't say that. But while you listened, all I did was caress your toes. If you hadn't liked it, you could've stopped me."

"And you would've stopped?"

"Absolutely! I even gave you an easy way out. You could've claimed to be ticklish."

"I see." Celestine's irony was unmistakable. "Just think about it for a moment. You asked why did I, a twenty-one-year-old girl—"

"Woman," he interrupted.

"Girl, woman—whatever. Why did I consent to sleep with a man who was older than my father?"

"Oh, my God, you're not going to give me Freud now, are you?"

"I could, but I won't. There are times when a cigar is simply a cigar. I don't believe for a moment that I was searching for a father figure in you. Maybe other young women would have. I presume there've been others?"

"Others?"

"Oh, Graham," she exclaimed, "don't act. For once, let's be honest. Have you had many others like me?"

"None like you, Celly."

"Graham!" Celestine didn't hide her irritation. "You know what I mean: young like me."

"A few."

"Okay. I won't ask how many are a few. Were there any after me?"

Lufkin looked momentarily at Celestine and then dropped his eyes. "One."

"I see." She spooned more sugar into her empty coffee cup and motioned to the waitress for a refill.

The pause was long enough to re-establish some sort of equilibrium between them. Celestine resumed the conversation. "I guess what I wanted in our relationship was parity. I couldn't very well compete with you intellectually but I didn't want to be just a sexual object. At least I wanted to matter to you, and when you suddenly sent me packing I resented it deeply."

"I know," he replied. "I knew you'd feel that way before I even said a word. But I also wanted parity. How long could I remain sexually attractive to you—"

"Don't be such a fool!" blurted out Celestine. "What sort of sexual attractiveness are you talking about? Your sex attractant, Lufkin's personal pheromone, is knowledge. It's intellectual mastery that draws a young woman to an older man. You abused that."

"How can you say that?" exclaimed Lufkin. "Let me tell you what you meant to me. Calling yourself a sexual commodity totally demeans our relationship."

"Ha!"

"Don't 'ha' me, Celly," he replied bitterly. "Don't you know what your youth meant to me? When we went to the opera in New York, most of the time I watched you through the corner of my eyes rather than looking at the singers on the stage. To you it was all new. Don't you know what that means to someone like me?"

"Yes, I know," she said quietly, "that was a great weekend."

"And our sexual pleasuring at that time didn't make it ugly, did it?"

"No, Graham, it didn't. Not at that time. But eventually it did. Maybe I'd feel differently if I'd been the only one. But you just told me there were others, before me and after me. What did they represent in your life?"

Lufkin said nothing. He looked down at his coffee cup, the middle finger of his right hand drumming an impatient patter on the plastic table top. Celestine still remembered the sign: it was his way of counting to ten. This time the drumming took so long that Celestine was almost ready to repeat the question. In the end, it was unnecessary. Lufkin started in a low, almost angry voice, his eyes fixed on his cup as if he were talking to himself.

"When I got tenure at Hopkins, I was a promising researcher. But the tenure decision was really made because of my teaching. I always took teaching seriously and even twenty-five years ago I was damn good at it. But my research never really took off. I didn't want to admit that to myself, not for the first dozen years or so, but it was true. Only gradually did it dawn on me that I would never become a star. I have never said that to anyone else. I don't think I've ever even said those words aloud to myself." He looked up suddenly from the cup: Celestine was struck by how red his eyes were, how old they looked. "You may wonder what this has to do with your question."

For the second time that morning Celestine reached over to touch Lufkin's hand. "Go on."

"As time progressed, it became clear to me that I wouldn't get a great deal of approval from those scientists I admired most. My research simply wasn't important enough for that. So I ended up focusing on my students rather than on my colleagues. Getting excellent student evaluations in my courses, seeing excited faces in class, hearing spontaneous laughter and good questions, at times even applause—these are all satisfactions. But in the end they weren't enough for me. Not as the years passed. Maybe it would've been different if I hadn't remained a bachelor, but it wasn't enough. So, instead, I focused on individual students."

Lufkin stared at his coffee cup, which he'd encircled with his hands as if he were warming them. Suddenly he put them into his pockets and looked across at Celestine. "Thank you for being so patient," he said with a wry smile. "You see, I'm working my way toward your question.

"I was only interested in the brighter students, the ones I imagined might turn into the type of scientist I aspired to become. Students like you, Celly." Again, his eyes rose to meet her gaze.

"I suppose they were all women?" she asked. Seeing his nod, she continued. "Why no men?"

"Why no men? Because sex was also important and I don't happen to be gay. What can be more convincing evidence of approval than sex? Demonstrating my attractiveness to a young intelligent woman in competition with young attractive males had become almost an obsession of mine. You put it right: the pheromone is my intellect. But the proof of its effectiveness—in the sense that I wanted to prove to myself that I'm not yet old and decrepit—is whether an intelligent young woman will prefer me over her physically much more alluring contemporaries. This may not be a pretty answer, but it's an honest one."

"Graham, let's agree for the sake of the argument that it's important for you to prove that you're attractive to young women—"

"No, it's more than that," he interjected. "A young fresh mind—"

"Young fresh mind! Graham, this sounds like the clinical description of an experimental subject."

"Celly, you know that is not what I mean."

"Let's skip it, then. What I wanted to say is this. You throw out your net, baited with racy lectures and sexy insects. You take care to throw back any students to whom you haven't yet given a grade or who happen to be below the age of twenty-one. Lo and behold, you haul in Celestine Price: young, intelligent, all that. You're so subtle that she never realizes she's caught. And you? You get your necessary reinforcement so as to forget your fear of lost youth or whatever other problem your male climacteric is creating in you."

Lufkin grimaced as if he were in pain.

She continued as if she hadn't seen. "You caught me, I came willingly, and we enjoyed each other. You taught me a lot and I'm not referring to what we did in bed. It lasted long enough that I didn't get the feeling that I was being used. And then, bang! One morning, just a few hours after a warm and affectionate evening, you sent me packing."

"Packing? Is that what I did? Don't put it that crassly," he pleaded.

"But that's what you did. So when you told me that we were through, just minutes after I had been crying out with pleasure, I felt so humiliated. You'd reduced me to a sex object, just a response to some technique you developed with God knows how many 'young fresh minds.' "

"Celly . . ."

"Don't 'Celly' me. Remember the reason you gave me when you informed me of your decision? *Yours,* Graham, not *ours!* Because you were about to fall in love with me! As if this were some disease you were about to catch. So far, you've only spoken about what this type of relationship did for you. Let me tell you what it represented to me. To maintain my self-respect, to be reassured each time you stroked me, caressed me, kissed me, encouraged me to please you, I had to be sure that there was something more than sex that had brought us together. I had to forget about our age difference because I had to feel that in some sense we were contemporaries, or at least equals, who offered *each other* something. I had to believe that you weren't just doing it with a face or a body or a texture of skin or the year on my driver's license. I had to believe that you were doing it *with me:* with an individual: with Celestine Price, somebody who in the long run matters just as much as you do." Celestine stopped abruptly as if she were suddenly exhausted. When she spoke again, her voice was resigned. "But I didn't, did I?"

"No, it isn't true. You weren't really paying attention to what I said. You want parity between a young woman and an old man—"

"Older man, Graham, not old." Celestine had started to calm down.

"Thanks for the correction. What about the parity between the older man and the young woman? *My* fear that our relationship will end because of *your* initiative? In fact, it was inevitable that this would happen, given our age difference. The deeper our involvement, the longer our relationship, the greater my ultimate pain."

"And you're telling me that's why you decided to end it all? Before it became too painful for you? When you might be too old to find a substitute for me?"

"Yes," Lufkin said, "that's it more or less."

"Graham," Celestine said flatly, "I just don't believe it's that simple." She pushed her seat back and rose. "Let's go. I told Jean I'd have you back at the department by eleven."

Celestine arrived at the lecture hall just a few minutes before four. She was impressed to find it nearly full. Her favorite seat—halfway up on the right-hand aisle, suitable for quick departures—was already occupied. She didn't recognize the squatter who'd displaced her, but it wasn't anyone from chemistry. Clearly, Lufkin's "One-Night Stands Among Insects" had brought in the customers. Celestine was curious to see how he'd deliver the goods. She realized that she'd never heard Lufkin give a research talk. Her earlier exposure had always been to Lufkin the teacher, with her playing the role of the admiring student. Now, as a sophisticated critic, she would be listening to Lufkin talk about his own research.

The first few minutes were vintage Lufkin. Virtually all sex attractants are secreted by female insects, he pointed out, but sporadic reports have surfaced in the entomological literature claiming the existence of antiaphrodisiacs among males. " 'Antiaphrodisiacs? In males?' you might ask." He pretended astonishment. "Why?" Some students in the audience started to snicker, but Lufkin maintained his usual deadpan mask when talking about risqué subjects. Part of his lecturing style was not to encourage flippancy. It was his combination of serious mien, measured tone and simultaneous description of outrageous sexual behavior in insects that Celestine had found so irresistible in his classroom lectures at Hopkins. Evidently he hadn't lost his touch. "Just reflect for a moment on the purpose of the human chastity belt. Certain insect species are simply cleverer than we. Instead of a clumsy chastity belt, they developed a chemical marker to enforce sexual monogamy in their female partners.

"The earlier evidence for antiaphrodisiacs among insects was circumstantial," proclaimed Lufkin. Now he was going to prove to this audience that they really existed. Celestine could almost sense the audience sit up as if someone had given them a collective prod. She smiled to herself. The usual chemical talks certainly didn't start that way. Lufkin was right. Sex is irresistible, especially so in science.

"Take *Lasioglossum zephyrum*," he pronounced the words slowly while writing them on the blackboard, "also known as the sweat bee. Some ten years ago, Barrows at the University of Kansas reported that male sweat bees patrol the nests and pounce on females. Such pouncing seems to be promoted by a female odor that can be equated with an aphrodisiac. Barrows was struck by the fact that there were many pounces but very few matings. Aha, thought Barrows, the female sweat bee mates but once."

Lufkin's eyes slowly swept over the audience. There was hardly a sound as they waited for the next disclosure.

"Along comes Penelope Kukuk from Cornell. Taking some tethered females and exposing them to passing males near the clay bank of a stream—a favorite habitat of sweat bees—Kukuk noted that at least half a dozen males would head for the tethered female. Within a minute or two all but one of the males would depart, leaving a mating pair. Repeating that process with that same tethered, but now deflowered, female showed that she was now unattractive."

"Deflowered tethered female!" How typical of Graham, mused Celestine, I bet half the class is thinking of bondage. But how does one tether a sweat bee?

"You may wonder how one tethers a bee," continued Lufkin, as if he were now indulging in a personal dialogue with her. "It's easy. You just tape her by the wings to an applicator stick using Scotch tape. May I have the first slide, please?"

The slides showed the natural habitat of the sweat bees; the tethered females seemingly crucified with Scotch tape on the wooden applicators; the small vials containing pollen, honey and water as well as a single captured virgin female bee. Each day, such a virgin would be transferred to another vial while the contents of the preceding day's jail—Celestine had passed judgment on the experimental protocol—were extracted with methylene chloride to furnish one FDE of sexual odor. Celestine hadn't caught what an FDE was. "A 'female day equivalent' of odor," Lufkin added.

After several hundred FDEs had been accumulated, *artificial* female models, made of black nylon wrapped around the tip of the applicator, were perfumed with a few FDEs. A number of such crucifixes were placed on the ground so that the perfumed plastic virgins projected just over the top of the vertical stream bank where the male bees patrolled back and forth. If one of the horny males approached a virgin bee to within half an inch and faced it for more than five seconds, his behavior was counted as a "hover." Pounces that involved physical contact with the nylon model were considered pseudo matings. Statistical analysis of the data clearly demonstrated that, once a perfumed nylon virgin had been touched a few times by a male, a significant reduction in "hovers" occurred around her. The antiaphrodisiac was plainly contributed by the males.

The isolation of the active antihovering factor, which had been Lufkin's personal contribution, proved to be both straightforward and yet exceedingly laborious to explain. In spite of the fascinating biological response, the ultimate chemical structure had turned out to be remarkably uncomplicated. Celestine was not surprised. She recalled having felt the same sense of disappointment when Lufkin had lectured in class about the incredibly difficult isolation of the first pheromone from the silkworm *Bombyx mori* and then disclosed that the pure chemical isolated by the German chemists was a simple, long-known, organic alcohol. At that time he'd made a slightly flippant comment which Celestine hadn't forgotten. "Let's remember that *Bombyx mori* synthesizes its pheromone to attract another insect, not to attract an organic chemist and test his intellectual mettle. We're dealing with sexual reproduction—the perpetuation of the species—rather than titillation of the human intellect."

This afternoon's audience apparently hadn't minded the chemical anticlimax. They had been stimulated as well as gratified, and their enthusiastic applause showed it.

Suddenly Celestine understood what Lufkin had meant at the airport coffee shop. Lufkin's talk—which had contained no reference to modern molecular biology; to recombinant DNA; to protein receptors or cloning or monoclonal antibodies; not even to novel aspects of analytical or spectroscopic techniques other than what all contemporary chemists now used—this lecture had captivated an audience that was both larger and more diverse than is usually encountered at the supersophisticated seminars given in this department. Judging from the raised hands of prospective questioners in the audience, the students clearly had appreciated Lufkin, reflected Celestine, but no wonder his scientific peers weren't impressed. From his talk, it wasn't even obvious what portion had dealt with data from the literature—from Kukuk's lab at Cornell—and what had been accomplished at Hopkins by Lufkin and his students.

"Professor Lufkin," Celestine asked in a loud voice, "I hope you don't consider this a theological question. But why did the male sweat bee develop such a chemical marker?"

Lufkin squinted toward the upper reaches of the auditorium. "Theological? You mean divinity students come to chemistry seminars?" It was a clever trick to give him time to choose his words. Several of the tittering students turned to look for the source of the question.

"I'm sorry"—Lufkin allowed himself a faint smirk—"I know you meant that seriously. I can only guess. One possibility is that the sweat bee is primarily concerned with propagation of the species rather than with sexual jealousy. One mating is sufficient to fertilize her. By marking her as having fulfilled her reproductive purpose, other males won't waste their reproductive potential on her but rather spend it on other virgin bees."

"In that case," countered Celestine, "why use terms like 'one-night stands'? Aren't these rather typical buzzwords describing human behavior?"

"Buzzwords? I like that word in the context of bees." Lufkin looked pleased at the snickering audience.

Celestine didn't appreciate the pertness of Lufkin's riposte. "Professor Lufkin," she called out, "the choice of words may not have been precise, but there is a point to my question."

Lufkin looked briefly and sharply at Celestine. Now he picked up his notes and, like an anchorman at the end of a newscast, tapped them into a stack. It gave him something to do while he thought of a response. Was this a continuation of their dialogue at the airport? If it was, he decided to cut it short.

"All right: let's take 'one-night stand.' Apparently you don't like the idea of it, and therefore you object to my using those words. Perhaps I misjudged by being somewhat flippant in my choice of title for a serious scientific talk, but it served its purpose, didn't it?" He waved his hand around the full auditorium. "But that's how far I meant to go. I was simply using that phrase as a synonym for a short, single event. Don't immediately assign male chauvinist motives to the sweat bee—or to me for that matter. The male bee hasn't really exploited the female. What I'm trying to say is that you make a mistake if you look at the sexual behavior of insects in anthropomorphic terms. If there are no other questions . . . ?" He gave one quick look at the audience, picked up his papers, and strode from the podium toward the first row where Jean Ardley was sitting.

15

They were driving back from Sol Minskoff's home in Paula's Volvo station wagon, the cello case securely strapped in the back. "Leonardo," Paula said, breaking a silence that had endured since Ravenswood Avenue, "you're like a weathercock, so different from my initial impression of you. You're so moody, it even shows in your playing. You were just terrible today—Dvořák probably covered his ears in his grave."

Cantor smiled wryly. "I know."

"Do you feel like telling me what's wrong? Just a couple of weeks ago, you seemed to be on cloud nine: the most important experiment of your life came out as you'd predicted. You told me yourself it was unheard of for somebody like you to have done all that lab work by yourself. And now?"

"Paula. First answer a question. Why do you socialize with someone like me?" He sounded wistful.

" 'Socialize'? My God, Leonardo, what a terrible word. Is that what we're doing? Socializing?"

Cantor sighed. "You name it then."

"What's wrong with 'friendship'?"

"Nothing. Nothing is wrong with friendship, but why me?"

"Oh, Leonardo," she said, and stretched out her right hand to squeeze his. "You fool. It's simple—or, at any rate, it was simple. You don't bore me."

"Maybe it's because we don't see each other all that often."

"Could be, but don't be so modest. You're a complicated man; a man of parts. You know how Sol described you? 'I.C. is a *mensch.*' Coming from him, that was a real compliment."

"Well, we've known each other since college."

"That makes it even more of a compliment. It's . . . what do you call it? Biostatistically even more significant."

"Not bad, Paula." Cantor's tense form seemed to settle slightly in the dark. "So it's because I'm a *mensch?*"

"Not just that." She responded quickly, taking her attention for a moment from the road. "I want to know what binds together your various personalities. And now, just when I think I'm beginning to understand you, something comes unglued. What happened? Or is it inappropriate for me to ask?"

Cantor said nothing. The pause became so long that Paula looked anxiously at her passenger, his face illuminated by the headlights of oncoming cars. She hesitated. "I guess I shouldn't have asked you that."

"No, that's not it." Cantor's voice lacked its usual masculine timbre. "Stop over there." He pointed to the side of the street. When Paula pulled up at the curb, Cantor reached over and turned off the ignition. "Stafford quit," he said brusquely, "he decided to go work with Krauss at Harvard and never told me. I only learned about it when Krauss called about a letter of recommendation."

"Oh, now I understand," Paula said sympathetically.

"No, you don't." Cantor gave the words an angry ring.

"But it's so ungrateful. . . ."

"Sure." He made a dismissive gesture. "But what about the letter of recommendation?"

Paula looked up, puzzled. "Be generous, Leonardo. You said he was one of your best men. And he did accomplish that very important experiment."

"That!" He gave a brief, sardonic laugh. "Don't you see, that's exactly what it's all about." With these words, the floodgate opened. "That experiment, which you called 'that very important experiment' was almost certainly faked."

Cantor proceeded to tell her about the envelope that he'd

found in his office; why he'd not mentioned it to anyone; why it had been essential to provide a second, independent test of his tumorigenesis theory; and that now, just when he'd succeeded, he was faced with a monstrous dilemma. If he refused to send a letter, he would have to explain himself to Krauss. After all, Cantor couldn't just claim that he wanted to keep Stafford around and, therefore, would not recommend his best student. But if he did write such a letter, Cantor would never be able to erase the Cantor-Stafford Experiment without implicating himself. An enthusiastic letter of recommendation to Krauss would permanently close the door to such a withdrawal. It was fiendishly clever blackmail that Stafford had challenged him with, and there was nothing left but to pay the ransom. "I always knew Jerry was very bright, but I never took him to be cunning." Cantor sank back in his seat and stared straight ahead through the windshield.

Paula finally broke the silence. "Leonardo," she said quietly, and touched his sleeve, "how do you know what Stafford was doing in your laboratory? How do you know he was cheating? Perhaps it was just a malicious gesture by somebody who was jealous of Stafford. Don't you think, in all fairness, that you should have confronted him?"

"Confronted him?" Cantor looked shocked. "If he'd confessed, I would have had to retract that *Nature* paper. No one would ever have forgotten that—even if I had published the second experiment. Once you're tainted by scandal . . ."

"But you weren't to blame!"

"Of course I was to blame. Everybody would have thought so, and so would I. When you publish together, you must share credit and blame."

"That social contract you told me about?"

"Precisely."

"But suppose Stafford had offered a perfectly plausible explanation for his presence in your laboratory that Sunday evening?"

"It's a bit like Othello. Once the seed of suspicion is planted . . ."

"But, Leonardo," she said gently, "that experiment is not Desdemona. And besides, you could have repeated Stafford's experiment on your own, couldn't you?"

"That would have taken weeks! And if it had not worked, what then? Was it another unknown variable? My inferior laboratory technique? Or Stafford's cheating? What I did was wiser."

"Safer. Not necessarily wiser."

"Let's not quibble," he began angrily. "There is no doubt that Krauss, or anyone else for that matter, will be able to repeat *my* experiment. That will settle any question about my tumorigenesis theory. Sometime in the future, I might return to Stafford's work and see if I can repeat it. If not, I may put some discreet footnote into some future paper indicating we've had trouble repeating Stafford's experiment. By then, no one will pay much attention: it will just be a historical footnote of no real consequence. But don't you see? The fact that Stafford has applied to Krauss, behind my back, clearly shows that he felt guilty."

"But are you sure? You yourself told me how you'd practically locked yourself into your laboratory; how you hardly saw anyone, including me. You never told Stafford about your work, did you?"

"No."

"Well? There you are. Your closest collaborator is left out in the cold. How do you think he felt all that time? Perhaps he sensed your distrust. Maybe he thought that going to Krauss—the man who had first raised doubts about his work—would clear him."

The following Monday, Cantor wrote the recommendation letter. By the end of July, Stafford had departed for Harvard.

16

For twenty-five minutes, October 11 was the best day of Cantor's life. Shortly after 6 A.M., while he was showering, the phone rang. The persistence of the caller finally drove him, dripping wet, to the bedside phone.

"Professor Isidore Cantor?" The man's accented voice was unfamiliar; furthermore, nobody had called Cantor "Isidore" for decades.

Despite the excitement rising in his chest, he decided to be noncommittal. "Who's calling?"

"Ulf Lundholm from the *Svenska Dagbladet* in Stockholm."

"Yes?" Cantor was barely able to utter this single word, so full of suspense, desire, triumph, and some deviousness. He wanted to pretend cool detachment, but his heart was pounding. He found himself wondering, in a part of his mind that continued to live its normal existence even while the rest of him was losing its composure, why the first call invariably came from a reporter. "Yes," he added more forcefully, "this is Professor Isidore Cantor speaking." Isidore Cantor? My God, this sounds like a total stranger! "What can I do for you?"

"I have the honor to congratulate you on winning the Nobel Prize in medicine." Cantor didn't mind the pompous words; in fact, they'd hardly registered. "I wonder whether you have any comments?"

"Comments? No, I don't. I don't even know whether it's true."

Cantor recalled the embarrassment of Vincent du Vigneaud, who had publicly acknowledged his pleasure when a reporter congratulated him on winning a Nobel Prize—prematurely, it turned out. In du Vigneaud's case, the reporter had been early by one full year.

"Professor Cantor!" Ulf Lundholm sounded outraged. "Surely you do not believe that I am telephoning from Stockholm to make a joke?"

"How do I know you're calling from Stockholm?" Cantor figured he could afford caution, even at the risk of insulting the caller. Furthermore, he was enjoying himself.

"I shall give you the number of the *Svenska Dagbladet,*" Lundholm shot back, "so that you can call me here in Stockholm."

"Never mind," replied Cantor, enjoying himself hugely now. "I'll comment, but for the time being it's off the record."

"How do you feel having won"—Cantor could almost see the man rise and bow from the waist down—"the Nobel Prize?"

"Frankly, I haven't thought about it, but if it's true, it's a great surprise. If it's true," he repeated for emphasis, "then it's not just an enormous honor but also recognition for the efforts of my entire team of collaborators over the years."

This was the sort of stilted answer that most reporters, especially Swedish ones, recognize as mere form. Even the institutional Ulf Lundholm required something meatier. He took another tack. "And what will you do with the prize money, Professor? Have you decided how to spend it?"

Cantor was taken aback. He had practiced that first speech often enough. But he had never really thought about the money. "No . . . no, of course not. I haven't even thought about it."

Although this answer was perfectly spontaneous, the reporter sounded skeptical. "But you do know how much money goes with the prize?"

Again, Cantor was surprised to find himself unprepared. His answer came out in the distracted tones reporters love at moments such as this—mistaking it, of course, for unworldly disinterest. "Well, I know it's a lot, but I don't know exactly how much."

As soon as the Stockholm reporter hung up, Cantor turned on

the radio. He missed the key words by just a second or two. ". . . this almost completes this year's Nobel Prizes. The winner of the literature award will be disclosed next week."

Dammit, thought Cantor, do I have to wait for the seven o'clock news to hear the name, or should I call the radio station? Actually, he didn't have to do anything. The first telephone call followed shortly thereafter. The caller was Kurt Krauss.

"I.C." His voice was warm and excited. Genuine pleasure seemed to flow over the telephone. "I hope I'm one of the first to congratulate you. You really deserve this Nobel. It also shows that I know how to pick the candidates."

Cantor started to say something modest, but to his irritation Krauss barely paused. "I know you'll be amused by what I'm about to tell you. Guess what Lurtsema said when he read the news just now on the radio?"

"I haven't got the foggiest notion," countered Cantor. "I don't even know who Lurtsema is."

"The announcer on WGBH. But that's not important. Come on," coaxed Krauss, "just guess what he said!"

"All right." Cantor decided to play along. " 'Midwestern cancer whiz wins Nobel.' "

"Wrong!" Krauss was triumphant. "Lurtsema started out with 'another Nobel Prize won by Harvard man.' Can you beat our local chauvinism? It's typical of Harvard."

"I don't get it." Cantor sounded puzzled. "Why should he've said that?"

"What do you mean, you don't get it? You Midwestern yokel, we're so damned anxious to add to our list of laureates, everybody here is including Stafford on the Harvard roster. Ridiculous, isn't it?"

It was 6:28 in the morning. Cold and half naked in the darkened bedroom, Cantor felt the day had taken a shape for the worse.

The Cantor-Stafford pairing probably seemed just to most people: the key paper—the one that succinctly, but unequivocally, described the generalized theory of tumorigenesis together with its first experimental test—had carried the names of both Cantor and Stafford. The seeds for Stafford's inclusion were probably sown in 1923, when Banting and Macleod won the Nobel Prize in Physiology or Medicine for Banting and Best's discovery of insulin. The outcry about the injustice to young Charles Best, who with Banting had performed the crucial experiment in Macleod's laboratory, persisted for decades. Since then, the Nobel committees had leaned over backward to recognize younger collaborators. Milstein and Jerne, together with a much younger Georges Koehler, in 1984 were only the most recent example of such a shared Nobel Prize for their work on monoclonal antibodies.

The telephone must have rung at least ten times before Leah reached for it in the darkness. "Hello," she mumbled sleepily.

"Leah? This is Jerry. I've got to talk to Celly." His tone was urgent, but Leah was too groggy to catch it.

"What?" she groaned.

"Leah! I've got to talk to Celly," he reiterated.

She reached over to turn on the light. "Jesus Christ! Do you know what time it is?"

"I know," he said in a guilty voice, "it's just past seven. But—"

"It's six o'clock, you jerk. Call back at a decent hour!"

Stafford's pleading stopped her from slamming down the receiver. "Please, Leah, please wait. I'm sorry I forgot about the time difference, but I've got to talk to Celly. Right now. It's urgent."

"Well, you can't, Jerry. She isn't here."

"What do you mean, she isn't there? At six in the morning?"

"That's what I said." Leah was still cross. "Now do you mind if I go back to sleep?"

"Wait! Don't hang up. Do you know where she is? I've got to get hold of her."

He sounded so urgent that Leah started to take pity on him. "I know where she is, but I don't know whether you can reach her. Do you want to leave a message?"

"No. I've got to talk to her now. Haven't you got the number where she is?"

"No, I don't."

"Oh, God, Leah." He sounded miserable.

"Wait, maybe I can find it in the phone book." She stumbled out of bed and went to the kitchen. *How the hell does Roger spell his last name?* she wondered. *It sounded like Dougherty, but it wasn't that.* Leah started to shiver in her nightgown. She was about to give up when she found it: Docherty, R.

"Whose number is this?" asked Stafford.

"A friend of hers. And now good night." She hung up before Stafford could ask for the name.

Stafford quickly dialed the number. After two rings, he heard the beginning of the guitar intro from *Gimme Shelter.* "Jesus Christ," he exclaimed, "one of those machines." A male voice cut in over the guitar. "This is Roger. If you must leave a message, wait for the beep. And make it snappy."

Unnerved by the command, Stafford said hurriedly, "This is an urgent message for Celestine Price. Please ask her to call Jerry right away at—" he rattled the number into the phone, repeating it twice. "Thanks." He hung up and waited. *This isn't going to work,* he concluded, *if they're still asleep. And who the hell is this jerk Roger? It might take hours before he gets the message.* He decided to continue phoning until someone woke up.

After the fourth time, a real voice interrupted the guitar. "Yes?" Stafford was so surprised, he had to be prompted by a second "Yes?" even more irritable than the first, before asking for Celestine Price.

"Celly, it's for you," he heard the muffled voice say, "do you want to take it?"

"Who is this?" Celestine's voice sounded anxious over the telephone.

"Celly, this is Jerry." He hurried on before she could respond. "I know it's very early but, Celly, you've got to help me. You're the only one who can."

"What's the matter, Jerry?"

"I can't tell you over the phone. I've got to talk to you in person. I'm already at the airport. I'm taking the 7:20 flight. Please pick me up."

"All right, but tell me—"

"Celly, please don't tell anyone that I'm coming. And please," he urged, "don't turn on the radio or TV until you see me. Promise."

Celestine sat straight up in bed. "Jerry, are you in trouble?" she asked in a low voice.

"I'll tell you when I see you. I've got to run to make the plane," he replied and hung up.

"Oh, Celly, thank God you came."

"What's the matter, Jerry?" Celestine asked as soon as he'd released her from his embrace. "Tell me."

"Not here. Let's drive out to Memorial Park. But who's Roger?"

"One of my options. Remember, this is not a weekend."

As soon as they arrived at the nearly deserted park Celestine pulled over to the curb. She turned to Stafford. "Now tell me, what happened?"

"Celly," he stammered, "I've won a Nobel Prize."

"Come on," she said flatly, "I'm in no mood for kidding. Not after you wake me up in the middle of the night."

"It wasn't the middle of the night, it was—"

"Cut it out, Jerry. You scared me the way you phoned. And dragged me out to meet you at the airport. If you're not going to be serious, you can hitchhike into town from here."

"Celly, I'm not kidding. It's true."

Celestine stared at him. And she saw genuine terror in his face. He was telling the truth. "You? You won the Nobel Prize?" she gasped. "You?"

"Me. Me and I.C. They called this morning from Stockholm. And then Krauss called. That's when I phoned you. Celly, I'm afraid."

She looked at him curiously. Her earlier concern had disappeared. "I don't get it. Every scientist dreams about winning a

Nobel Prize, and now that happens to you . . ." She broke out laughing. "You must be the youngest guy who's ever won it. And instead of jumping up and down for joy, you look as if you're about to be shot. What's gotten into you?"

"I have to get out of this car," he said abruptly, flinging open his door. They walked down a path until, without a word, he pointed to a bench. When Celestine sat down, he faced her, straddling the seat.

"I don't deserve it."

"Hold it, Jerry." Gently, she placed a hand over his mouth. "Don't overdo this righteous Baptist bit. I know, I know: it was Cantor's idea. But that's not what's bothering you, is it?"

Stafford flinched as if struck. Celestine reached out, took his shoulder and pulled him closer. "You're just scared, Jerry. That's all it is. This much success so soon—it would make anybody nervous. But you *do* deserve it. As much as anybody. Sure it was Cantor's idea, but he couldn't have published the *Nature* paper if it hadn't been for your experiment." She leaned back suddenly, a wry smile on her lips as she looked out across the park. "I wish I had your problem."

"Don't say that," he exploded. "Don't you remember, Krauss's man Ohashi couldn't repeat the experiment. And he's a good man, I've gotten to know him at Harvard."

"But, Jerry, you repeated the experiment with Cantor."

"And?"

Celestine shook her head in wonder. "And nothing. It worked the second time around."

"But Krauss never repeated it again."

"I didn't know that. Why not?"

"Because Cantor came up with the second experiment. The one he did all by himself and didn't tell anybody about." He leaned forward until she could feel his breath. "Not even me, Celly. And after it worked, he persuaded Krauss to drop my work and focus on his second experiment. Krauss did just that. But that's really beside the point. What matters is *I* got the point: Cantor didn't trust me.

That's why I wrote to Krauss and asked him to offer me a fellowship."

"You wrote him? But you told me that he'd called you out of the blue."

Stafford looked down on the ground. "I lied."

"Again? Why this time?" she demanded.

"I wanted to find out whether Cantor had written to Krauss. About why he didn't trust me anymore. Evidently, he hadn't, or Krauss wouldn't have given me the fellowship."

"Why didn't you tell me any of that?"

"I couldn't."

"Why not?"

"Because there was something else."

"Go on, Jerry. And make it good."

"Celly." He halted and dug the nails of one hand into his palm. "When Krauss couldn't repeat my experiment, I got scared. I thought it was due to my sloppy notes . . . that I'd missed something important. When we repeated the experiment in Cantor's lab, I tried to be extra careful. But after a while, I.C.'s continuous looking over my shoulder and checking every detail against the notebook got me real edgy. The day before we were supposed to be finished— a Sunday—I had just gone home, when suddenly I realized that earlier in the day I had added too little kinase."

Celestine suddenly noticed the digging of his nails. She took his hand and held it. "Go on," she said gently.

"So I returned to the lab, without informing I.C., and added some more enzyme. I don't think this was real fudging. I calculated how much kinase I had missed earlier and then just made up for it. I know I should've told I.C., but I didn't have it in me. First my sloppy notebook, and then that stupid mistake. I don't know how, but I.C. must have suspected something, because right after that, he started on his second experiment. From then on, he was never the same with me. When he announced his success and I went to congratulate him, he almost came out and said it. That was another reason why I wanted to work in Krauss's lab. I was hoping that he'd have somebody repeat *my* experiment and I'd be there to see it happen."

"And add some more enzyme?" she asked quietly.

"I would never do that again. And even if you don't believe that, don't you see, when Cantor's experiment worked, in a way it also vindicated my first one? I should've had confidence in it without worrying all the time about what I.C. was thinking of me. By then all I wanted was for Krauss to take another look at it."

"And has he?"

"Not yet, but last week I persuaded Ohashi to start on it."

Celestine looked out across the park again; she stared a long time, as if making up her mind. "So what happens now, Nobel laureate?"

"Please, Celly. Don't kid now."

"Kidding? You *are* a Nobel laureate. You can't change that."

"Can't I?" Stafford rose and paced nervously in front of the bench. "Celly, you've got to help me. You're the only person I can talk to. I want to see Cantor today." He turned to her. "Will you go with me?"

"Me?" Celestine looked dumbfounded. "What good would I do?"

"Please let me finish," he pleaded. "I haven't seen or spoken to I.C. since I left his lab. I feel terribly uncomfortable and . . . guilty. I want you there not just for moral support but to have a witness present. I intend to tell Cantor what really happened, and then I'll explain to him that I'm going to decline the Nobel Prize."

Celestine gaped up at him. "You'll do that?" she finally asked. "Turn down a Nobel Prize? What are you going to say?"

"I already told you."

"No, not to Cantor. What will you say in public? That you cheated? Isn't that overdoing it a bit? After all, you got the Prize because of your first experiment. Unless you're not telling me the truth, that first one worked, didn't it?"

Stafford nodded. "Yes. And I'm sure it'll work again."

"So why crucify yourself in public? Jerry. You'll be through in science. You'll never be able to get a job again. Isn't that an absurd price to pay for one transgression? Purgatory, maybe; but should you roast in hell forever? Come, sit down"—she patted the bench—"and let's discuss it calmly."

The logistics of seeing Cantor in private were not as simple as they'd imagined. Bedlam reigned in Cantor's lab. There was no way to get through on the telephone. It had been ringing when the secretary arrived and had continued to ring constantly ever since. Stephanie finally took it off the hook and left to join the big party that was under way in the seminar room. Colleagues, deans, even the president of the university, were there, pressing around Cantor, whose flushed face glowed among the crowd. Temporarily, he'd even forgotten that he was sharing the Prize.

Stafford had realized right away that he couldn't very well march into Cantor's office. He would bump into too many people who knew him. That was why he had tried to reach Cantor by phone and arrange a meeting in some neutral territory. When he was unable to get through, he wrote a note. Celestine took it over. Now she was standing at the periphery of the crowd, wondering whether Cantor would even open the envelope she was clutching. It only said "Professor Cantor, PERSONAL." She took out a pen and added in big letters: "From Jeremiah Stafford." That should do it, she thought, and indeed it did. She pushed her way through the crowd and thrust the envelope under Cantor's nose; he did a classic double take. After tearing open the envelope and reading the note, he glanced around for the bearer of the message. "Is there any message for Dr. Stafford?" she asked in a low voice.

Cantor motioned her into the corridor. "Who are you?" he demanded curtly.

"Celestine Price," she responded.

Remembering names was not one of Cantor's fortes. Even if it had been, recalling that her name had been mentioned months ago by Paula Curry, and once on the telephone, would have been unreasonable under the present circumstances. "I'm a friend of Jerry's," she added.

"Tell him to come . . ." Cantor began, and then looked

around as if he were searching for something, "to my house. Right after lunch is really the earliest I can make it. Tell him at two o'clock."

"Isn't it weird," Stafford said to Celestine as they waited at the front door, "that it's taken me six years to see the inside of this house?" He groaned as he heard the latch being released on the other side of the door. "Now I wish we were anywhere else."

"Come in, Jerry," said Cantor as he opened the door, and then he stopped. Clearly, he'd been taken by surprise to find a third person.

"Thanks for seeing me so promptly," Stafford said nervously. "This is Celestine Price, my . . ." He paused to look at Celestine, who stood to his left and slightly behind. "My fiancée," he blurted out. "I hope you don't mind her joining us. And, Prof," he rushed on, "let me congratulate you. You must be enormously pleased. You really deserved this Prize."

"Yes? And what about you?" Cantor hesitated for a moment, just long enough for Celestine to wonder what the question really referred to. "Aren't you pleased?" he finally said, an ambiguous smile on his face.

"That's why I came," said Stafford quickly as he entered the house, "I've got something to confess."

Cantor's reply was abrupt and to the point. "This is not a time for confession, Jerry. This is a day for celebration. Come in. Sit down. Can I offer you something?" He looked at Celestine. "Miss . . . ?"

"Price," she added quickly, "Celestine Price."

"Oh, of course, Miss Price. Shall I get some champagne? We must celebrate Jerry's Nobel Prize," he said, displaying the same equivocal smile, "and your engagement. Is that recent?" he asked, looking from Stafford to Celestine and back to Stafford. "I didn't know you were engaged . . . at least not while you were in my lab."

Stafford blushed. He couldn't look at Celestine. He didn't know how she would deal with her new role as fiancée. "Well, you know," he mumbled, "we never talked much about our personal lives."

"True enough," conceded Cantor. "Perhaps we should make up for it now. But first let me bring some champagne."

"Well," said Celestine, as soon as Cantor had left the room. "I didn't know I was engaged to a Nobel Prize winner."

"Please, Celly, don't get angry. I didn't know what to say."

"Who says I'm angry?" she replied. "I was just wondering how big a diamond ring a Nobel Prize winner can afford."

"Celly!" A combination of pleading and warning sounded in his voice. "Remember why we're here."

"Oh, I forgot," she continued, "you're about to refuse the Nobel Prize. Well, a postdoc will hardly pay for a diamond, even the smallest."

"Here we are," announced Cantor as he put the tray with three glasses and an ice bucket on the coffee table. "We'll have to wait just a moment, while the champagne chills. In the meanwhile, tell me, when is the great event?"

Stafford looked puzzled. "Event?"

"The wedding, of course." Cantor laughed somewhat stiffly.

"Oh," he gasped.

Celestine rescued him. "We've left that open. It depends on our professional plans—where we'll get jobs, that sort of thing. Jerry will be looking for a faculty position—"

"Well, that shouldn't be difficult," interrupted Cantor, "not for a Nobel Prize winner. What about you," he said, looking at Celestine, "what do you do?"

"I'll be getting my Ph.D. next year. Organic chemistry. I'll also be applying for academic jobs."

"You mean postdoctorate fellowships?"

"Actually, no." Stafford looked at her in surprise, but Celestine refused to meet his gaze. "I've already been offered an assistant professorship. In fact, two of them." She smiled self-consciously.

"And where are they?" Cantor had become curious.

"The University of Wisconsin, and"—she paused, because she knew what the response would be—"at Harvard."

"At Harvard?" Cantor and Stafford blurted simultaneously.

"Yes," she replied, pretending diffidence.

"So you'll both be in Boston," said Cantor. "How fortunate."

"Why do you say that?"

"Come now, Miss Price. You're forgetting you'll be marrying a Nobel Prize winner. If he doesn't get an appointment at Harvard, he'll get one at MIT—"

"Or Boston University. Or Tufts. Or Brandeis," she interrupted. "But I'm not sure where I'll end up. I don't have to make any commitments until February. Who knows? I may get another offer or two before then."

"And you'd consider them over Harvard?" Cantor leaned forward. "What did you say your field was? Who have you been working with? He sounds like a very well-connected man."

"Professor Ardley, Jean Ardley."

"Ardley? Gene Ardley? I don't know any—" He stopped. "Oh yes. I've never met her. She's in chemistry, isn't she? But then, Miss Price, you must be—" Suddenly he rose. "Let me get a napkin," he said quickly, "it's time to open the champagne."

"Celly," whispered Stafford, "you never told me about these offers. When did all this happen?"

"You never told me about yours. But relax," she said, patting his arm, "I only got those phone calls a couple of weeks ago. I was going to surprise you on my visit to Harvard. They all seem to be excited about my allatostatin work. Especially since we've managed to carry out the virus incorporation. To chemists I now look like a hotshot biologist: an irresistible combination." She looked at the door behind them. "You know, when Cantor comes back, we'd better start talking about you."

"Prof." Stafford wasn't up to the informal "I.C." "Hold the champagne. I told you that I came to confess something."

"And I responded that this was no time for confessions," Cantor said dryly. "I'm not prepared to assume the role of confessor. Enough of that." He reached for the bottle, but Stafford put his hand forward.

"Please, I.C."—the pain was clear in his voice—"listen. I can't accept the Nobel Prize."

Cantor's mouth opened, but no sound came out.

"I.C.," Stafford rushed on, "I don't deserve it. You know that as well as I do. The theory was your idea, you thought of the experiment, you did it yourself—"

"Jerry!" Cantor's tone was peremptory. "The Nobel Prize was awarded for what we published in *Nature*. *We,* Jerry: Cantor and Stafford. Let's not second-guess the Swedes."

"But, I.C.! That's what I have to talk to you about. The first experiment—the one we published together."

"And that's precisely what I don't want to hear about," exclaimed Cantor. "Not here"—he looked at Celestine and then Stafford—"not ever. I know all about that experiment and it's water over the dam."

Stafford looked around in desperation. "All right, forget about the experiment. But the Nobel Prize: you worked for it for years, you expected it—"

"Come now, Jerry."

"Okay, we in the lab expected it, Krauss expected it—he told me so himself. It shouldn't be shared with someone who—"

"Who what, Jerry? Whose experiment couldn't be replicated the first time around? It's all right, Jerry. A lot of people have that kind of trouble, especially with an experiment as . . . difficult as yours." Cantor's tone shifted abruptly from sarcasm to something else—half a plea, half reproach. Why doesn't Jerry just shut up? Celestine wondered. Can't he hear what Cantor's saying?

"Forget about that damned experiment! I simply can't accept the Prize. I'll refuse it and ask the Academy—"

"The Karolinska, Jerry," Cantor observed mildly.

"I beg your pardon?"

"The Nobel in medicine is given by the *Karolinska Institutet,* not the Academy. They are responsible for chemistry and physics."

"Well, whoever! I'll tell them that they made a mistake and that it should all be awarded to you."

"Jerry, calm down." Cantor's voice was firmly paternal. "That boat has sailed. That fact can't be changed anymore. The Nobel Prize can't be refused."

"It can't?" Stafford and Celestine chorused.

"No, Jerry. It can't." Cantor smiled at Celestine. "Let me tell you how I know. It might even be useful for you, Miss Price, since you're such a promising chemist." He turned back to Stafford. "Of course you were right that I was hoping for the Nobel. What scientist doesn't? I've met a lot of Prize winners in my time. I've read quite a bit about the Prize. On more than one occasion, a couple of the Nobel committees have even solicited me to nominate candidates. By the way, Jerry"—Cantor winked at his morose student—"now we can nominate candidates every year—one of the fringe benefits of being a laureate. And don't think it's a negligible one. You'll see how, suddenly, all kinds of people will be very nice to you. Krauss, for instance. . . .

"But let me explain why you can't refuse the Nobel Prize. You can give somebody your half of the money, of course—Banting gave Best half of his. By the way, that's a story you might want to read sometime. Not only because Macleod, the department head, whom Banting hated, shared part of his money in turn with his other collaborator, James Collip—which complicated the issue of credit even further—but also because of the difficulty in reproducing some of the early experimental results on insulin. You see, Jerry? Even Banting and Best had problems with their own experiments. And Macleod never did any work in the lab!" He shot a meaningful glance at Stafford.

"Yet if you look at the official list of Nobel Prizes, you won't find the names of Best or Collip. They shared in the money, but not the prize. The Prize, you see, isn't really yours to accept or reject. Actually, I don't know of any scientist who ever refused a Nobel. Oh, there were those three Germans—Kuhn, Domagk and Butenandt—but they didn't accept theirs simply because Hitler forbade it. They changed their minds quickly enough after the war and collected their medals. Not the money, though! You've got to pick it up within one year or you forfeit your claim. Think about that, Jerry. I don't know whether the reporters have caught up with you yet, but if they haven't, you'll hear about it soon enough. Your share is over $150,000. Better ask your fiancée how she feels about your turning *that* down."

"So nobody ever turned down the Prize purely on principle?" Celestine asked.

"Actually, one person did: Jean-Paul Sartre, in literature. He did it on philosophical grounds, and never accepted the medal or the money. But here's my point: if you look at the list of Nobel Prizes for 1964, you'll find Sartre's name right on it, next to Konrad Bloch's in medicine, Dorothy Hodgkin's in chemistry, and all the rest for that year."

"Then what am I going to do?" Stafford's question sounded so helpless that Celestine intervened.

"Professor Cantor," she said, "you've heard how Jerry feels. What do you think he should do?"

Cantor slowly stroked his chin while staring at Stafford. I wonder what he's really thinking about? thought Celestine. "The one thing you can't do," he said slowly, "is turn it down. I wouldn't let you do it—for my own sake as much as for yours. I'm not interested in raising questions, Jerry—not after I worked so very hard to lay them to rest. So you might as well accept the Prize in good grace and"—he paused—"modesty, if you wish."

"But how can I do that? What am I going to say in Stockholm? I'm supposed to give a lecture there—what am I going to talk about? *My* experiment?"

"Ah," said Cantor, and smiled, an open, uncomplicated smile of satisfaction that did not escape Celestine. "I knew you'd come to your senses. Now we're talking about a real problem, not a hypothetical one. To be quite frank, I thought about it this morning, just after Kurt Krauss called. By the way, did he phone you?"

Stafford nodded.

"And?" Concern reappeared in Cantor's face. "What did you say?"

"Nothing much. I just thanked him and told him I was flying back here."

"Good." Cantor uttered the word with relief. "Now, to my

proposal. We're sharing the Nobel Prize for a joint discovery. Not like Banting and Macleod, as enemies in the same department; nor like Guillemin and Schally, who started their hypothalamic hormone research together in the same lab but then finished it as bitter competitors in different institutions. We'll be talking as collaborators, from one laboratory, who published together. Regardless of what you said right here—and I trust that will remain within these four walls"—Cantor looked meaningfully at his two young listeners— "with us there is no public question about who deserves credit for what."

"Everybody knows it was your idea," offered Stafford.

"Be that as it may," replied Cantor, "we can divide our presentation in whatever form we wish."

"That's exactly what bothers me," muttered Stafford. "You'll talk about the theory, which is truly a brilliant concept, and I'll then follow with a description of an experiment which has so far not been repeated anywhere else. The best I'll be able to say is that failure of confirmation is not necessarily confirmation of failure."

"Wrong!" triumphed Cantor. "*You* will give the first talk and discuss *our* theory, which we published together, and I will follow you by discussing *my* second experiment, which I haven't even submitted to *Nature* yet. See? The solution is simple and clean and, in addition, I'll be reporting something new and unpublished. Now then: it's time to open the champagne and drink. Skoal, Jerry! You might as well learn how the Swedes toast." And with these words he popped the cork.

"Finally! Is that really your voice, Leonardo? Do you know that you've been unreachable all day?" Paula didn't give him an opportunity to respond. "Isn't it marvelous? You must be thrilled. What does it feel like, becoming immortal?"

Cantor was pleased. "Immortal? Oh, come now, Paula. I'm not very different from the person you saw the last time."

"We'll see! I can't wait to celebrate with you. Has Sol got through to you yet? I didn't think he could. But he had a fabulous idea. He promised to find another violist. We'll do one of the Mozart quintets. He suggested Köchel 516, which is damned decent of him. Do you know that one? In the minuet the viola leads both violins. I already looked at the score—you'll love it, especially the adagio. And when will I see you next?"

Cantor was stretched out on his bed, content and tired, the telephone cradled at his neck. The day had been hectic; his face almost hurt from smiling. But he was at ease, especially after the session with Stafford. He was in a mellow mood, ready to go over it all again with an appreciative audience. "God knows when I'll come to Chicago. I've only just started to think about what I'll have to do during the next eight weeks. That's when I'm due in Stockholm."

"Then you have plenty of time. What do you have to do other than see if your tuxedo still fits? You do have one, don't you?"

"Tuxedo? Yes, I have one, but it won't do. I'll need tails! Remember, the Prize is presented by the King."

"And a top hat?" Paula's delight was audible. "And will you practice bowing from the waist?"

"I'll have to practice dancing. There's a big dance after the formal Nobel dinner."

"Now how do you know all this?" Paula's tone reflected her surprise. "Don't tell me the Swedes told you about tails and dancing this morning."

"No," he chuckled. "I heard about it from no less than three different Nobelists who called to congratulate me. One even told me where I'd be put up—in a corner suite at the Grand Hotel. It has a view of the water, the Strömmen inlet, and the old Royal Palace on the other side of the bridge. He'd not only brought his wife and children but even his mother-in-law. At least they'll save some money with me—no wife, no children, no in-laws."

"It must be nice," Paula said wistfully, "I've only been to Scandinavia once, and never to Sweden. But tell me about the rest of your day."

"Well, you can imagine the number of people who came to the lab. Even the university president. I don't remember ever having seen him before in the Life Sciences Building. And guess who else was there?"

"I've no idea."

"A relative of yours."

"Relative? My niece Celly? How did you meet her?"

"She came to my house with Jerry Stafford."

"Stafford? I nearly forgot. How do you feel about sharing the Nobel with a student of yours?"

"Most Prizes are shared." Cantor tried to sound offhand. "Husband and wife; father and son; professor and student; bitter competitor and bitter competitor—you've got every kind of combination. I would think that professor and student—and father and son—are the nicest."

"Father and son? Are there many of those?"

Cantor, glad to pursue that tangent, dropped into his lecturer's mode. "There have been several sons who followed their fathers' footsteps in getting Nobel Prizes, and even one daughter: Irène Joliot-Curie. But at least one father-and-son pair has won it together —the Braggs, in 1915. In fact, the son, William L. Bragg, was the youngest Nobel laureate in history; just twenty-five years old. He beat Stafford by almost three years." That last sentence had just slipped out. Cantor could have bitten his tongue, but it was too late.

Paula did not let the subject rest. "What was Stafford doing there? I thought he'd abandoned you for Harvard and that man . . ."

"Krauss. Yes, he's still with Kurt Krauss, but when he heard about the Prize this morning, he flew straight here."

"To celebrate with you?"

"Not exactly," Cantor replied cautiously.

"Then why?"

I might as well tell her, Cantor thought. She's the only one who knows the background. "Actually, he came to inform me that he'd decided to refuse the Prize."

"What?"

Cantor was pleased to hear Paula's surprised exclamation. "He felt he didn't deserve it for doing just one experiment. As a matter of fact, he kept insisting that he wanted to confess something, but I stopped him. I could guess what he wanted to say. I was certainly not prepared to hear it."

"You mean you're still determined to hear no evil? Even after winning the Nobel Prize?"

"Now even more so."

Something in his tone warned Paula away. "So he wanted to turn down the Prize. How did you stop him?"

"I pointed out that it was impossible for him to refuse. Some people had tried in the past—"

"Didn't Pasternak turn down the Nobel Prize in literature?"

"Why, yes." He halted. Cantor was taken by surprise. He'd forgotten about Pasternak. "Wasn't that for political reasons? Still, it doesn't matter: I'm sure Pasternak is on the list of Nobel Prize winners in literature. Anyway, I convinced Jerry that he couldn't do it. I think he got the message that there was no way to get out of it. Not without causing a great deal of damage."

"Damage to whom?"

"Well, to himself, of course. Although also to me, but I didn't bring that up. But that wasn't what was bothering him. Not really. Do you know what he was worried about? The Prize lecture. He was worried that he would have to get up and describe an experiment that no one had reproduced. In the end, I solved the problem quite simply." Cantor proceeded to describe to Paula how he'd apportioned the order and subject matter of their respective lectures.

"And he agreed?"

"Why shouldn't he? What's wrong with my suggestion? I'm letting him speak first and cover what, quite frankly, is the more significant part: the theory. Why should he refuse such an opportunity?"

"Why?" Paula asked softly. "Didn't he realize why you made that offer, I.C.?"

If Cantor noticed the sudden switch to "I.C." he didn't let on. "I'm sure he did. Or at least I hope he did. Paula, there are some things that needn't be said in order to be understood."

17

"I suppose there must be some advantages to motherhood. Like a real tête-à-tête between a mother and a grown-up daughter." Paula Curry was stretched out on the sofa in her living room, wiggling her bare toes.

"Unless she's a grimalkin," replied Celestine.

"Or she has to ask her daughter about some big words. What's a grimalkin?" Her smile was one of pure delight.

"Since you're not my mother, but only my favorite aunt, I'll tell you to look it up. That's the answer I got from my roommate when I asked her the same question. But you're right, it's nice to be together like this. I talk to Mom over the phone every week, but it isn't the same. I wish she were here in person for a real gab among the three of us. Did you invite me for a specific reason or because you missed me?"

"Both, Celly. Both. First, I have to confess something."

"Ah, that I like," said Celestine, sliding closer to her aunt. "Confess!"

"I wanted to tell you that I know Professor Cantor, the man who won the Nobel Prize with your friend Jerry."

"Is that all? I was hoping for something more juicy. Besides, I already know. You've gone out with him."

Paula sat up. "Who told you?"

"No one. I saw you with him. It was a few months ago, at a performance of the Kronos Quartet."

"I'll be damned," said Paula, "and amazed. You're really full of surprises. Why didn't you come and say hello?"

"I wasn't sure you'd be comfortable."

"Why shouldn't I be? We met playing chamber music. He's a pretty good violist."

"Cantor a violist?" It was time for Celestine to be surprised. "I bet Jerry doesn't know that. Paula, what else do you know?"

"Oh, nothing much. Other than that you're engaged." A deep flush colored Celestine's cheeks. "My goodness, Celly," exclaimed her aunt, "how perfectly Victorian! My unflappable niece displaying crimson cheeks." She leaned over to hug her. "You are going to invite me to the wedding, aren't you? Or were you going to elope? And does my sister know?"

Celestine started to recover. "How did you hear that story?" she demanded.

"Story? Isn't it true? I.C. told me that you'd get married as soon as you found a job. He even told me you'd be going to Harvard. Have I got it right?"

"Jesus!" Again she flushed, this time out of irritation. "I'm *not* engaged and I have *not* told Mom, although she does know about Jerry and me. And I haven't made up my mind about any job. I did get an offer from Harvard," she added in a calmer voice.

"Then how did I.C. get the facts so wrong?"

"Oh, he isn't to blame. I can understand how he assumed all that. Jerry introduced me as his fiancée out of embarrassment—I don't think he can pronounce the word 'lover' in front of a third person."

"So you don't think Jerry meant it?"

"I didn't say that. It's just that we haven't talked about it. Right now his head is full of the Prize. Can you imagine, winning a Nobel two years out of graduate school? I wonder what it'll do to him."

The women exchanged long stares. "Yes, I wonder," Paula said finally. "To him and his professor." She picked meditatively at the upholstery before looking up again. "I.C. told me something about your conversation at his home. It mustn't have been easy for Jerry."

"Cantor told you about that?" Celestine looked at her aunt with bewilderment. "How well do you two know each other?"

"Pretty well," Paula said, a faint rose appearing on her cheeks. Celestine was watching her aunt carefully. "Aha," she said.

"Aha nothing," broke in Paula. "We happen to be good friends."

"Sure, sure," Celestine said with a smirk. "That's what Jerry calls me."

"Celly, enough of that." Paula's tone turned businesslike. "There's something else we should talk about. How would you like to go to Stockholm for the Nobel Prize ceremony? With me," she added after just the slightest pause, "as my guest."

"Paula!" exclaimed Celestine. "You must be kidding. How could I? Why?"

"How? Because I'm inviting you. Why? Because you're Jerry's friend, or lover, or maybe even fiancée, and"—she hesitated—"because I need a chaperone."

"How was it?" Stafford was standing in the kitchen of his small apartment just off Harvard Square, drying his hands on the apron he always wore when he cooked. It was his domestic version of a lab coat. "How did your talk go? Have you made up your mind?"

"Jerry, I'm famished. I didn't have anything to eat all day." Celestine dropped her bag in front of the refrigerator and immediately started to scavenge among its contents. Between mouthfuls of cold chicken she said, "I gave my talk on allatostatin during lunch. While the faculty and students ate, I talked." She drained several inches from a carton of milk. "There were so many questions afterward—especially about the virus angle of our work—I was late for my interview with the dean. All I had was some coffee. What's for dinner?"

"If you have any room left, it's a surprise and not quite ready. I can see why housewives complain about their husbands: they come home at any old time and expect to find food on the table. So while your enzymes work on the chicken, tell me how you made out with the chemistry department. Did they all get a shot at you?"

"And two deans." She grinned. "Harvard is finally considering affirmative action, but not too seriously. They still don't have a single woman on their tenured faculty in chemistry."

Stafford opened the oven, releasing a burst of delicious smells. A moment later, he produced a bubbling casserole and set it steaming on the table, whose other function was that of a writing desk, since the room also had to accommodate the sofa bed, his one easy chair, and a chest of drawers. He had cleared the table of all papers and had set it for dinner. He had even bought some real napkins for the occasion.

"Ah," Celly said gratefully. "I'll forgive you, houseboy, for not having the food on the table as I opened the door."

"How about house fiancée?" Stafford interjected.

"Houseboy will do," she said quickly.

"But is a houseboy permitted to fuck the houseguest?" He blushed but did not look away.

"Why, Dr. Stafford! What language! A Nobel Prize winner, and a Baptist at that, using four-letter words? Tsk, tsk." She grinned. "Is that what living alone for the past five months has done to you? But the answer is yes."

"Right now?" he asked, taking her in his arms.

"No!" She pushed him away. "Only on a full stomach."

There were a new tablecloth and candles on the table. He had surprised Celestine with an ethnic meal—all Greek—a cuisine he had never tried before. He confessed that the stuffed grape leaves, with which they started the meal, and the concluding baklava, dripping in honey, were store-bought, but the Greek salad and especially the moussaka were pure Stafford. "Boston is quite a place for Greek food," he pointed out proudly. "Just taste those black olives, and the feta. You'll like it here, Celly. Boston and its environs aren't all that bad to live in."

Celly eyed him curiously. "This is a wonderful dinner you put together, Jerry. But who taught you Greek cooking? And you sound like the Chamber of Commerce."

"Aren't you going to accept their offer?" he asked.

"So that's it. Jerry"—she leaned over and gave him a kiss—"I might as well tell you. I've pretty well decided to turn them down, but I want to discuss it once more with Jean." She laughed, looking at his blank expression. "You've been here only a few months, but you're already like all Harvard men. They think this is the ultimate place; they only have to whistle and you come."

"But, Celly, this is Harvard. The best in the country."

"For whom? Shh. . . ." She put out a hand and hushed the exclamation on his lips. "Let me tell you why I say that. I had quite a day today: I saw nearly all their superstars in organic chemistry, one after another: Kishi, Schreiber, Corey, Evans, Whitesides. I was warned about George Whitesides, but he was particularly nice. He's doing a lot of enzyme work and was pleased to see an organic chemist interested in biological problems. But it was obvious to me that, even though they were excited about my work and its possible practical applications, they'd never have considered me at this stage—not yet a Ph.D. and no postdoc experience—if I were not a woman."

"But, Celly," Stafford interrupted, his impatience showing, "so what? You know you're good, extremely good. Why not take advantage of the situation? Besides, don't think it'll be any different anywhere else."

"I realize that. I'm not a fool. I'd rather get a job because I'm a woman than be refused one because I'm not a man."

"Well, what is it then?"

"Something that doesn't have anything to do with being a woman. They all made it plain that starting out as an assistant professor meant that I really didn't have a chance of getting tenure in their department. Not unless I won the Nobel Prize." She quickly put her hand back over his mouth. "Jerry, one of them actually said just that. He even used you as an example. They're actually proud that they don't promote from within. The implication was that you should be satisfied to have started out at Harvard. When you're ready for tenure, you'll just have to look someplace else."

"Well, what's wrong with that?" asked Stafford.

"What's wrong with that?" Celestine retorted. "No other chemistry department tells you ahead of time that in the long run you couldn't possibly be good enough for them. I think your Nobel Prize has gone to your head. There've been some damn good people here at Harvard who were treated that way. Gilbert Stork, for instance. One of the greatest organic chemists in the world and as good as any of the present Harvard bunch. He had to go to Columbia to get tenure. Or Wilkinson. He got his Nobel for the work he started as an assistant professor at Harvard. Of course, he only got the Prize after they booted him out and he returned to England." A long pause ensued before she continued in a calmer voice. "I learned all that from Jean. She warned me about the situation here. You know what she told me?"

Stafford shook his head.

"She said, 'If you start at the top you have nowhere to go but down.' She gave me several examples of how doing important work in a lower-ranked university can actually call more attention to you. How other institutions will search you out, because publishing an exceptional paper from an unexpected source is more dramatic. Wayne State, for instance—hardly one of the leading universities: that's where another one of your Nobel Prize winners, H. C. Brown, launched his academic career. Or that other man, what's his name, out at Stanford." She wrinkled her brow. "Even you must have heard of him, he publishes so damn much. Never mind, he started out at Wayne too. According to Jean, the most important factors are a good physical and collegial environment, not too much teaching, a fair distribution of graduate students—"

"Fair?" asked Stafford. "You mean fairly good?"

"I mean fair. That one or two of the leading faculty members don't hog all of the incoming graduate students. You've got a maximum of six years to accomplish a lot or you won't get tenure. You can't do that alone."

"So what will you do?"

"I've already been out to Wisconsin. It's a good school, a big department, and I'd be tenure-track: if I do well, I'll get promoted— not sent packing, like at Harvard. The other good thing about them is they've got a first-class ag school. If I'm going to continue my insect work, a good entomology department close by is a real plus."

"So it's on to Madison?"

"I'm not sure yet. There may be something at Cornell. That wouldn't be a bad place for me—they've got Eisner, Meinwald and Roelofs: they're tops in the insect field. Or Cal Tech. Jean tells me they're really expanding their chemistry department, what with all the money they just got from Beckman."

"You've certainly got it all worked out," remarked Stafford admiringly. "There aren't many graduate students your age—"

"Look who's talking: Dr. Jeremiah P. Stafford, who didn't get his Nobel until the ripe old age of twenty-eight!" She reached across the small table and pinched his cheek. "Come, my stomach is now full."

As far as Cantor was concerned, the most important aspect of the Nobel Prize ceremonies were the scientific lectures to be given by him and Stafford. The newspaper and magazine articles, the TV and radio coverage, even the award ceremony itself, all that was ephemeral, and in any event outside his immediate control. But the lecture, that was for the record: its text would appear in the annual volume, *Les Prix Nobel,* issued by the Nobel Foundation. He didn't want to leave anything to chance—especially since Stafford was going to speak first. Therefore, he decided to prepare, with even more than usual care, the manuscript for Stafford's lecture in addition to his own. And it wasn't only the written text he was worried about: there was the presentation as well. The week before Thanksgiving, Cantor phoned Stafford in Boston.

"Jerry, I've been thinking about the arrangements for our flight to Sweden. First of all, I think we ought to arrive together. There'll be a lot of press coverage, right from the start, and the first interviews are important. To simplify matters for you," he continued, after hearing no response from Stafford, "I'm flying via New York so that we can link up at Kennedy. From there, we'll both take SAS to Stockholm. They have a one-stop flight via Copenhagen. We ought to arrive on Friday, because the ceremony will be held on Sunday. That will give us time to adjust our physiological clocks. Now: who is accompanying you?"

"What do you mean?" inquired Stafford.

"The Swedes must have asked you how many rooms they should reserve at the Grand Hotel. They wrote me. What about your parents?"

"Unfortunately, they can't make it."

"What about your fiancée?"

"I asked her, but she told me she was in the middle of her final experiment for her thesis and couldn't make it."

"But you shouldn't have taken no for an answer!" Cantor sounded surprised. "An experiment can always be postponed."

"Ha," Stafford said hollowly.

Cantor ignored him. "Does she know what she's missing? She's unlikely to be invited soon to another Nobel Prize ceremony."

"I told her that," replied Stafford, "but she said she'd simply have to wait until she won the Prize on her own."

Cantor sighed. "So we'll both be alone. Never mind, you'll have plenty of company there. By the way, are you aware that our lectures are scheduled for the following Monday at the *Karolinska*—"

"Yes," Stafford interrupted. "I've hardly thought of anything else. I've been working on it for the last couple of weeks."

"You have?" Cantor was chagrined. "Actually, I've prepared a draft for you."

"You have?" Stafford's tone was irritated. "Why?"

"What do you mean, why?" Cantor started to stutter. "I thought—"

"I.C., surely I should compose my own Nobel lecture," he broke in. "Don't you agree?" His voice had become unmistakably frosty.

Cantor was stumped. "I might as well send my draft to you," he conceded. "You may find it useful."

Paula Curry's discreetly inquisitive nature paid off. She had little difficulty in learning when the men planned to depart and where they would stay. Hadn't Cantor proudly shown her the "Memorandum on the Nobel Week" that the Nobel Foundation had sent? She had been amused by the precise, even pedantic style of the section entitled "Hotel Accommodation":

> *Room reservations will be made by the Nobel Foundation at the Grand Hotel. The Foundation pays the cost of room and breakfast for the Laureate, spouse and non-adult children (below 21 years). Adult family members or professional assistants, accompanying the Laureate are welcome as paying guests. In principle, the number of guests may not exceed 6. Hotel rooms will be booked by the Foundation, if requested in time. Please indicate your wishes on the questionnaire.*

Getting a reservation at the Grand Hotel for the Nobel Prize week turned out to be impossible for the travel agent, but not for Paula. She called the concierge in Stockholm and pointed out that they were close friends of two Nobel laureates, who would otherwise be unaccompanied. "One double room for the two of us will do," she remarked, "but do keep it completely confidential. It's a surprise." She got them both bargain-rate tickets on Icelandair via Reykjavik. "The men are going to be in tails and we'll need evening gowns. That's where we'll spend the money. Don't forget that you need a passport," she reminded Celestine, "and take your fur coat."

"My fur coat?" her niece exclaimed. "You must be kidding. Do you think that's what graduate students are wearing these days?"

"Then I'll rent one for you here in Chicago. No niece of mine will go to a Nobel ball in an evening gown and a parka."

18

Cantor knew from his Nobelist friends that everything associated with the Prize ceremonies, starting with their reception at Arlanda Airport, would be truly *distingué*. He planned to arrive in style, and made his airline reservations accordingly. Stafford, on the other hand, had never flown anything but economy class, and this trip—his first to Europe—was no exception. As a result, at Kennedy Airport the two men boarded the plane together but then were immediately separated. Up front, Cantor, when he chose to leave his seat that was practically a chaise longue, was free to go slumming *ad libitum*, whereas Stafford was restricted to steerage. The first time Cantor attempted to visit him, the narrow aisles were blocked by serving carts. The second time around, Stafford was fast asleep, wedged in between two large blond businessmen. Cantor had been anxious to discuss with him some last-minute items concerning their arrival press conference; he concluded it would have to wait for their layover in Copenhagen. It didn't work out that way.

Shortly after take-off from New York, the captain had announced that this time, contrary to the usual plane change in Copenhagen, they would stop only for refueling and continue on the same aircraft to Stockholm. Cantor had underestimated the soporific effect of the six-course dinner, the two wines and the glass of port. When the plane landed in Copenhagen, he was dead to the world, a sleeping mask over his eyes, while Stafford, wide awake, wandered past the duty-free counters of Kastrup Airport.

Stafford failed to hear the first departure call for his flight. He caught the second one and headed back for his gate. Suddenly, he stopped in his tracks, smiled to himself, and turned around. He had not even finished the delicious pastry and the coffee with real cream in the coffee shop—his first Scandinavian breakfast—when the final departure of his flight was announced. Slowly he sauntered to one of the transfer desks, not minding in the least that a Turkish-speaking passenger took nearly ten minutes to complete his simple transaction. Finally, the young woman behind the counter turned to him. "Yes?" she snapped, her day's quota of patience having been exhausted by the Turk.

Upon hearing that he had missed his plane to Stockholm, she raised her eyes to the ceiling and sighed audibly. "I'll see whether there is any space on the next flight. I doubt it," she warned, "the weekday morning flights to Stockholm are often full. You may have to go on standby. Why didn't you stay on the plane?"

Stafford shrugged, a contented look on his face. "I don't mind waiting. Just see what you can get for me. The name is Stafford. Initial J."

The agent reached for his ticket and conversed with her computer. Suddenly, her expression changed. She picked up the telephone and spoke rapidly in Danish, all along eyeing him curiously. When she finished, she rose from her stool. "Please excuse me, sir," the young woman said, "I didn't know who you were. Let me escort you to the VIP lounge." She laughed nervously as they walked down the long corridor. "You're the first Nobel Prize winner I've ever met. And so young!" she cooed.

As soon as the seat-belt sign was turned off, Cantor went back in search of Stafford. His seat was empty. Cantor sat down and waited; the only place where Stafford could be was in one of the toilets. When ten minutes had elapsed, Cantor headed for the row of lavatory doors. After another ten minutes, he had seen each one open and disgorge its occupant. No Stafford.

"Miss," he addressed a passing stewardess, "I'm looking for a passenger who was sitting in that seat over there. Do you have any idea where he could be?"

"There's no one there," she replied.

"I know that," he barked, then caught himself. "That's why I'm asking."

Flight attendants on SAS are trained to be polite, and this one was no exception. "I'm sorry, sir. I meant the seat was unoccupied when we took off."

"But that's impossible," he sputtered. "The passenger was sitting there all the way from New York. A young man, clean-shaven, brown hair: you must've seen him."

"I'm sorry, sir," she said patiently. "I only joined the crew in Copenhagen."

"But he has to be here," he insisted, his voice rising in desperation. "Where could he be?"

"Perhaps he's in Copenhagen," suggested the stewardess. "Why don't you let me get the purser?"

The purser, who knew of Cantor's elevated status, was of no help. "Professor, please don't concern yourself. We'll be in Stockholm in twenty minutes. I'm sure the ground crew there will have information on your colleague." He gave Cantor a respectful wink. "SAS has never yet lost a Nobel Prize winner."

Cantor looked sullenly out the window. It was one of those brief Scandinavian December days, the sun hardly above the horizon before it was on the way down; the landscape below was barely dusted with snow, the Stockholm archipelago lay just ahead. A cheerful voice broke in on him. "Don't worry, Professor. The captain has just spoken with Copenhagen. Dr. Stafford will be on the next flight to Stockholm. He must've missed this plane."

"How could he've done that?" muttered Cantor.

The passengers standing in line, straining to get out, stared enviously when Cantor was asked to deplane first. As he emerged from the narrow gangway he was momentarily blinded by bright lights shining straight into his eyes. Waiting for him—and partly responsible for the lights—was Lars Sjöstrand, photographer for the *Svenska Dagbladet*. Sjöstrand called himself a photo journalist, not a *paparazzo.* He felt that the function of a news photographer was to burrow beneath his subject's surface. That was why he was the only *Svenska Dagbladet* photographer who didn't use a Hasselblad on such occasions. He carried a motor-driven Nikon with a 600-mm zoom lens, a specially designed holster, together with his powerful left arm, taking the place of a tripod. He made it a habit to focus on his subject's nose: if he could count the hairs peeking out of the nostril, he knew that he'd catch every nuance of his victim's expression, every droplet of sweat not recognizable through a regular lens. His photographic bazooka was aimed straight at the doorframe of the passage through which the plane's passengers would spill. Ulf Lundholm, the *Svenska Dagbladet* reporter, was standing next to him. "Remember, Lars," Lundholm reminded his colleague, "I want one with his mouth open. The man was too arrogant. Have him look silly."

When the picture appeared the following day, Cantor's mouth was gaping. He did in fact look silly. At the moment Lars's bazooka fired, Cantor had just caught his first sight of Paula Curry: tall, blond, wrapped in fur with matching boots—and a slightly wicked gleam in her eyes. In the succeeding photographs, which Lundholm had rejected, Cantor's open mouth had become just an accoutrement to unmitigated pleasure. The shot showing Paula Curry embracing the professor also ended up on the cutting-room floor. It would have been too similar to the accompanying picture featuring a slightly tousled Stafford kissing Celestine.

Lundholm congratulated himself on his acumen in getting that shot. The various wire services, and the local competition—the *Dagens Nyheter, Aftonbladet* and *Expressen*—each had sent only one team to meet Cantor's and Stafford's flights. When the official welcoming party, consisting of a representative from the Swedish Ministry of Foreign Affairs, the American cultural attaché, the rector of the *Karolinska Institutet* and two Swedish professors, had swept Cantor toward the special reception area provided by SAS, all the reporters followed except for Lundholm, who had held his photographic sidekick back. Lundholm suspected—correctly, it turned out—that Cantor's interview would contain few surprises. He had accumulated enough background on Cantor, who was listed in *Who's Who in America* and the other standard references. He'd even had their Washington correspondent dig up some clippings for him. It was the young cowinner, Jeremiah Stafford, who'd piqued his interest. The information the Nobel Foundation provided on Stafford had been so sketchy as to border on the useless: place and date of birth, educational history, and the titles of four scientific articles—all but one also bearing the name of I. Cantor. Lundholm knew the Swedish readership. A human interest story, featuring the second-youngest Nobel laureate in history, seemed to him much more promising.

When the next Copenhagen flight arrived fifty minutes later, in addition to Lundholm and Sjöstrand only the Swedish Foreign Ministry attaché and an attractive young American woman were there to meet Stafford. The attaché was practicing American colloquialisms with the woman, who was wearing a black down-filled coat, footwear resembling after-ski boots, and no hat. Her hair was light brown and unusually short. She looked excited.

Sjöstrand had taken one last look at the head shot of Stafford that accompanied the Nobel Foundation's brief press release. He raised his bazooka and took his stance. But in contrast to Cantor's carefully orchestrated arrival, Stafford's had been completely informal. He'd been sitting in the back of the crowded plane and was one of the last to saunter down the gangway, anorak in one arm, an airline bag and small book in the other. Suddenly he stopped, so suddenly, in fact, that the passenger immediately behind bumped him, and completely spoiled Sjöstrand's first two pictures. The third one, however, ultimately graced the front page of the *Svenska Dagbladet*. It showed Stafford, his airline bag and book lying on the floor, kissing Celestine. His hands were around her waist, while hers encircled his neck. Lundholm had bent down to pick up the volume. The title surprised him: *T. S. Eliot. Collected Poems 1909–1961*.

"Celly darling," Lundholm heard Stafford exclaim after the couple had stopped kissing and were giggling at each other. "I can't believe it! How did you get here? How did you fool me so completely—you and your important experiment?" He was about to kiss her again when he heard a discreet cough. It came from the Foreign Ministry emissary, but Lundholm transformed it into his own cue.

"Welcome to Stockholm, Dr. Stafford," he said in his most ingratiating manner. "I'm a reporter for the *Svenska Dagbladet.* Please let me carry this for you." He held up Stafford's bag, which he had retrieved with the Eliot volume. "May I ask you just a few questions before this gentleman leads you to the reception area?" He gestured toward the attaché, who had so far been unsuccessful in approaching Stafford.

"Sure," replied Stafford good-naturedly, his left arm still around Celestine's waist, "shoot."

"Is this your first trip to our city?"

"Absolutely! My first to Europe altogether. What about you, Celly?" He nuzzled his companion.

"My first to Scandinavia," she replied. "I've been to Europe a couple of times with my family."

"Are you prepared for all the festivities? To meet our King?" Lundholm straightened unconsciously as he named the royal majesty.

"I'm not sure I'm prepared, but I'm looking forward to it."

"Do you know his name?" the reporter asked, a foxy look in his eyes.

"I'm afraid not," admitted Stafford. "But I'll hardly need to, will I?" he asked. "Won't 'Your Royal Majesty' do for addressing the King or Queen?"

"Jerry, her name is Silvia Renate," Celestine interrupted, wishing to spare Stafford further embarrassment.

"Now how did you find that out?" Stafford exclaimed.

"I've been here a whole day. And guess with whom?"

"Leah?" he asked.

"No," she replied, "although that would've been fun. Imagine getting a Bakhtinian perspective on the Nobel ceremony. Guess again."

"I give up. Who is it?"

"My aunt, Paula Curry."

"No kidding. Why her?"

"Just wait. You'll find out." She moved aside for Lundholm. "But I think this gentleman would like to ask you some more questions first."

"Quite right," said Lundholm. "For instance, who's this young lady?"

"She is my—" Stafford began, but Celestine broke in.

"My name is Celestine Price. We're friends. From the same university," she added lamely.

"Ah," said Lundholm, jotting in his notebook. "How do you spell Price? Like the Nobel Prize?"

"No," laughed Celestine, "with a *c*, like an expensive price."

"Or like priceless," added Stafford. "That's really what she is."

"Ah," Lundholm said a second time, writing quickly.

"And this book? You dropped it when you came." He handed the slim volume over to Stafford. "Is this part of your preparation for the festivities?"

"Who knows?" Stafford mimed diffidence, but his blush gave him away.

"What were you reading, Jerry?" demanded Celestine, reaching for the book. "T. S. Eliot? Well, I'll be damned."

Lundholm, having jotted down the author's name, considered that subject finished. "Dr. Stafford?" He called Stafford's attention back from Celestine. "Do you think you deserve to win the Nobel Prize with Professor Cantor?"

Again Celestine came to the rescue. "Don't answer that, Jerry!" She turned to the reporter. "You know, that isn't a fair question."

"I am only interested in Dr. Stafford's opinion."

"Well, you wouldn't want Jerry to second-guess the Nobel Committee, would you? That's hardly polite."

Lundholm bowed his head slightly. "I can see why you're priceless, Miss Price. One last question, Dr. Stafford, may I? Have you decided how you'll spend your portion of the Nobel award? It's quite a lot of money, especially for so young a scientist as yourself."

"I was wondering that too," laughed Celestine. "What are you going to do with all that dough?"

"Yes, I have thought about it," he said to her dryly. "I'll tell you before I leave Stockholm." He turned to the reporter. "In spite of what my priceless friend here said, I'll answer your previous question. But then we must go: I can see that this gentleman is getting impatient." He smiled at the Foreign Ministry emissary, who had been listening quietly to their exchange. "You asked whether I deserved to share the Nobel Prize. Of course Celestine is right, you should ask the Nobel Committee. Apparently, they thought the tumorigenesis theory merited the Prize. The original concept was Professor Cantor's, but if they'd given it for just that, they would have taken quite a chance. Do you know that, in 1926, Johannes Fibiger received a Nobel Prize for proposing that malignant tumors were caused by parasites? He turned out to be wrong, of course, and for forty years thereafter, no Nobel Prize was awarded for any work in the cancer field."

Lundholm scribbled furiously; Celestine, however, looked at Stafford with open astonishment. "Where did you learn all that?" she whispered.

"Professor Krauss told me," he answered *sotto voce*. "It seems there's very little about cancer and the Nobel he doesn't know." Stafford turned again to Lundholm. "But let me return to the question you asked. A hypothesis, in any field, is a sleeping beauty. She needs a prince to wake her up. With this sleeping beauty, the prince is the experimental test. I provided that first test, and to that extent I brought her to life."

"So you're the prince!" Lundholm's eyes shone with delight. "That's marvelous: the prince and his priceless friend arriving in Stockholm—"

"Wait a moment," laughed Stafford. "Miss Price is priceless, but I didn't say I was a prince. I just meant that's why I was coauthor of the original publication. And that's presumably why—"

"Jerry," interrupted Celestine, her discomfort showing clearly. "I wouldn't—"

"Aha," broke in Lundholm, who was hearing exactly what he was after and was not going to let it escape. "And Professor Cantor came to you to provide that experimental test?"

"Yes, he did."

"Because you were the only person capable of doing it? At age twenty-eight?" He raised his eyebrows.

"Of course not." Stafford dismissed the question with a shake of his head. "If I were the only one capable of performing that experiment, it would have no operational meaning." He was pleased with that phrase, even though he had a feeling he'd heard it before. "An experiment is only meaningful if it can be repeated by someone else. You need at least two princes to convert a hypothesis into fact. Therefore, by definition I couldn't be the only one capable of accomplishing it."

"I see," murmured Lundholm as he jotted vigorously. "And who repeated your experiment?" he asked without looking up from his notebook. "Who's the other prince?"

"We've really got to go and join Professor Cantor," replied Stafford, taking Celestine by the hand. "I bet he's wondering what happened to me in Copenhagen."

As they followed their Swedish guide down the hallway, Celestine whispered furiously, "Jerry, have you gone mad?"

"Relax," he whispered back, "I know what I'm doing." He squeezed her hand. "That's why I missed the plane in Copenhagen."

"Well, well, the long-lost sheep," proclaimed Cantor, shaking Stafford's hand. "Let me introduce you to our Swedish hosts. And then let me present you to all these reporters." He made a sweeping gesture at the microphones, cameras and reporters. After the formal handshakes, all duly recorded on film, Cantor pointed out Paula Curry, who was sitting on a sofa observing the scene. "And this is—"

"Why, Miss Curry!" exclaimed Stafford, stepping forward to greet her. "Celly's mystery companion: what brings you here?"

"Paula, you know each other?" Cantor's voice came puzzled from behind. "Where have you met?"

She shrugged, hoping her reply would sound innocuous. "Oh,

in Chicago. My niece brought him along. But you two must be bushed. Finish with your interview and then let's get to the hotel."

"You're right," replied Cantor, the remnants of mistrust barely extinguished. "While we were waiting for you, Jerry, I've talked to all these people." Turning around, he began in a loud voice, "Gentlemen, I trust—" and then caught himself. "And lady." He bowed with an apologetic smile toward the single woman reporter in the crowd. "This is my colleague, Dr. Stafford, who seems to have been delayed in Copenhagen. I trust I've answered all your questions on our joint behalf. I think it's time for us to go to our hotel and take a nap."

"Excuse me, Professor," called out Lundholm, "I was not here during your interview. I have one question, which I addressed earlier to Dr. Stafford." A lupine smile crossed the reporter's face. "Unless, of course, you've already covered it here with my colleagues."

"Go on," said Cantor, flashing a glance of suspicion.

"I wanted to know why your twenty-eight-year-old collaborator shared the Nobel Prize with you. What, precisely, was his contribution?"

Several microphones, which had been hanging listlessly in reporters' hands, suddenly rose and moved closer to Cantor. Pencils poised over paper. "What did you say?" Cantor turned to Jerry.

Stafford was about to reply, but Lundholm held up his hand. "I'd be interested in *your* answer, Professor Cantor. I already have Dr. Stafford's." He raised his notebook.

"Now wait a moment," Cantor began angrily. He stopped, and struggled to change his tone. "We were collaborators. Throughout the project. That's why Dr. Stafford and I published the work together. That's why we share the Prize."

"Professor, we all know that," said Lundholm with exaggerated patience, "that's what the Nobel press release states. But my question to you is about his specific contribution, what he—"

Cantor contained himself with an effort. "True collaborators don't divide credit. We were partners on the entire project." A few weeks ago, Cantor would have been livid at the reporter's insolence. Now, tempered by the Nobel glow, he only simmered. "May I suggest you come to the scientific lectures on Monday? I think there you will find all the answers to your question."

"Thank you for that suggestion, Professor," Lundholm replied smoothly. "I'll be there."

19

A stack of envelopes in a red leather folder awaited Stafford in his third-floor, corner suite at the Grand Hotel. He'd never before found himself with so many invitations. Among them were the Saturday dinner at the Grand Hotel with the *Rector Magnificus* and some of the more distinguished Karolinska professors; Monday evening's banquet for the Nobelists and their families, given by the King and Queen at the old Royal Palace (Stafford could see the lights from his window); lunch with the American ambassador on Tuesday at his residence on Nobelgatan 2; and Wednesday's Lucia dinner, to be hosted by the head of the Medical Students Association of Stockholm. With the possible exception of the luncheon, for the next five days Stafford would be unlikely to get out of his rented tails. The tails themselves had been waiting for him when he arrived: they were hanging, freshly pressed, in his closet. He'd sent his measurements ahead of time on the form the Swedes had so thoughtfully provided: waist; crotch to right foot; crotch to left foot; chest; shoulders; left arm; right arm.

Two of the envelopes in the stack were thicker. One dealt with the arrangements for Sunday afternoon's presentation of the *Nobelpriset* in the Concert Hall in Hötorget. It could hardly be called an invitation. It was a summons, a timetable so detailed that the only item not mentioned was a toilet break. A note attached to the envelope suggested that these directions be brought to the 11 A.M. dress rehearsal. The other bulky envelope contained the invitation to the formal Sunday banquet in the City Hall. As Stafford looked with astonishment at the guest list, comprising 1318 names and titles, their locations at sixty-six tables indicated precisely in an accompanying diagram, his head started to swim. He'd had no idea of the scale and formality of the event.

The telephone woke him. The room was dark, as in the middle of the night. Some moments passed before Stafford gained his bearings. "Jerry, did I wake you?" He recognized Celestine's voice.

"What time is it?" he asked, groping for the switch of the bed lamp.

"Almost four o'clock."

"Why are you waking me up at four in the morning?" he whined.

"Dummy," she countered good-naturedly, "afternoon, not morning. You're way up north and it's the middle of December. Let's go for a walk—just the two of us, before the press catches up with Prince Stafford."

"Where do you want to go?"

"Let's cross the bridge to the Old Town. But put on everything you've brought, it's bitterly cold outside. It'll clear your brain. I think you need it, Prince."

Stafford had almost finished dressing when Celestine knocked on his door. Her face sparkled with enthusiasm and affection.

"God, it feels wonderful having you here, Celly. Just a few hours ago, I thought I'd spend all these days just by myself."

"Jerry, you never told me why your parents aren't here."

Stafford winced. "I might as well tell somebody. I.C. asked, but I simply said they couldn't make it. You know about my father: Scripture is revealed truth; Darwinian evolution is blasphemy. Maybe I should've gone into chemistry, like you, so the subject of evolution could be avoided. But biology? Ever since my undergraduate days, I had to keep quiet or argue. It just got worse in grad school. My father's harping on creationism produced an enormous gulf between us. If you think the Nobel Prize helped, you're mistaken."

"Oh, Jerry, I'm so sorry."

"So am I. The Prize only reinforced my father's disapproval. When I invited my parents to come at my expense, my father turned me down flat. As far as he's concerned, I've succumbed to another temptation. All he had to say to his son, the Nobel laureate, was: 'Pride goeth before a fall.' Since I've already fallen, let's go out and enjoy it."

Paula Curry's and Celestine Price's roles as unofficial consorts of two laureates had become known so late that their names could not be added to the printed invitations. It was probably just as well, because their formal status was never clarified. The ambiguity of "friend" did not simplify matters, but the Swedish hosts improvised graciously. Two tickets for the award ceremony—otherwise unobtainable at so late a date—were delivered to their room. Their seats were in the middle of the fifth row just behind the Swedish cabinet and the diplomatic corps.

The Nobel banquet was more difficult: the booklet containing the precise seating arrangements had been mailed out days in advance. According to the attached chart, the royal family, the Nobel laureates and their families, and some of the most important government and academic officials—86 persons in all—were grouped around the enormous head table. The rest were divided into two groups: 720 guests, with titles like *Ambassadör, Friherrina, Ceremonimästare,* and *Professor,* were allocated to twenty-four long tables, arranged perpendicular to that of the honorees. Another 512 less important guests—journalists, specially invited students, and last-minute additions, including a sprinkling of professors with foreign names—were assigned to an outer circle of forty-one smaller tables. The relative importance and status of all the guests had already been nicely gauged by their distance from the head table, and especially from its royal center. It was simply not feasible to displace anyone for Celestine's or Paula's sake.

The Nobel Prize winners are provided with escorts for the period of their official stay—from arrival at the airport until December 14, the day after the *Luciadag* celebration, when the laureates are awakened at 7 A.M. by eight white-gowned young women, who sing the Santa Lucia hymn and serve them breakfast in bed (all recorded by an intrusive TV crew). The escorts handle all logistic details and also dispense advice on matters of protocol and decorum. Cantor's and Stafford's respective guides were now assigned the additional duty of taking care of the two "friends," to whom they had to explain why they would find themselves at the very end of one of the tables. "At least, it's Table Number 25 in the center," one of the men had added consolingly, offering, by way of compensation, a pair of collapsible opera glasses, "and you will eat the same food as the King and Queen. Let me confide a secret," he leaned over conspiratorially. "It's supposed to be a surprise. The main course is a local delicacy: saddle of Swedish hare with calvados cream sauce and apple rings."

"How come you know that if it's supposed to be a secret?" asked Paula.

"Don't tell anyone," he replied, placing his right index finger over his lips. "I know one of the chefs at the *Stadshuskallaren*. That's the restaurant where the whole banquet is produced."

The only special recognition that the "friends" received on Sunday was that they shared their respective laureates' stretch-limousine Volvos on the way to the ceremonies at the Concert Hall and from there to the banquet. It was practically their only time alone until well past midnight. Little was said on the afternoon trip from the hotel. Stafford was too nervous, his slight smile the only sign that he'd felt Celestine's reassuring squeeze of his gloved hand. His mood had changed completely, however, by their second private meeting—the ride from the Concert Hall to the *Stadshuset*, Stockholm's lovely reddish-brown City Hall with its Italianate tower and green copper roof. Stafford, the newly crowned Nobel laureate, was relaxed; Celestine was bubbling over.

"Jerry," she blurted out the moment the car door slammed shut behind them, "I got goose pimples when the trumpets sounded and you all marched in. You looked wonderful in your tails—and even younger than the students leading the procession!" She leaned over and kissed him on his cheek. "You've got to buy yourself some tails when we get back home. I'd love to go out with you, dressed up like that."

"It's a deal," concurred Stafford, "provided you wear the dress you have on just now. I didn't know you owned anything like that." He leaned back, ogling her at length.

"I didn't either. It was Paula's gift. She's the one who treated me to this trip." Celestine opened her fur coat and stretched out her legs. "The saleswoman said I had just the right build for it." Celestine went on, her voice soft in the darkened interior of the car. "What I'll never forget, Jerry, is when they called out your name, and the fanfares sounded, and everybody rose as you approached the King." She turned to face him, grinning. "What did he say to you?"

"It's a state secret, but maybe I'll tell you someday."

"Like tonight?" she asked coyly.

"Maybe," he replied in the same voice.

"Jerry, where did you learn to walk backward?" she asked. "Nobody else did that. Was that so you wouldn't turn your back to the King and Queen?"

"Yes," he beamed, "that's what my escort suggested to me at the dress rehearsal. He said, 'Walk backward, with your eyes on the royal family before you bow to them. The Swedes in the audience will appreciate it.' I guess I was the only one to do that. He promised to give me a videotape of the ceremony."

Their privacy was interrupted by their escort. "Miss Price, we are about to arrive at the *Stadshuset.* As soon as I turn Dr. Stafford over to his dinner companion—he will be sitting between the Queen and the wife of the *Talman,* who heads our Parliament—I shall lead you to the *Bla Hallen,* the Blue Hall, which is not really blue but white. You are at Table Number 25 on the far end, across from Professor Cantor's friend. You will find a place card with your name; you are Number 806 on the diagram."

During the afternoon award ceremony, amidst the pomp and the trumpet flourishes, the speeches and orchestral interludes, the deepest imprint left on Celestine's mind was that of the serene expression on her lover's face as he walked confidently backward, the medal in its red box and the red leather folder in his hands. She had expected pride or excitement, not peaceful composure.

During the banquet, with Stafford several hundred feet away, her attention focused on an impersonal detail: the unbelievable military precision with which the white-gloved, uniformed waiters and waitresses served the various courses, as some of the laureates made brief speeches. Cantor was one of them and his turn came early, right after the fish course. "I.C. is lucky," remarked Paula. "Now he can relax and enjoy the rest of the meal."

Cantor spoke with precision and true elegance. " '. . . what you do not know is the only thing you know/ And what you own is what you do not own,' " he intoned, "as a great poet once wrote, who subsequently won the Nobel Prize in literature." Who was that poet? Celestine wondered; she could see from some of the heads moving together, the whispers in her neighborhood, that others were also occupied with that question. Cantor went on, "It was he, of course, who said in another context, 'To arrive where you are, to get from where you are not,/ You must go by a way wherein there is no ecstasy.' While these sentiments can also pertain to scientific research, tonight I am using the poet's words with reference to the Prize you have so graciously bestowed on me. I do not own it, because the contribution you honored with the Nobel Prize is not the work of one or two individuals. It is the culmination of years of research, often tedious and seemingly unsuccessful, at times touched by ecstasy, of many . . ." Celestine had stopped listening. She was speculating about what Jerry would have said if he had been asked to make one of the dinner speeches.

The most dramatic performance of the serving staff came with the dessert. As trumpets sounded, the lights gradually dimmed, until the whole hall was bathed solely by the flickering light of the candles on the long banquet tables. The waiters, each holding a silver tray high up in the air, marched to their positions at each table and stopped. They were about to dispense the *Nobel Is*—the traditional Nobel ice dessert crowned with a frozen "N."

At a wave of the hand by the staff commander, the waiters moved in unison, serving each guest at exactly the same speed, so that they arrived at the end of each table at precisely the same moment. At Table Number 25, Celestine and Paula received the last two portions of the *Is*. Celestine was startled suddenly to hear Jerry's voice, amplified by the public address system: at first, she had thought he was standing by her side. She looked up and saw him, resplendent in his formal clothes, his face radiant as he leaned over the microphone. Celestine raised her opera glasses. Why hadn't he told her he was going to speak?

"Your Majesties," he began, bowing in the direction of the King and Queen as if he'd been addressing royalty since childhood, "Your Royal Highnesses, Your Excellencies, distinguished cabinet ministers and ambassadors, ladies and gentlemen. Since Professor Cantor started his address with some lines from Eliot's *Four Quartets*," a remark producing widespread nods and smiles among the dinner audience, "I consider it appropriate to follow my mentor and professor by also quoting T. S. Eliot: 'The Nobel is a ticket to one's funeral. No one has ever done anything after he got it.' " A visible wave of astonishment passed through the great hall; low mutterings followed. Did he intend a joke? Stafford himself provided the answer as he continued after a brief pause.

"Eliot, of course, did not utter these words here when he accepted the Nobel Prize in literature. It would have been enormously discourteous. He said them in private, when he complained about the demands and expectations placed on him—already world-famous and sixty years old—when he received that highest honor. But I, who until a few weeks ago was utterly unfamous"—again he stopped for a short pause, just long enough for Paula to whisper to Celestine about his consummate timing—"and still can look forward to many decades of active work: I have to think of these words. What will the Nobel Prize do to me when it is bestowed so early in my life? I offer my answer to you in the same manner in which Eliot ended his very last poem: 'These are private words addressed to you in public.' "

Celestine pressed the opera glasses against her eyes until they hurt. She wanted to catch Stafford's eyes as they swept slowly over the audience.

"In spite of the generous words addressed to his many students and collaborators, Professor Cantor can with justification consider the Nobel Prize the ultimate recognition of his enormously productive scientific career. I, however, stand here because I had the good fortune to be trained by him and to participate—at his invitation and at just the right time—in a crucial experiment. Only a few weeks ago, I was planning to apply for an independent academic post after the completion of my postdoctorate training. But if I am now to receive such an offer, will it be because of my Nobel Prize, which I share with Professor Cantor, or will it be because of my past record and future promise? I shall never know.

"I imagine that, in preparation for their trip to Stockholm, many Nobel laureates have studied the records of their predecessors: what words they voiced here; what their experiences were in subsequent years. As I did so, I was particularly struck by the careers of two physicists, who won the Nobel Prize early in life. The youngest, W. L. Bragg, received his at age twenty-five, together with his father, for their contributions to the field of X-ray crystallography. He spent the rest of his life in that field. Donald Glaser was in his very early thirties when he was so honored for the invention of the bubble chamber. I perceive him as a particularly appropriate model. First, he spent part of his honorarium on a honeymoon." Celestine found herself blushing at the ripple of laughter passing through the audience. By keeping her opera glasses to her eyes, she didn't need to respond to Paula's nudge.

"But he is also an appropriate model for me because of a decision he made after he won the Prize. Glaser switched his area of research from bubble chambers and cosmic rays to molecular biology and biophysics. I have resolved to do likewise—to move into another field; to start a new line of research all on my own. But I have also chosen to go a step further, to follow a course which, I trust, is still consistent with Alfred Nobel's will. Originally, Nobel thought that the financial reward accompanying the Prize would make the winner independent. Nowadays, that is only true in that the Nobel Prize usually assures the recipient of research support from governmental institutions or foundations. However, I would like to use the bulk of my honorarium in the narrower sense in which Nobel first envisioned it nearly ninety years ago: to offer me the wherewithal to achieve professional independence. I shall go back to school"—Stafford paused to let the phrase sink into the audience—"to medical school, in order to earn the degree of Doctor of Medicine, which will enable me eventually to explore the clinical implications of the tumorigenesis theory conceived in Professor Cantor's laboratory.

"Since Professor Cantor first introduced me to Eliot's poetry, I trust that he will not mind if I end with a quotation from the poem he selected for his beginning: 'We shall not cease from exploration/ And the end of all our exploring/ Will be to arrive where we started/ And know the place for the first time.' "

As Stafford walked back to his seat next to the Queen of Sweden, Celestine wiped the tears from her face with her napkin. She had forgotten to bring a handkerchief.

The banquet had taken nearly three hours; Celestine had not been able to exchange a single word or glance with her lover, who had practically proposed to her in front of hundreds of guests. She hoped to make up for it on the dance floor, but even that meeting was delayed. The dance given by the university students was held in the upstairs *Gyllene Salen.* This year's head of the Students Association, a woman who could have stepped out of the pages of a Swedish Tourist Board advertisement, led Stafford from the Queen's side directly to the dance floor. Celestine had to content herself with waltzing with the Swede who'd accompanied them in the car. The next dance, a fox trot, was usurped by Cantor.

"Miss Price," he announced with gracious formality, "I'm sure you'd rather dance with Jerry, but he seems to be too much in demand. The fox trot is just about my style. May I have this dance?"

Cantor proved to be a slightly stiff but otherwise competent dancer who led her to the periphery of the swirling crowd. Celestine began to congratulate him on his acceptance speech, but the professor interrupted her. "Let's talk about Jerry's speech instead. Were you prepared for what he said?"

"Absolutely not."

"Neither was I, but I must say I was impressed. And I never knew he took my advice about Eliot so seriously. I'm impressed," Cantor repeated. "But you know, I believe you have a lot to do with his decision about medical school."

"How so?"

"Winning a Nobel, and then deciding to go back to school as a student?" he mused. "He may be right. He certainly got me thinking with that remark of Eliot's about the Prize. I'd never heard it before." Cantor moved his head back so as to face his dance partner. "When I congratulated Jerry down there"—he motioned with his head in the direction of the Blue Hall downstairs—"I asked him whether he'd decided yet on a specific medical school. You know what he said?"

Celestine shook her head.

"I would've thought he'd pick Harvard: Jerry is already there and Kurt Krauss could take care of everything. Instead, he told me he'd sent out applications to Wisconsin and UCLA. Didn't you mention the University of Wisconsin as one of the places that offered you a job?"

"Yes."

"But why UCLA?" Cantor wondered. "It's a good school, but there are at least a dozen in that rank."

"I've no idea," replied Celestine, her eyes searching for Stafford. "Maybe he's got a friend at Cal Tech."

It took a Bee Gees number to remove some of the older dancers from the floor and to bring Celestine face to face with Stafford. "Finally!" he exclaimed. "I had a hell of a time finding you. And now when we finally meet, we can't even touch each other." They moved their hips, shoulders and arms to the disco tempo. Every time they approached each other, a brief question shot out.

"So you're considering UCLA?"

"Who told you?"

"Cantor."

"The bastard!"

"No, he just couldn't understand why."

"And you?"

"Yes!" she shouted. "You want to spend some of your Nobel money near me."

"And on us," he yelled back.

That's when she stopped dancing and embraced Stafford. "To hell with the dance."

In the car on the way back to the hotel, their escort turned around and asked, "Dr. Stafford, did Eliot really say that about the Nobel Prize and his funeral?"

"Yes. It's in his latest biography."

"Your talk was very daring." He looked at Celestine. "Miss Price, did you know that Dr. Stafford planned to go to medical school?"

"No."

"And what do you think about it?"

"It's very daring," she broke out laughing. "And quite wonderful. I only hope he gets admitted."

The man looked shocked. "With a Nobel Prize?"

"It depends how you mean that," observed Stafford. "Let me tell the two of you something but please keep it quiet. In addition to Wisconsin and UCLA, I also applied to Harvard. Just in case." He winked at Celestine. "You know what happened? A couple of days before my departure for Stockholm, I got a card through the mail. A printed card from the admissions office, not even signed."

"What did it say?" asked the escort.

"That Harvard couldn't consider my application. I had missed the deadline."

"But . . . but," the man started to sputter.

"I know what you'll say," interrupted Stafford. "They obviously didn't know that I'd won a Nobel Prize. But isn't that the point I made during my acceptance speech?"

"What's it like, making love to a Nobel Prize winner? Now that it's official, that is," he murmured in Celestine's ear. It was well past three o'clock, but both were still too excited to fall asleep. Their formal clothes were strewn over Stafford's bedroom floor. They were lying in bed, the lights from the street barely defining their features.

"It was quite an evening, wasn't it?" he said with a satisfied masculine touch to his voice. "I wish you'd sat next to me at the banquet."

"You would have missed talking to the Queen. What was she like?"

"Very nice and very beautiful."

"That doesn't tell me anything! What did you talk about?"

"You'll never guess."

"So tell me." She pinched him. "Come on, Jerry. I've never conversed with royalty."

"You will tomorrow night. At the palace—you're coming with me."

"I know, but I'd like to hear what you talked about at the banquet. Just one example."

"Okay. The cutlery."

"Cutlery?" She pinched him again. "Be serious, Jerry."

"Cross my heart. You saw the settings at the banquet. Did you count the knives and forks and spoons? Especially the knives?"

"No."

"Well, I did. I've never used a fish knife in my life. When we had the gravlax, I just cut it with the fork. Until I saw how the Queen ate. Then I copied her. Apparently she noticed but didn't say anything when the rabbit was served. . . ."

"Not rabbit. Hare. Saddle of Swedish hare."

"How dare you correct a Nobel Prize winner?"

"Sorry, my Nobelist," she snickered. "Go on with your story."

"I cut the meat the usual way—as I've eaten all my life. That's when the Queen finally spoke about knives and forks. She was very kind and polite about it, but I could see she was amused."

"About what?"

"The way I used my knife and fork. The Queen said the Western world could be differentiated by the manner in which people handle their eating utensils. Most Europeans hold the fork in one hand and the knife in the other, and never switch. The acid test comes when they eat peas."

"Come on, Jerry. The Queen talked to you about eating peas?"

"Yes, seriously. With peas, according to the Queen, the Europeans—except for the English—hold the fork in the position in which it is designed to support the food: with the curved side facing the plate and the prongs pointing upward. The peas are then shoved onto the fork with the knife. The British, the Queen pointed out, also hold the fork in one hand and the knife in the other, but they carry the never switching to an absurd extreme: the prongs of the fork are kept pointed toward the plate, the way one does when piercing a piece of meat. As a result, the only way to eat peas in England is to mash them with the knife blade against the fork, which is easier if you employ mashed potatoes as glue or cement so that the peas won't fall off."

Celestine started to giggle. "Jerry, I can't believe it! What got the Queen talking about the peas?"

"My eating. She observed that I was the typical American— the third variant of eaters—who uses cutlery in what she called the most time-consuming manner. She pointed to the way I cut my meat: putting the knife down; taking the fork into the other hand; eating a morsel; then switching back, and doing this until the meat was finally consumed. You know what she ended up asking?"

"Go on."

"Why we Americans, who are supposed to be so efficient, have never employed a time and motion expert to conduct an analysis of how American productivity would escalate if everybody ate the way the Europeans do. I countered that Americans want to eat slower to encourage dinner conversation. She liked that."

"Is that all you talked about? Knives, forks and peas?"

"No."

"What else?"

"When I came back from the microphone after I gave my talk, she asked about my honeymoon comment: was it hypothetical, or did I have someone specific in mind?"

"What did you say?"

"I told her that I meant it, that the candidate was actually sitting in the audience, but that I hadn't quite brought up the subject."

"You hadn't? What about your remark in front of a few hundred people?"

"I thought it might have been too subtle."

"Perhaps for the Queen. But not for the candidate."

"Jerry, come take a look," called Celestine. She was wearing Stafford's robe and gazing out the window.

"What time is it?" came his lazy question from the bed.

"I don't know," she replied, "probably late. At least ten o'clock. The sun is up, it's another clear day. But come here," she gestured, pointing down to the street.

They could see Cantor and Paula Curry standing by the water, looking at the sea gulls land on the shore of the *Strömmen.* They were holding hands.

"It's strange to see I.C. with a woman," mused Stafford, "I never thought of him that way. I wonder whether they're lovers."

"I hope so."

"He seems happy," he continued pensively, as if he hadn't heard her.

Celestine turned to him in surprise. "Why shouldn't he be? Aren't you?"

"Not really. Today is Monday."

"And?"

"This afternoon we give our formal lectures."

"You aren't worried about that, Jerry, are you?" She took his face into her hands. "You've got a manuscript and slides—and you certainly know what you'll talk about."

"Yes, I know. Still, I'm not unworried."

The main *aula* of the *Karolinska Institutet,* Sweden's principal medical school, was packed. The senior faculty occupied the front rows, but many of the students had to be content with the steps in the aisles. In addition to journalists and photographers, their insolent flashes popping, many other nonacademics had flocked to this pair of lectures. In spite of their technical nature, cancer and the Nobel constituted too tempting a combination for many guests who had never before sat through a talk at the Karolinska. Stafford and Cantor sat in the first row, on either side of Professor George Klein, one of the world's top cancer biologists. As a senior member of the Karolinska faculty, it fell to him to introduce the two speakers. While Cantor and Klein had known each other for years, Stafford had met him only on Saturday. Given these circumstances, and the fact that Cantor was so much better known and recognized, Klein handled the introduction with masterful diplomacy. What could he have said about Stafford, other than that he'd received his Ph.D. with Cantor—everyone knew that—and that he was now in Kurt Krauss's laboratory at Harvard? He chose to introduce them in one package—a small but elegant one.

"Today, we have the privilege of listening to two 'uncommon men,'" Klein began, raising two fingers of each hand to simulate quotation marks. "I use these words in the sense defined by Gerald Holton, the Harvard physicist and philosopher of science: men who *make* science, as distinguished from most members of the scientific community, who *do* science; who do most of the 'mopping up,' a phrase coined by another philosopher of science, Thomas Kuhn. The biographical and professional *vitae* of our two laureates were already presented at yesterday's Nobel festivities and I shall not recount them today. Since their Nobel lectures describe one collaborative effort, I suggest that we listen to them without interruption. Professor Cantor"—he smiled at his friend sitting in the first row— "I hope that you will not mind taking off immediately when Dr. Stafford finishes. It will be like Wagner's *Fliegende Holländer,* an opera that needs to be heard without an intermission. Dr. Stafford" —Klein stretched out his hand—"I understand you're first."

Stafford strode to the podium, adjusted the height of the microphone and commenced his talk. He was like a swimmer who did not scrutinize the water but dove in instantaneously. Except for a nod in Klein's direction, he dispensed with the expected formalities—even the "ladies and gentlemen."

"May I have the first slide," were his starting words. Testing the laser pointer on the screen, he began: "We've decided to present our work in chronological order, which, fortunately, also makes logical sense. Let us first turn to the theoretical construct. . . ."

Cantor slouched back in his seat, not only because it offered the most convenient angle for looking at the slides from his seat in the front row, but also because he was relaxed. After the exotic glamor of the Nobel ceremonies, he was once again in his element: the matter-of-fact technical sentences, the beam of the slide projector cutting through the darkened room, the rhythm of the speaker's voice all lulled him into the familiar half-attentive state of a listener at a lecture already heard. He still remembered the words "theoretical construct"—they appeared in the first paragraph of the draft that he'd sent to Stafford in Boston. As Stafford proceeded, Cantor closed his eyes. He didn't have to look at the slides—it was clear that Jerry had stuck closely to Cantor's text.

The two women were sitting halfway up the steep amphitheater, near one of the aisles. While Celestine paid avid attention, Paula started to doze. The subject matter was much too technical for her, many of the words almost incomprehensible. But when Stafford had spoken for nearly half an hour, she suddenly found herself hearing words she could understand. Or was it a change in his tone of voice? Beside her, Celestine too had straightened. She was leaning forward, but in the darkened room could discern only the outline of Stafford's face, lit from below by the lectern's lamp, haloed above by the light of the slides. The expression on his face was impossible to make out. "Let us now turn to the relation of theory to facts," he was saying. "A scientific theory cannot be proved but only disproved. In other words, it must be tested experimentally."

Cantor opened his eyes and looked at his watch. The words sounded like an impending cue to announce his lecture, but Stafford had only spoken for twenty-eight minutes. Cantor was surprised that Jerry would not spread his talk over the allotted forty-five minutes. "Therefore, I would now like to address myself . . ."

Cantor's mental radar started to detect the first blips of irregularity. Was it the use of the first person singular?

". . . to the first experimental test to which we subjected this generalized theory of tumorigenesis." Only two persons in the audience reacted to this sentence, but to them it was like being doused with ice-cold water. Cantor sat straight up, while Celestine covered her mouth. "Oh no," she whispered.

"What's the matter?" Paula leaned anxiously toward her niece.

"Just listen!" Celestine groaned under her breath.

Switching back to the first person plural, Stafford proceeded in a straightforward manner to describe his first experiment, the one Cantor had imagined he'd finally buried. Celestine was still wondering what had possessed Jerry to bring up that topic, when an even bigger surprise arose. "But testing one's own theory is not enough. There must be external controls. In our case, Professor Kurt Krauss of Harvard chose to provide such confirmation by asking Dr. Ohashi in his laboratory to repeat our experiment."

What has gotten into the man's head? Cantor wondered frantically. Has Jerry gone mad? Celestine closed her eyes. She felt like a person driving down a one-way road who suddenly finds herself confronted by another car hurtling toward her. All she could do was to slam on the brakes and shut her eyes.

Just when she expected the crash, she heard Stafford say, "Initially, he had problems repeating our work. Only when each step was scrutinized carefully was the discrepancy discovered. In the end, it was really quite trivial." A hint of a smile crept into his eyes as he looked for the first time at Cantor, who was staring at him from the front row. "If there is one lesson to be learned from this experience, it's that even the smallest details should be put into one's notebook." Cantor winced at the echo of his own oft-repeated words. " 'You never know which details may turn out to be crucial.' "

Celestine opened her eyes. Stafford's smile was plainly visible. "Fortunately, Dr. Ohashi replicated our experiment only a few weeks ago. But, as it happened, his confirmation was unnecessary because, in the meanwhile, we had conceived of a second test, which worked beautifully." He waited to let the remark sink in. "Incidentally, that experiment is now also under careful scrutiny in Professor Krauss's laboratory. I have no reason to doubt that eventually it will also be replicated." For the second time in his talk, Stafford rested his gaze on Cantor. But this time he didn't smile. To the stunned Cantor—and most likely to Cantor alone—it looked like a warning. "That ingrate," he swore under his breath. And what does he mean by "eventually"?

Before Cantor could digest the implications of that menacing word, Stafford tossed the ball to him. "So we actually have two independent tests in support of our theory. I trust that none of you will consider this just a superfluous crossing of a *t*, the unnecessary dotting of an *i*. After all, 'tumorigenesis theory' has two *t*'s. And the work itself was performed by two *I*'s: myself, and then Professor Isidore Cantor. He will now tell you about that second experiment."

As the lights went on and the audience broke into applause, Stafford waited for Cantor to rise. The podium could be mounted by two sets of steps, one on either side of the platform. When Stafford saw Cantor move slowly toward the right, he descended on the opposite side.

Celestine was staggered. If Jerry was telling the truth—and how could he lie in public, in the context of a lecture that would practically be set in stone in the archives of the Nobel Foundation? —then, quite subtly, he had converted Cantor from an "uncommon" man into just another scientist, one who would now be reduced to describing the minutiae of what might almost be called a confirmation of a test. Yet he had done so in a way that would only be understood by Cantor and Celestine.

Cantor had less than a minute's warning for this change of circumstances. Later that night, Celestine and Stafford commented with admiration on how well he had improvised.

" 'Words strain,/ Crack and sometimes break, under the burden,/ Under the tension, slip, slide, perish,/ Decay with imprecision, will not stay in place,/ Will not stay still.' " Cantor's cadence emphasized the rhythm of Eliot's words, his eyes focused on Stafford. He waited until Stafford finally looked away. "But this will not be my problem today," he continued, looking up at the audience, "because my colleague here has made it easy for me to finish our joint presentation. As he stated so correctly, to validate a theory, one must test it. For a significant theory, two tests are far superior to one. To quote for the last time from T. S. Eliot, 'Old men ought to be explorers/ Here and there does not matter.' By comparison with Dr. Stafford and my other students, I certainly qualify as old. Perhaps that was why I was tempted to conduct with my own hands the experiment which I shall now describe."

At the conclusion of his lecture, as soon as Klein had closed the proceedings, Cantor turned to his host. "George, I just realized I must make a very urgent call to the States. It'll be very short. Could I use your office?"

"Kurt," Cantor started the moment Krauss answered the telephone, "I'm calling from Stockholm. I know it's early—"

"Never mind," boomed Krauss. "Congratulations! How did your lecture go?"

"Why don't you let Jerry Stafford tell you when he returns to Boston?" he answered archly. "Speaking of Stafford, he tells me you've been able to repeat our first experiment after all. I was wondering: how come it finally worked?"

"I guess I should've called you, but Ohashi only succeeded a couple of weeks ago and Jerry wanted to surprise you. He kept pestering Ohashi to give it another try—even though I'd told them it wasn't really feasible to finish both confirmations before December 10."

"Go on," Cantor said automatically. He knew what was coming.

"Ohashi must have been two thirds through your experiment, I.C., but Stafford kept insisting that we look once more at that first experiment of his. He said that, for the sake of history, the first experiment should be replicated before December 10 of *this* year, and not postponed to some future time. After all, that was the one for which you two got the Prize. He even offered to help. So I gave in and told Ohashi to give it one more shot. The explanation turned out to be ridiculously simple: apparently, Ohashi had been using a brand-new scintillation counter whose calibration hadn't been checked. You know how it is, some piddling detail . . ."

"Yes." Cantor whispered the word almost inaudibly.

"I.C.? Did you hear me?" shouted Krauss.

"Yes, I heard you."

"There is one problem." Krauss hesitated. "Ohashi won't be able to finish *your* experiment. He got a marvelous job offer from Kyoto, but that means he'll quickly have to tie together some loose ends in his own work. So I decided to hand it over . . ."

Cantor never heard the rest. His left index finger pressed firmly on the telephone plunger as if he were extinguishing a burning cigarette.

For the trip back to the Grand Hotel, Cantor suggested that Paula and Celestine ride in the same car. He wanted to talk to Stafford.

"Jerry," he began, "why didn't you tell me ahead of time what you were going to say? Aside from elementary courtesy, don't you think that would've been the fairest thing to do?"

Stafford avoided his stare. "I couldn't, I.C."

"Ha!" sniffed Cantor. "Why not?"

"You would've told me not to mention that work." He finally looked at Cantor, a pained expression on his face.

Cantor gazed back at him. "Yes, I probably would have."

"But don't you understand, I.C.?" cried out Stafford. "I couldn't have come to Stockholm if that first experiment hadn't been repeated in Krauss's lab. I don't think you would've believed me if I hadn't announced it in public."

"You're right, Jerry," he conceded. "I had to pick up the phone today and ask Krauss directly."

"You did?" Stafford's tone was sharp. "When?"

"Right after the lecture. From Klein's office."

"Would you've phoned Krauss if I'd just told you the facts in private?"

"No," admitted Cantor, "I would've been afraid to. As it is, Krauss is probably putting two and two together. But you forced me, Jerry."

"I knew it," murmured Stafford, "I knew it."

Cantor gazed out the car window, brows knitted. Finally, he turned back. "Jerry, what did you do in my lab that Sunday evening? The day before we completed the experiment together."

Stafford looked up. "How did you know I was there?"

Cantor shrugged. "Never mind. It's not important."

"You're right," agreed Stafford. "What is important is that I added some additional enzyme to the incubate. That's what I came to tell you at your house, and to explain why I had done it. But you wouldn't hear me out."

Cantor momentarily closed his eyes and swallowed hard. For a long time he said nothing. "And the first time?"

"Do you still have to ask?" Stafford shot back. "Didn't Krauss settle that for you?"

"Yes . . . but . . ."

"But I was also there at Harvard, when Ohashi finally succeeded? Is that what you wanted to say, I.C.?"

Cantor nodded silently.

Stafford looked out the car window at the early evening traffic. "I.C., I knew that I'd never be able to live down what I did that Sunday night—not in your eyes, and not in mine, for that matter. That's the real reason why I'm going to medical school. Instead of just turning a page, I'm starting a new book."

"I thought it clever."

"Clever?" Stafford shouted the word so loudly that their escort in the front seat turned around. Stafford had forgotten about the company up front. Quickly, he pretended to examine his feet stretched out in the long limousine. "So that's what you thought," he finally whispered, "it was just 'clever'? You didn't perhaps consider it penance? And you never thought about your role in that entire episode? How you'd really made it impossible, that second time, for me to disappoint you in the lab?" The pitch of his voice had increased again. Cantor put an index finger over his lips.

"In the end, all you really cared about was what the Krausses of this world would think. You'll never forgive me for having put you in a position where he might prove you wrong. Isn't that right?"

It was Cantor's turn to look out of the window. " 'Never forgive' is too strong. 'Never forget' is probably more accurate."

"So instead of calling me in, you kept me totally in the dark. All you wanted was an experiment that Krauss could repeat. Isn't that right, I.C.?"

For just a flicker, Cantor glanced at his companion but said nothing.

"Without Krauss's approval"—Stafford's voice turned sarcastic—"your tumorigenesis theory was not complete. Isn't that the truth? Answer me, I.C.," he demanded, "isn't that true?"

"Yes."

"And now you're thinking as well that Ohashi's verification of my work hasn't done the trick because of my presence at Harvard. Right?"

"Right."

For a long time the two men were silent, staring out opposite windows. The wintry street rolled by too slowly. When Stafford spoke again, his voice was unnaturally casual. "And did Krauss tell you, by any chance, what happened with Ohashi?"

"Yes," replied Cantor, "he said something about a lousy calibration of the scintillation counter."

"I don't mean that," snapped Stafford. "Did he tell you that Ohashi is about to return to Japan?"

"Yes." Cantor sounded weary. He felt a sudden, unhappy urge to sleep. "He said he'd assigned it to someone else in the lab."

For the first time that afternoon, Stafford's voice showed compassion. "I gather you don't know who that person is."

20

"This is quite a place you've got here, I.C. How come you never let on? It makes me wonder what else you're keeping up your sleeve."

Cantor was flattered: with Krauss, such a statement qualified as a compliment. "I may have plenty of faults, Kurt, but secretiveness isn't one of them. Ask my students."

Krauss threw Cantor a crafty look. "Maybe I will. After all, I've got your Stafford. But I'm not talking about science; what I meant is that, while I may know practically everything you've done professionally during the past dozen years—or whenever it was that you saw the light and joined us in our noble battle against cancer—I've just realized that your private life has been a closed book to me. You never told me, for instance, that you have this place here in Chicago. Or this." He pointed to the four chairs and music stands. "You've never so much as whistled a note in my presence. And you're a collector of English antiques to boot. What else are you hiding around here?" Miming suspicion, Krauss craned his neck ostentatiously around.

"You never asked. Whenever we meet it's usually all shoptalk. So you know about English furniture? And are *you* interested in music?"

"I haven't got time to play an instrument, but yes, I like music." He nudged Cantor conspiratorially. "I've even been seen at Tanglewood."

Cantor was mildly annoyed: this kind of kidding wasn't like

Krauss. He decided to ignore it: he had a feeling he would find out what it was about in due course. "Do you want to stay tonight and listen to us play? We don't usually have an audience, but I could probably convince our fierce first violinist to make an exception."

"I can't," Krauss said flatly. "My plane leaves O'Hare at 7 P.M. I've got to be back in the lab bright and early—somebody has to crack the whip, you know. Not like you, I.C. Now you can afford to lie back, be magnanimous with your students and play your fiddle."

"Viola," Cantor interjected with a grimace.

"Don't be so literal. What I mean is you've got it made. While the rest of us still have to . . ."

Krauss's voice trailed off, as if he'd suddenly thought of something else. "Did you get my c.v. and bibliography? I recently had occasion to revise them both, and I thought you might find them useful."

Cantor mimicked a pensive frown. "Why, yes, I did get them. They nearly got buried. You wouldn't believe how much mail I've been getting lately."

"Well, I'm glad they surfaced. I wouldn't want all that effort to be for naught."

"Yes," Cantor said dryly, "I've never seen a more elegantly printed c.v. Your secretary must have used at least three different fonts. How do you get your laser printer to handle that heavy letterhead?"

Krauss looked up guardedly. "I don't know. We have people to handle that sort of thing. But I wasn't referring to the c.v. so much as to my bibliography. I decided to rearrange it by main topics and then subheadings. Like most of us, I've been guilty of some 'salami publishing,' but this time I've discarded all but the thickest slices—you know, seminal stuff."

"I noticed."

"I thought it would make things easier."

"Easier?"

Krauss continued as if he hadn't even heard the question. "Have you sent in your nomination yet?"

Cantor had been sitting in one corner, legs casually crossed, one arm thrown over the back of the sofa. Krauss perched in the other corner. Suddenly Cantor rose. "Kurt, I never even offered you a drink. Would you like something before you leave for the airport? White wine? Sherry? Or maybe Perrier?"

"Nothing, thanks. I've a dinner flight and there will be plenty to drink. When I fly on business, it's always first class."

"I'm going to get myself some sherry," said Cantor as he moved to the Queen Anne sideboard.

"Well, have you?"

Cantor was staggered by the bluntness of the question. "No," he said, pouring the sherry as if it were a dangerous chemical in the laboratory. "I hadn't even thought about nominations."

"I'm not talking about nominations"—Krauss drew out the word as if it carried three *s*'s—"for the usual sort of awards. I'm asking about *the* nomination. After all, one of the real privileges of a Nobel Prize winner—maybe the only lasting privilege—is that he doesn't have to wait for the committee to ask him for a nomination." He gave a hard, short chuckle. "You were lucky, I.C., that last year was my turn. . . ."

Back in his corner of the sofa, Cantor choked on his sherry. Krauss reached over and clapped him on his back. "Take it easy, I.C., we can't afford to lose you now."

At that moment a key turned in the front door lock. "Leonardo dear," a woman's voice rang out, "I managed to get away earlier than I—Oh," Paula Curry exclaimed as she reached the entrance to the living room, "I didn't know you had company."

Cantor jumped up to relieve Paula of her shopping bag. "This is Kurt Krauss from Harvard," he said, motioning toward Krauss. "He just dropped in on his way to the airport. You've heard me talk about him before. Kurt, this is Paula Curry."

"Aha," Krauss cried, peering up at Paula. "I knew there were more secrets in reserve. How do you do, Miss Curry?" He rose slowly and clumsily bowed. "Or is it Dr. Curry?"

Paula looked down on Krauss, who was nearly six inches shorter. "Just Paula Curry." It was very unlike Paula to stare, but the surprise was simply too great. She had heard enough about him, first from Cantor and later, in Stockholm, from Stafford, to form a rather precise mental image of the man: a powerful, Prussian officer-type figure, not this gnome with an oversized head, an Einstein-like cloud of hair, and small, glinting eyes. Now she could only think of Alberich, the king of the dwarfs in the *Ring*. "Don't let me interrupt you," she finally said, "I'll go change before Sol and Ralph arrive."

"You're not interrupting us at all, Miss Curry." Krauss had returned to the sofa. Once seated, his giant head dominated his small body even more. "What role do you play here?" he asked with characteristic bluntness, his hand sweeping around the living room.

"Cello. In the quartet. What do you play, Dr. Krauss?"

Cantor permitted a slight smile to cross his face. He was pleased to see Krauss for once on the defensive.

"I don't have time for playing."

Paula arched her eyebrows. "Surely one can also play in science."

"Science is more of a battle than a play, Miss Curry. But don't let me keep the two of you from playing," he continued in a mocking voice. "There's just one more thing, I.C." He turned to Cantor as if he had dismissed Paula. "I might as well tell you that Stafford is having a bit of difficulty repeating your experiment."

Cantor felt the flush appearing on his face. Did it show? he wondered.

Krauss realized that he'd scored a hit. "Well, you know how things go," he continued with a faint smile, "this can happen to the best of us. Probably some overlooked detail in the stuff you sent us. I suggested to Stafford that he come back here and do the experiment with you in your lab. Paid by *my* NIH grant, of course." He spread his hands magnanimously. "But Stafford would have nothing to do with it. He said he wanted to repeat the experiment like an *independent* researcher in a distant lab, not like some prodigal son returning home. But don't worry, I.C."—Krauss lifted himself up from the sofa—"no one will hear of it from me. And Stafford is certainly much too embarrassed to noise it around. Remember what you told me once, that he's the best man you've ever had? If he can't duplicate your work, then you're lucky it's happening in my lab and not elsewhere." He bowed to Paula and started to move toward the vestibule. "I better catch a cab for O'Hare." But then he hesitated. "You know, I.C., we should be thankful for Federal Express. Today is the twenty-fifth of January."

"What a peculiar man," remarked Paula, as soon as the door had closed behind Krauss, "and what was that cryptic remark about the date?"

"That blackmailing bastard!"

Paula had never seen such an angry expression on Cantor's face. Nor had she ever heard him call anybody "bastard."

"What Vesuvian fury, Leonardo." Paula tried to mollify him. "Come, sit down on the sofa and tell me what happened."

Cantor continued to stalk around the room. "The gall of that man. I'm the first to concede that big problems attract big egos. And cancer is a big problem. But if anyone had told me what just transpired, I wouldn't have believed it. Not even of Kurt." Hands in his pockets, he stared over the dark expanse of Lake Michigan. He turned to face Paula, leaning back against the windowsill and shaking his head. For a moment he stood there, brooding. When he spoke again, his tone was so quiet she almost missed the words. "You see, Paula, nominations for the Nobel Prizes must reach Stockholm by January 31. It's amazing how many scientists are aware of that deadline."

Paula walked up to him at the picture window. "Were you?"

Cantor nodded. "Yes. I knew about the deadline, but I wasn't so crude as to approach somebody to nominate me. That's what Kurt had just asked me to do when you appeared. He implied that I owed it to him, since he had nominated me. How do I know that other people didn't put up my name as well? But they didn't arrive with their begging bowls." Cantor lowered his voice again. "I'm sorry, that was nasty. I suppose you must be disappointed: you don't often see scientists washing their dirty lab coats in public."

"Washing off dirt isn't disappointing. It's human. And you yourself have shown me how human even famous scientists can be."

He smiled at her. "Still, I was shocked by Kurt's sledgehammer hint."

"Will you do it?"

"No," he said almost explosively, "I will not."

"But why?" protested Paula. "You've told me before what a great scientist he is. Didn't you say a sarcoma was named after him? Hasn't he been almost your mentor? Although now that I have seen him in the flesh, I'm not quite sure why you picked him, of all people. But still, doesn't he deserve the Prize?"

Cantor raised his hand, as if to prevent further questions. "The answer is yes to all your questions, but I won't nominate him—certainly not this year. I've been too preoccupied until now to even think about Nobel nominations—for Kurt Krauss, or anyone else. Incidentally, the question is not necessarily whether he deserves the Prize. Certainly he does. For his sarcoma, and several other things as well. But many more people deserve the Nobel than get it. Krauss should've gotten it years ago. Though by now so many other discoveries have been made that he's farther down in an ever increasing queue. Besides, the Swedes are unlikely to give two successive Prizes for cancer research."

"But that's not the real reason, is it?"

"No. The real reason is that I simply won't be blackmailed."

"Oh, come now, Leonardo. Kurt Krauss suggesting that you owe him a nomination may be a somewhat crude quid pro quo. But how can you call that blackmail?"

"You heard him. He said Stafford is having problems. With *my* experiment."

"But—"

"I know what you're going to ask. 'How is Jerry involved in all of this?' Don't you see? It couldn't have been a coincidence that out of his huge research group he selected Jerry to duplicate my experiment. Didn't you see the nasty glint in his eyes when he assured me he wouldn't mention it in public? It's the same look he gets when he knifes a seminar speaker. What he meant was, he wouldn't mention it provided I . . ." Cantor didn't find it necessary to complete the sentence. "But why didn't Jerry call me if he had run into a snag?"

Paula took his right hand in both of hers. "Now you're asking the right question. Surely Krauss must've realized what had happened between you and Jerry when you telephoned from Stockholm." She patted his hand reassuringly. "Don't get angry," she added, "if I ask you something that I was tempted to ask in Stockholm, except that it didn't seem the right time. Didn't you find it sad that Jerry thought it necessary to talk to you through the medium of the audience in Stockholm, and that even then you didn't trust him? Krauss must've picked up on that."

"I suppose so," Cantor said sullenly. "But still, why didn't Jerry call? I wish I *knew* what happened in their lab."

"So call him."

"And say what? 'Kurt Krauss mentioned you've had some problems repeating my experiment. Can I help you?' Impossible! It would be too humiliating."

Paula slowly shook her head, more out of compassion than disagreement. "In that case, ask Celly. Maybe she knows. I haven't told you yet, but she's arriving tomorrow on her way back from Los Angeles. I hope you didn't mind that I've asked her to stop by after lunch, before she heads back to the university by bus. I haven't seen her since Stockholm."

Cantor perked up. "I liked what I saw of her—Jerry made a good catch."

"Bravo, Leonardo! You're getting more broad-minded all the time. I bet Krauss would've said, '*She* made a great catch.' "

"Let's look at you, Celly." Paula held Celestine by her shoulders, arms stretched out, and swiveled her slowly around. "If I didn't know this was my sister's daughter, I would say I'm looking at a Chicago yuppie with an MBA. Look, Leonardo," she called out laughingly, "blue skirt down to mid-calf, matching jacket, sensible heels, white blouse, and the obligatory fluffy bow tie. Celly, what's come over you?"

"Give me a break, Paula." Celestine grinned. "May I catch my breath and sit down before defending myself?"

"Of course you may, my dear. Let me bring some coffee. And then let's hear how you suddenly turned conventional."

Cantor, left alone with Celestine, was in no mood for banter. Ever since the previous evening, he had been wondering how he could bring up the subject of Jerry Stafford and his current work. "What brings you to Chicago?" he finally asked.

"Oh, didn't Paula tell you? I flew out to L.A. for an interview at Cal Tech."

Cantor remembered their dance following the Nobel Prize banquet. "Did Cal Tech also offer you a job?"

Celestine nodded, a broad smile on her face.

"That's quite impressive. First Harvard, and now Cal Tech."

"And before that, Wisconsin," she added.

"And?" The girl was stringing this out intolerably, Cantor thought, but he still couldn't find a graceful way to bring up Stafford. With Krauss's recent bad example before him, he was not going to force the subject.

"I made up my mind on the flight home. Cal Tech."

"Well, I arrived just in time," Paula said, bringing in the tray.

"You're turning down Harvard?" Cantor's curiosity got the better of his impatience. "Why?"

"Simple. Cal Tech's department is fairly small and very collegial; the grad students are first class; and they don't have a single tenured woman chemist."

"You'll find plenty of other institutions in that category," Cantor observed dryly.

"True," admitted Celestine, "but they seem to be willing to do something about it. There are even rumors that Jacqueline Barton from Columbia is going there as a full professor. Jack Roberts, their grand old man, went out of his way to tell me about his physician daughter. He offered to help me and Jerry find housing near the campus."

"When are you and Jerry getting married?" Cantor seized the topic.

"I don't know. I told Jerry we ought to live together for a while first and see what it's like."

"You've already done that," observed Paula.

"Not under the right circumstances: professional independence, you know." Cantor wasn't sure he did, but he was willing to let it pass. He was trying to think of a more pertinent question about Stafford, but Celestine wasn't finished. "I mean, how do I know what it's like to live with a Nobelist? He's handling it pretty well right now, but what about later? What do *you* think, Paula?" Celestine grinned at her aunt's sudden discomfiture.

"If you marry," Cantor interjected, "would you publish as Mrs. Stafford?"

Celly looked at him, not knowing whether he was joking or serious. Paula broke in. "I know what Celly will say."

"You do? All right then, Aunt Paula"—she gave the word "aunt" a funny ring—"tell me."

"You'll keep your own name, of course."

"It's possible, but I doubt it."

"What? You'd consider going as Celestine P. Stafford?"

"No, I didn't say that. I'd consider changing my name if Jerry did the same."

"Jerry? 'Jerry Price'?" It was Cantor's turn to be astonished.

"Hmm. I like that. But I was thinking more along the line of hyphenated names."

"Hmm." Cantor tried again to assume control of the conversation. "You were telling us about your Cal Tech interview. How did you bring up Jerry's name? Did he—"

"Oh yes," Celly said eagerly. "I told them that my fiancé planned to go to medical school and that he had a Ph.D. in cell biology. When I told Harry Gray, their department head, that Jerry had applied to UCLA, he said he knew their med school dean and picked up the phone. It really was funny. I guess the dean must have asked, 'What's his name?' 'Jeremiah Stafford,' I said, 'he's a cell biologist.' Gray repeated this over the phone and I could see him, and you could almost hear the dean on the other end of the line do a classic double take. 'The man who . . . ?' I just nodded demurely, wearing this very suit with my bow tie."

It was clear that Celestine was enjoying herself as she drew out every detail of her story. Cantor had stopped listening. Celestine's mention of Stafford had given him his opening. "What's Jerry working on these days?" he asked. "How does he like it in Krauss's lab? Come to think of it, I never asked him in Stockholm."

"Well, he says it's different from your lab."

"What does that mean?" Cantor's nostrils flared as if he were sniffing the wind.

Celestine looked at him with an amused expression. "During the time we shared an apartment, it seems you saw him at least once a day, if not more often."

"Well?"

"According to Jerry, he's lucky if he sees Krauss a couple of times a month. He's pretty well on his own. Which suits him fine. He's developing a new assay for anticancer activity by trying to expedite the response of Krauss's sarcoma to different therapeutic agents. But that sarcoma isn't easy to grow in tissue culture," she added in an aside to Cantor. "At the same time, he's picking up as much new methodology on screening techniques as possible. He thinks this will be particularly useful for the clinical work he wants to do in medical school."

"Is that all he's doing?"

"I think so," said Celly. "At least, he didn't mention anything else the last time he was here."

"Jerry was here? When?"

Celestine looked up, surprised at Cantor's peremptory tone. "Two or three weeks ago. He's coming out again for Washington's Birthday."

Cantor took out his pocket calendar. "Paula, why don't we spend that weekend down in the sticks? We'll have Jerry and your niece for lunch." He tried to sound offhand. "The last time I saw Jerry in my house was under rather unusual circumstances. It's time we congratulate the lucky couple properly, don't you think?"

Paula and Celestine exchanged a glance—one that Cantor, preoccupied, did not notice.

"Guess who I saw earlier today?"

"I.C."

"What? How did you guess?"

"Pure intuition."

Celestine could hear Stafford's chuckle over the phone. "Well, I'll be damned," she said. "And can you guess what we talked about?"

"No, I can't. But before we get to Cantor, I want to know what happened at Cal Tech. Did they offer you the job?"

"Yes, they did. A fabulous offer."

"And?"

Celestine hesitated. She was certain that he'd prefer it if she decided in favor of Harvard. But she also knew that the Nobel Prize had changed Jerry in many respects. The most important, and least anticipated, was the way he'd used the Prize to move a step below her. Just when Celestine was starting to rise in her career, Jerry had chosen to descend to the level of student. Both of them had joked about it: how many medical students start out with the Nobel Prize? But he was also worried about it, she knew. How would the professors treat him? With deference? Or would they try to take him down a couple of pegs? And, even more important, how would his fellow students respond? Celestine guessed this would put a strain on their relationship, and she was already wary. "I'll probably accept," she said. "It's really the best situation for me. There are plenty of medical schools in the L.A. area," she hurried on. "You know perfectly well you'll get into any school of your choice."

"If I tell them about the Nobel Prize. But unless I do, I'll bet there aren't many admissions committees who'll put two and two together. It's just not likely."

"Jerry, don't be a purist. You know how little admissions decisions have to do with real worth. You might as well take advantage of your prize. UCLA is probably your best bet if I go to Cal Tech, so we'll pick a place halfway and split the commute. Let's talk about that when you come out in a couple of weeks. You're still coming, aren't you?"

"Sure, I'm coming."

"You don't sound very happy. You really prefer Boston so much, or is it Harvard?"

"Probably both." She could hear him make an effort to change his tone of voice. Was it really okay, she wondered, or was he saving it up for later? "At least you picked a good day to tell me about California. It's miserable here—cold, with a lot of dirty slush. But you were telling me about I.C. Is he still seeing your aunt?"

"He sure is. I didn't have a minute alone with her to ask, but I wouldn't be surprised if they're actually living together."

Stafford let out a low whistle. "I'd never have thought that of I.C. So what's he up to these days?"

"I don't really know. He kept pumping me about your work. When he heard that you're coming to see me, he invited you to lunch."

"Why didn't he invite me himself?"

"Jerry, don't be stuffy. One stuffy man at lunch is enough. And after all, he's your professor."

"He was my professor." Stafford sounded testy.

"No, he still is. You haven't exactly cut the umbilical cord."

"Umbilical cord? Between two men?"

"Don't play dumb with me, Dr. Stafford: you don't need an M.D. to figure that one out. Or haven't you noticed that painful tugging at your belly lately?"

"I thought that was you," he said mischievously.

"I wish. . . ." Her voice sounded wistful.

21

"Is that what you're going to wear?" asked Stafford as he straightened his tie in the mirror.

Celestine, who was sitting on the side of the bed, had just pulled up one boot. She looked up, surprised. "You know, Jerry, I don't think you've ever asked me that question. Not even in Stockholm. Why today?"

Stafford gazed at her in the mirror before turning around. "Let me help you with the other boot," he said finally. She stretched out her other foot. "You're right," he went on, tugging distractedly at her cuff, "why am I worried about our appearance today? Why am I wearing a tie? It's not like I'm going to church."

Celestine slipped back on the bed all the way to the headboard and crossed her booted legs. During the last couple of months, Jerry had become much more introspective. She liked listening to him in that mood.

"Maybe it's because I've been thinking back to the other time we were in I.C.'s house. Do you remember how scared I was? I wouldn't have made it through that day, Celly, if you hadn't gone with me. It's only four months ago, isn't it? It feels like years. As though it happened to a different person."

"What made the difference? The Prize?"

"Not entirely. During the last few months, for the first time in my life, I've made some major decisions on my own. When I left South Carolina to move up here, I essentially traded my parents for

I.C. I'm not saying that was bad. I learned an awful lot. But in some sense I was being manipulated. I don't think that I.C. did that consciously. Krauss, for instance, is much more deliberate in his maneuvering of people, even though we see less of him than we ever saw of I.C. in his group. Maybe this is just the way things are in grad school—for years, you have intimate contact with just one professor. Especially if he likes you, it's like a parent who wants to replicate himself through his son. Has that been true of you and Jean?" Stafford had been wandering up and down in front of the bed. Now he sat by Celestine's side.

She reached for his hand. "Less so. But I'm not sure if that's because we're only ten years apart or because we're both women."

"It'll be interesting to see what happens to me in med school. I don't need a mentor anymore—I know exactly what I want to do there and where to go. The Nobel has given me a sort of independence that's quite different from financial security."

"Don't forget the money, Jerry. You'll be the only one in your class who isn't up to his stethoscope in debt."

Stafford continued as if he hadn't heard. "I've a feeling that, when I see I.C. today, it'll be almost as peers. Maybe that's why I'm wearing a tie and jacket. He's such a fastidious dresser."

Celestine was looking forward to some woman-to-woman talk with her aunt. As soon as the young couple arrived at Cantor's house, Celestine marched her aunt into the kitchen. "Let me help you with lunch," she said in a voice so insistent that Paula acquiesced without protest.

"Can I get you something, Jerry?" asked Cantor. He was surprised at how awkward he felt, alone with his former student.

"Thanks," replied Stafford, "not just now." He walked over to the *Sitzmaschine* and sat down gingerly. While Cantor poured himself a drink, Stafford looked around the walls. When he'd been there a few months ago, he'd been unable to see anything but his own immediate problem. Now he found himself face to face with one of Schiele's erotic watercolors. As Cantor had pointed out so correctly to Paula, most visitors—and Stafford was no exception—were unacquainted with the Austrian painter. However, one didn't need to be an art connoisseur to be impressed, even at first sight, by Schiele's craftmanship.

"Well, what do you think of them?" Cantor had moved unnoticed to Stafford's side.

"They're . . . what shall I say?" he stuttered.

"Not what you expected?"

Stafford laughed. "No, I.C., that's not what I was going to *say*, but you're right, that's what I was thinking. They're very . . . um . . . original."

"It's amazing how many people use that word. What they really mean is that they're erotic."

Stafford openly scanned Cantor's face. Had he ever looked him in the face before? He didn't think so. Not in quite this way. He held the older man's gaze for a moment. They broke it off at the same time.

"I.C., I can't help being amused at the sight of the two of us. I've known and admired you for years, but only recently have I begun to realize how little I know about you. Here I come, wearing my best suit and a tie, and for the first time in my life I see you without a tie."

Cantor glanced down as if he'd just noticed his open shirt and sweater. *"Mea culpa,"* he murmured, raising one hand with his palm up. "I should've invited you earlier, Jerry. Dress optional. How's life in Boston agreeing with you?"

"Not bad," Stafford replied cautiously. "Of course, it's not the same as in your lab."

"How?" The question had lost much of its sharpness.

"Well, Krauss's group is a lot bigger. That may be one reason why I don't see much of him."

"That's too bad," Cantor said with almost no inflection in his voice.

"Not really. I rather enjoy it."

"Oh?"

"Don't get me wrong, I.C." Stafford leaned forward. "I learned a tremendous amount from you. But the time's come for me to use that knowledge on my own."

"And what is it you're working on?" Cantor hardly cared if Jerry's remark had veiled any criticism. He was pleased that they'd arrived, sooner than he'd anticipated, at the topic uppermost in his mind.

"Primarily acquiring methodology. I figured it would be rather unlikely that I'd run into a super experiment like the one I did last year. . . ." He looked down at Cantor's feet. "I thought it would be most productive if I picked up some new techniques and looked at some problems that might be useful in my work after med school."

"I understand you're going to UCLA."

"Oh?" Stafford was taken aback. "How do you know? It's one of the schools I've applied to, but I haven't heard from them."

"You aren't worried, are you, Jerry? It would be preposterous to reject an applicant who's just won the Nobel Prize."

"Shared *in* a Nobel Prize," Stafford corrected him. "No, I'm not worried. But I didn't put it on my application. I'd rather like to be admitted without their knowing that."

"There is one thing I'm wondering about, Jerry. Why UCLA? I gather your fiancée has an offer from Harvard. Why not convince her to accept it? It's hardly a compromise."

"It might be for her."

Cantor didn't seem to have heard. "You said you're working on the cellular microecology of Kurt's sarcoma."

Stafford frowned. "Did I say that?"

"Well, maybe not in so many words." Cantor realized that he was using information he'd heard from Celestine. Maybe she hadn't told her fiancé about their earlier conversation. "But what else are you doing?" he rushed on. "Surely, that doesn't take up all of your time?"

"Why shouldn't it? It takes as much time as I give it. But frankly, I.C., I'm not working as hard as I did with you. Things have changed. It just isn't crucial that I publish some hot paper during my year in Krauss's lab; it probably doesn't even matter *whether* I publish."

"You've certainly changed. I wouldn't have thought it would happen so quickly."

"Even after what happened last year?"

Cantor nodded, unsure what else to do. He felt an uncomfortable sensation, familiar somehow, though for a moment he couldn't place it. Then he remembered the feeling—he had felt it during Stafford's Nobel lecture.

"I.C." Stafford drew himself upright in his seat. There was something in his tone, as well, that reminded Cantor of that lecture. "You've never asked me *why* I went back alone to your lab that Sunday evening."

Cantor nodded again, his face a mask. "True—I haven't."

"Don't you want to know?"

"If you want to tell me."

"But you wouldn't have asked?"

"No, I wouldn't have."

"Afraid?"

"I suppose so."

Stafford stared at his professor while slowly shaking his head. He said nothing.

Cantor's eyes were fixed on the floor. "I saw Kurt Krauss last month," he said. "He visited me here in Chicago."

Stafford stiffened but still said nothing.

"He said you had some problem repeating my experiment." For a long moment, Cantor was silent. "Why didn't you phone? I probably could've helped."

"Problem? I had no problem."

"Krauss said you did. When you didn't mention it, I was sure you were hiding bad news." He looked up, relief beginning to dawn in his face. "You aren't?"

"I didn't mention it because I'm not working on it anymore."

"Who *is* working on it?" Cantor asked, perplexed.

"No one. Why should anybody still be working on your experiment?"

"I don't understand."

Stafford looked at his former professor, whose head was thrust forward from his open shirt, a confused expression on his face. He felt brief pity for his mentor. "I told you," he said gently, "that I had no problem repeating your work. Why should I have had any? You keep an awfully neat notebook, I.C." Stafford felt a sense of embarrassment by this sudden reversal of roles, as if he were addressing a concerned student. "It's strange. You've always preached to us about keeping proper records, but I never saw yours while I worked with you. When you sent the Xeroxed pages to Krauss—don't get me wrong, I.C., but it looked a bit like a student sending his notes to the professor—and when Krauss gave them to me, I was almost touched. I say 'almost' because, frankly, I resented the fact that I learned about the details of your work through Krauss rather than directly from you."

Cantor displayed no emotion.

"There isn't much more to say. Your notes were clear and concise. And you know, I got some awfully good training in your lab. I breezed through your experiment the first time through."

"You finished it?" Cantor couldn't suppress his astonishment. "When?"

Stafford vacillated; whatever answer he gave would violate his confidence with either Krauss or Cantor. "Around the middle of January. I remember the date because Krauss doesn't come breathing down our necks the way you always did. I'd finished duplicating your experiment and I was wondering when he'd ask me about it. A week passed before he showed up in the lab. So I told him. It was almost eerie, because it reminded me so much of a conversation you and I once had. When you came back from your Harvard lecture—the one where the audience laughed and you told me about the experiment—you said something like, 'For once, I'll ask you to keep this confidential.' You remember that, don't you?"

Cantor leaned forward as if he were about to spring. "What did he say?"

"First he quoted Enrico Fermi: 'Experimental confirmation of a prediction is merely a measurement. An experiment disproving a prediction is a discovery.' But then he said, 'Let's keep this on ice for a while. I'm not yet ready to publish it. After all, we just submitted Ohashi's paper dealing with the confirmation of *your* experiment. Just as Fermi said, there isn't much mileage in just repeating other people's work.' "

"The bastard!"

Stafford was stunned. He'd never heard such language from Cantor. "Why do you say that?" he finally stuttered. "Krauss has a point. What's the hurry about publishing a second confirmation? You—we—already had the Nobel; Ohashi and Krauss had duplicated that experiment. I announced their confirmation in Stockholm; *that* paper will appear in a few months. What's the hurry?"

"But aren't *you* anxious to publish *your* confirmation of *my* experiment?"

"Why should I be? You know, I was tickled when Krauss asked me to take over after Ohashi dropped the work because, by repeating what you'd kept secret from me, I vicariously became your colleague. I.C., your experiment is a beauty and you certainly did justice to it in your Stockholm lecture. But why have me publish a confirmation? Isn't it sufficient for you to know that the work has been duplicated in another lab? Or are you bothered by the fact that I was the one who had to do that? If so, my publishing it won't solve your problem. Do you get the feeling that Krauss has staged this? It would be like his sense of humor, wouldn't it? He must've realized that something had happened between the two of us. Maybe he thought that this way he might find out."

Paula had appeared several times at the living-room entrance but each time had withdrawn discreetly. The men had not noticed. Now she called out: "I think you two have talked long enough. It's time to have lunch. You must be famished."

"I'm hungry," Stafford said quickly and rose. He'd been searching for a diplomatic closure to their conversation.

"I've lost my appetite," announced Cantor.

22

Curry & Cantor Antiques, Inc.
Fine English Furniture
Post Office Box 3759, Chicago, Illinois 60626

March 1

Dear Kurt:

Jerry Stafford visited us recently and reported on his excellent progress in your laboratory. I was delighted to learn that he had not lost his magic touch at the bench. But this, of course, is not the real reason for this letter.

When you were out here in what you, in your inimitable style, called the hinterland, you expressed surprise that I am a collector of antique furniture. I did not know myself that you had an eye for such things. This only shows how little we really know about each other.

I have indulged in such collecting for quite a while, but Paula Curry is the real expert in this field. As you can see from our letterhead, Paula and I have now formalized our interest. With your sharp eye, I am confident that you will interpret correctly the order in which our respective names are listed. After all, both of us know about the subtleties of senior authorship.

To get to the point: it occurred to me that you might be interested in acquiring an exceptional piece that Paula came across recently. It is a nineteenth-century rocking chair, made by Michael Thonet, and in mint condition. It comes from the collection of Billy Wilder of Hollywood fame—not a bad provenance! You might want it for your Harvard inner sanctum—I do not recall seeing such a piece of furniture in any of your colleagues' offices. But you must agree that a rocking chair is the ideal seat—or should I say throne?—for someone waiting.

Paula sends her best wishes and asked me to assure you that a special price could be arranged for so noble a piece of furniture.

Regards,

I.C.

P.S. I seem to have misplaced your c.v. and bibliography. I am sure they will surface one of these days.

11 Chatwick Circle
Boston, Massachusetts 02146

March 9

Dear I.C.:

Only after reading your recent missive did it dawn on me that, other than Christmas cards, we have never exchanged personal letters. Frankly, yours was a bit too cute for me. You seem to have quite a lot up your personal sleeve: a fancy pad on Lake Michigan, chamber music, antiques, an imposing female giant. Is there anything I have skipped? And who is Michael

Thonet? Is that just a manifestation of one-upmanship on the furniture front or am I missing something more subtle?

I think the time has come for us to shed our fencing masks. What I really asked of you in Chicago was to nominate me for the Nobel—not just this year, but to keep it up until I get it. We all know that your case was a relatively rare one as was that of those lucky physicists in Zurich who got the physics prize within months of discovering their fancy superconductors. Most of the other winners get nominated repeatedly before the message gets through to the Nobel committees.

Frankly, I rather object to your acting so icily pure. True, you didn't *ask* me to nominate you, but you did *expect* it, didn't you? You certainly responded promptly when I asked you for *your* bibliography and c.v. And what about that unsolicited and rather florid paragraph you enclosed, summarizing your tumorigenesis theory? Didn't you trust me to do justice to your work in my own inimitable style?

Speaking about Nobel Prizes and tumorigenesis, what about that famous second experiment of yours that you haven't published yet? And the full paper of the first experiment with Stafford that you still haven't written? There is an unpleasant odor of volatile amines around that work—admittedly faint, but not so faint that my perceptive nose is not detecting something fishy. It would be a pity if it contaminated your tumorigenesis theory, which is not only inherently plausible but also a real intellectual tour de force. Still:

When I asked Stafford to take over from Ohashi, he initially refused. Only when I pressed him did I learn that you had never told him about your second experiment until you announced it in public. Is that an example of your lack of secretiveness? You even had the temerity to suggest I consult your students about that stellar quality of yours. I myself would have trumpeted such news to my favorite postdoc—especially if I decided to do the work on my own. In fact, why did you perform that experiment yourself? To show us that you are still working in the lab, while the rest of us are just pencil pushers and PR types? Why do a second experiment when the first already proved the point?

Was there something not quite kosher about that first Nobel Prize experiment? And if there was, who did that experiment? And who was in my lab when Ohashi finally succeeded on the third try? Admittedly, Ohashi himself told me about the scintillation counter calibration, but we all know only too well the save face syndrome. Maybe he just made that up to explain why he failed the first two times in Stafford's absence.

For the time being, I am willing to let that sleeping dog lie, because I am not yet certain whether we actually have a dog here. I gather from your letter that you have missed this year's January 31 deadline. I shall forgive you for this lapse (an inadvertent one, I trust), primarily because the chances for a Nobel in the cancer field are slight right after yours. But next year, and the one after that . . .

My request is the following. This November, you will send me the nomination form, the one that says "Strictly Confidential" on the right top, and starts with the words, "We, as members of the Nobel Committee, have the honour of inviting you to submit proposals . . ." I will simplify life for both of us by completing the entire form and then sending it to you for your signature. You will then return the signed page to me, and after attaching my bibliography and other supporting documents, *I* will mail the whole package to Stockholm. I am quite aware of the fact that somewhere on that form it says that the person nominating a candidate is requested neither to make known his nomination nor to inform his nominee of the nomination. But we both know how few people abide by that request.

Jerry Stafford announced in his Nobel lecture that we did confirm his experiment but, fortunately for everyone concerned, our article has not yet appeared. I trust you will not be too shocked to learn that I have just withdrawn Ohashi's paper from publication. You need not worry—it was done in a very low-key fashion by just indicating to the editor that we wanted to check a few outstanding points. After all, it never hurts to be overly cautious. We'll let this dangle for a while—say for the period while I wait for the rocking chair you will send me as a gift for my sixty-fifth birthday this coming November 21. The lab is throwing a big shindig and you will, of course, get an invitation. Please bring your musical playmate with you.

Cordially,

Kurt

P.S. On rereading this letter, I just realized that I neglected to write about the confirmation of *your* experiment. Given the faint cloud hovering over Stafford (which, incidentally, you could dispel instantly), I suggest that we let that one dangle as well. There really isn't any hurry—after all, you, like Stafford, have already reported your work in a Nobel lecture.

AFTERWORD

There are several species of impositions that have been practised in science, which are but little known, except to the initiated. . . . These may be classed under the headings of hoaxing, forging, trimming and cooking . . . they [our men of science] may rest assured that not a fact they may discover, nor a good experiment they may make, but is instantly repeated, verified, and commented upon. . . .

—CHARLES BABBAGE (1830)

Outright fraud in scientific research is rare. Moreover, in science there can be no perfect crime, no permanently unsolved murder, because there is no statute of limitations. If the subject is important enough, sooner or later the experiment will be repeated, the theory subjected to independent verification. *Cantor's Dilemma*, however, does not deal with such a black-and-white issue; it maps out much grayer territory into which we scientists, deliberately or inadvertently, sometimes stray.

Original science—what Thomas Kuhn called "paradigmatic science"—usually involves the construction of a working hypothesis, which must then be substantiated experimentally. The hypothesis, when such arrives, seems so beautiful, so obvious, that it must be right. We design an experiment to test it; the results seem to bear us out. I say *seem.* At times a few inconsistent data show up: the two points out of eight that do not fall on a straight line, the one rat out of seven that did not survive. We ascribe them to experimental variability, to statistical aberration—these are the inescapable conditions of science. So we publish the massaged results, our paper causes a sensation, colleagues and competitors rush to repeat our work and to test it by other means. "Normal science" takes over, and our paradigm takes its place in the pantheon.

Suppose our insight was clairvoyant, our reasoning impeccable: what about the ethics of our data trimming? Such activity was noted and condemned a hundred and fifty years ago, by the inventor of the modern computer, the English mathematician Charles Babbage. Certainly it enjoys a long and glorious tradition: Gregor Mendel assuredly, Sir Isaac Newton probably—and no doubt Francis Bacon himself—smoothed their data with an eye toward something more than the truth. But what about our collaborators, our students? Have they been tainted? Have we been doubly tainted by ignoring the example we set our disciples? Science is both a disinterested pursuit of truth and a community, with its own customs, its own social contract. What harm is caused to its culture when the elite displays such occupational deviance?

Gray issues such as these are what I wanted to illuminate behind the scrim of fiction. Yet I could not start, and now cannot end, with the usual throat clearing of an author: a disclaimer that all characters are fictitious, any similarity to real events coincidental. Nor is this book science fiction. For instance, essentially every detail about insects is true: male scorpion flies really do display transvestite behavior; the female sweat bee's sexual behavior is indeed restricted by a chemical chastity belt; believe it or not, *The Wall Street Journal* does prevent sexual maturation and causes early death in the bug *Pyrrhocoris apterus,* whereas *The Times* of London is innocuous— according to an experiment conducted before that paper was acquired by Rupert Murdoch.

Cantor's Dilemma deals with science *in* fiction and, with one exception, all of the science it describes is real. Professor I. Cantor, Dr. Jeremiah P. Stafford and Celestine Price, as well as many of the subsidiary characters like Professors Graham Lufkin, Kurt Krauss and Jean Ardley (née Yardley), are creatures of my imagination. My Jean Ardley changed her name from Yardley to climb up the alphabetical ladder of authors. So did a scientific acquaintance of mine—jumping some twenty letters to move to the front by the stroke of a judge's pen. Can I guarantee that Cantor, Stafford and the rest never existed? In over four decades of research experience I have encountered them in many guises. Most of the other names are those of real people: the many Nobel laureates; the organic chemists on the Harvard University faculty; distinguished scientists like McConnell, Nakanishi, Roelofs, Röller, Stork and Williams; journal editors like *Science*'s Koshland and *Nature*'s Maddox. At one time or another I have met them all; some are my good friends. None are in any sense responsible for appearing in my book, except that I admire their work.

Publications, priorities, the order of the authors, the choice of the journal, the collegiality and the brutal competition, academic tenure, grantsmanship, the Nobel Prize, *Schadenfreude*—these are soul and baggage of contemporary science. To illustrate them, I had Cantor and Stafford work on a totally fictitious theory of tumorigenesis. It is almost as improbable that convincing proof could be adduced by just one or two straightforward experiments lasting a few weeks or months as happened with Stafford and then Cantor. While their research is made up, their laboratory background, their ethics and their ambitions are not. Only by giving myself, the scientist-author, the assurance that *their* science is pure fiction could I write about behavior and attitudes surely more common than we like to admit.

ABOUT THE AUTHOR

Carl Djerassi, Professor of Chemistry at Stanford University, is an internationally recognized scientist, best known for the synthesis of the first oral contraceptive, for which he has won numerous awards, including the National Medal of Science, the first Wolf Prize in Chemistry, and election into the National Inventors Hall of Fame. He is the recipient of eleven honorary doctorates, a member of the U. S. National Academy of Sciences and the American Academy of Arts and Sciences, a foreign fellow of many academies, and honorary fellow of the Royal Society of Chemistry. He also heads the Djerassi Foundation, a resident artists colony near San Francisco that supports working artists.

He is the author of *The Futurist and Other Stories* and his literary work has appeared in numerous magazines such as the *Hudson Review*, the *Michigan Quarterly Review*, the *Southern Review*, *New Letters*, *Cosmopolitan* and *Grand Street*. *Cantor's Dilemma* is his first novel.